AFTER THE RAIN

A Selection of Recent Titles by Nicola Thorne

THE PEOPLE OF THIS PARISH SERIES

THE PEOPLE OF THIS PARISH (Book I)
THE RECTOR'S DAUGHTER (Book II)
IN THIS QUIET EARTH (Book III) *
PAST LOVE (Book IV)*
A TIME OF HOPE (Book V)*
IN TIME OF WAR (Book VI)*

THE BROKEN BOUGH SERIES

THE BROKEN BOUGH *
THE BLACKBIRD'S SONG *
THE WATER'S EDGE *
OH HAPPY DAY *

AFTER THE RAIN *
COPPITTS GREEN *
A FAMILY AFFAIR *
HAUNTED LANDSCAPE *
THE HOLLY TREE *
THE HOUSE BY THE SEA *
THE LITTLE FLOWERS *
ON A DAY LIKE TODAY *
REPOSSESSION *
RETURN TO WUTHERING HEIGHTS *
RULES OF ENGAGEMENT *

* *available from Severn House*

AFTER THE RAIN

Nicola Thorne

This first world edition published 2012
in Great Britain and in the USA by
SEVERN HOUSE PUBLISHERS LTD of
9–15 High Street, Sutton, Surrey, England, SM1 1DF.
Trade paperback edition first published
in Great Britain and the USA 2013 by
SEVERN HOUSE PUBLISHERS LTD

British Library Cataloguing in Publication Data

Thorne, Nicola.
After the rain.
1. Wellington (N.Z.)--Social conditions--20th century--
Fiction.
I. Title
823.9'14-dc23

ISBN-13: 978-0-7278-8193-9 (cased)
ISBN-13: 978-1-84751-446-2 (trade paper)

All Severn House titles are printed on acid-free paper.

Severn House Publishers support The Forest Stewardship Council [FSC], the leading international forest certification organisation. All our titles that are printed on Greenpeace-approved FSC-certified paper carry the FSC logo.

Typeset by Palimpsest Book Production Ltd.,
Falkirk, Stirlingshire, Scotland.
Printed and bound in Great Britain by
MPG Books Ltd., Bodmin, Cornwall.

Dedicated to the memory of my mother who was born in New Zealand and always felt like an exile from her native land.

Author's Foreword

I was a small child when I visited Wellington with my mother, who had left after her marriage to my father and settled in England. So in writing this book I have been greatly assisted by my New Zealand first cousin Dolores Watson, daughter of my mother's eldest brother, and her husband Robin whose hobby is genealogy. But for their patience, enthusiasm and, above all, persistence in unearthing all sorts of obscure and interesting facts for me about family history and life in the twenties this novel would have been impossible. They even read the typescript for me, making more valuable suggestions. I owe them an enormous debt and I cannot thank them enough.

Nicola Thorne

One

1921. Wellington, New Zealand

Lottie, summoned to stay behind after school, looked anxiously at her class teacher perched on her high stool behind her desk. Miss Carson was correcting a pile of exercise books and finished her task before putting down her pencil, upon which her rather stern features relaxed into a smile.

'Don't look so frightened, Lottie. I just wanted to have a talk with you.'

With one of the exercise books in her hand, Miss Carson got down from her stool and, taking Lottie by the arm, led her to the front row of desks where each took a seat facing the other. She opened the exercise book and spread it out on her lap. Looking at the book, Lottie's sense of apprehension deepened.

'I want to talk to you about your essay.' Miss Carson gave a reassuring smile. 'It is very good indeed.'

'That's a relief.' Lottie brushed back her hair, returning the smile, her tense body beginning to visibly relax. 'I wondered what you were going to say.'

'I was also going to say that I was concerned to learn from the Head that you want to leave school at the end of the year?'

Lottie nodded.

'I think that's a very big mistake.'

'I don't want to leave, miss, but my mother wants me to take a job.' Lottie bent her head in an effort to conceal the fact that she was blushing. Then she raised it again and looked straight at her form teacher. 'Since Dad came back from the war he hasn't had a job. Times are very difficult, Miss Carson. We need the money.'

Miss Carson also coloured. 'I appreciate that, Lottie. But if you had some kind of profession you would earn more money and be in a better position to help your family. You're nearly sixteen so there's not much longer to go.'

Lottie shook her head but said nothing.

'For instance,' Miss Carson continued, 'if you took the high school examinations you could become a teacher or a doctor. Think of how proud your family would be of you then, and you would also earn more money and be in a much better position to help them.'

Lottie's eyes gleamed with excitement. 'I'll ask my mum.'

'Would you like me to talk to her if she says no?'

'Perhaps. I must go now, miss. Bella will be waiting outside for me.'

Miss Carson got to her feet and put her hand on Lottie's shoulder. 'I would hate for one of my best pupils to miss a chance to better her life. What a waste it would be.'

'I'll ask my mum, I promise.'

Bella, Lottie's younger sister, was waiting outside in the playground kicking her heels in front of her, a sulky expression on her face. She was eleven, almost five years younger than Lottie, on whom she was very dependent, although she was perfectly capable of going home on her own as it was only a short distance from the school. When she saw the bright, eager expression on her sister's face her expression hardened and became even more petulant. 'Where have you been?'

'Sorry.' In an ebullient mood, Lottie reached for her hand. 'Miss Carson wanted to see me.'

'Are you in trouble?'

'Not at all. She wants me to stay on at school, says perhaps I could become a teacher or a doctor.'

'But Mum says you are leaving.'

'I thought I was leaving. Wait until we get home and see what she says.'

'She won't be pleased, if you ask me.'

The euphoric expression vanished from Lottie's face as they drew nearer home. 'I don't think she will be very pleased either. But Miss Carson says if I get a better job we'll get more money and . . . Well, we must wait and see.' She suddenly felt more apprehensive than excited and slowed her pace.

Home was a terraced house in Mount Cook, a rather poor, downtrodden part of Wellington, where the family had lived all their lives. The houses were so close together that you could reach out and touch the one next door. The front door of each led directly on to the street and at the back was a small yard, usually with a single washing line strung across, and an outdoor toilet. Lottie's mother, Ada, who considered she had married beneath her, had always hated the area, resenting her modest house in a mean, shabby street. To Lottie, however, it was home, and she threw open the front door to tell her news.

As usual, her father, Desmond, was slumped in front of the fire, his paper on his chest as though he had fallen asleep, but he started up as she came in, rubbing his eyes as he looked at the clock on the mantelpiece.

Her father had served right through the war, surviving until the end, but he had returned home a virtual invalid with chronic breathing problems which prevented him from working. As a result Ada, who already took in washing to help the family, had started cleaning the houses of the more affluent, often having to cross Wellington in order to do so. She was a permanently dissatisfied woman who felt she had been dealt a bad hand by life, and accordingly her family suffered from her frequent ill-tempered outbursts.

Lottie and Bella divested themselves of their coats and hats as Ada came in from the kitchen, wiping her hands on her cloth, her habitual harassed expression on her face. 'You're very late,' she said, looking at the clock.

'Miss Carson wanted to see me!' Lottie burst out. 'So I had to stay behind.'

'I hope you haven't been in any trouble.'

'No . . .' Rather breathlessly, Lottie sat at the table, glancing first at her father wheezing away in his chair while her mother stood in the doorway leading to the kitchen. 'Miss Carson wants me to stay on at school! She says I could be a doctor or a teacher.'

Lottie paused as she took in the expressions on her parents' faces. They were very different. Her father's was one of surprise, her mother's of incredulity bordering on anger.

'And when are you going to be a doctor or a teacher, may I ask?' Ada folded her arms in a familiar and forbidding pose and leaned against the door. She looked tired to the point of exhaustion: grey-faced and older than her thirty-six years.

'After I've studied.' Lottie paused uncertainly and looked placatingly at her mother. 'Perhaps being a teacher would be better?' she ventured at last.

'And how long do you think this will take?'

Sensing her mother's hostility, which was not unexpected, Lottie now was reduced to silence, but her mouth set in a stubborn line.

'You want to forget all this nonsense,' Ada said, 'and find a job as soon as you can after school ends. Mrs Ellis knows plenty of ladies who need cleaners so you won't be out of a job for long, and you'll be bringing in money, my girl, of which there is a short supply in this house. Now come and get your tea.' She looked over at her husband and said sharply, 'Desmond, did you hear? Tea's ready; get up.'

Lottie lay in bed that night, reviewing the events of the day. She knew she was clever at school and she enjoyed her work. Not only was she a favourite of Miss Carson, but also of some of the other teachers who, knowing her background, admired her. Poverty was not unusual in the Mount Cook area of Wellington and many of the homes of the children had been affected by large-scale unemployment and the aftermath of the war. But Lottie was exceptionally bright and had an engaging personality; besides which she was a tall, attractive girl with thick, fair hair that in the sunshine seemed tinted with gold, deep-set blue eyes and a fine bone structure. In appearance she took after Ada before the rigours of her life had claimed and embittered her, destroying her looks.

If Lottie was aware of all these things she was unspoilt by them, her vanity kept in check by the hostility of her mother, who clearly preferred docile, obedient Bella but doted above all on their young brother, Jack who, at just eight years old, had no memory of his father until he came home from the war. Jack was a very small child, very beautiful with large blue eyes, a head full of fair, bubbly curls, a cheeky, waspish smile, and above all a sweet, lovable nature. Although he was very much his mother's boy, because he always did what he was told, he was adored by his sisters, who also spoilt and protected him.

Perhaps Ada resented her elder daughter's independent nature, her academic success, her closeness to her father. Perhaps, in many ways, they were too alike and this caused an ongoing conflict between them which had been accentuated since her father had returned from the war. He was a sick man, depressed and deeply disillusioned, not only by his experiences on the Western Front but by the subsequent treatment by the government of the men who had travelled all that way and undergone so much suffering, and in many cases death, for another country, to which many of them felt no allegiance at all.

In the bed beside her Bella stirred and gave a little sigh, as though the events of the day and the subsequent storm that simmered throughout the evening had disturbed her, too.

In the dark Lottie turned towards her sister, sensing she might be awake, but she seemed fast asleep. She was very protective towards Bella, who was totally unable to defend herself against their mother's frequent onslaughts and outbursts.

Although smaller-boned and petite, Bella was every bit as attractive as Lottie: fair-haired and blue-eyed, with a very pale, translucent complexion. However, in character, although she appeared mild and docile, she had a stubborn streak and was capable of outbursts of temper every bit as violent and unpredictable as her mother.

It was not a happy home and Lottie longed to leave it, but knew she was trapped by her loyalty to her father, sister and her little brother, all of whom were dependent in various ways on her as being the only one able to stand up to Ada and protect them from her erratic and uneven moods.

Also, in a way that was hard to explain, she felt trapped by the grudging respect she had for her mother because she had worked so hard to keep the family together to enable it to survive away from the workhouse. Particularly during the war, when she was the only breadwinner, that was very difficult indeed. She could understand her mother's anxiety that she should contribute to the family income, especially after her father had proved unfit to work when he returned from the war a broken man.

Yet to be a teacher, like Miss Carson . . . an ambition which she had never consciously entertained, except in her dreams. Perhaps that was something that would indeed eventually be of greater help to the family than being a drudge, cleaning the houses of other people in Island Bay. Maybe, with two incomes, they would be able to move to a nicer area, have a house with a garden, an indoor toilet – perhaps even a bathroom – and have the sort of better life to which her mother she knew, above all, aspired.

Ada had on her best hat for the interview with Miss Carson which was eventually arranged, somewhat to Lottie's surprise. Miss Carson had handled the whole thing both well and delicately, writing first to her parents to explain the benefits of further education and invite them to come and see her.

Naturally, Ada, who wanted to be in control of the situation, left Desmond at home and Lottie had to wait outside the room in which the meeting took place. Ada intended to take the lead, to be outspoken, even aggressive, but was seduced, as so many people were, not only by Miss Carson's persuasive charm but also the ease with which she got her word in first. She began by telling Ada how much she sympathized with her and what a wonderful job she had done and how grateful they should be to her for keeping the family together while her husband went to war.

Thus Ada had the wind taken out of her sails almost before she had time to get started with her objections. She even felt a sneaking admiration for Miss Carson, and an affinity with her.

'A teacher's training course is quite short you see, Mrs O'Brien. Only a couple of years, and the benefits will be enormous not only to Lottie but to the family.' She gave a winsome smile. 'It would be such a pity to waste the talents of a girl with so many gifts. She is one of our outstanding pupils and,' she added, 'Bella is not far behind, so you have two clever daughters, and I'm sure Jack will be equally as clever as his sisters.'

'Jack is only eight,' Ada protested, gratified beyond expectations by all this praise for her troublesome, willful and disobedient elder daughter.

'Plenty of time for him to develop,' Miss Carson said.

Abruptly pulling herself together, determined not to be seduced by all this charm, Ada's face assumed its customary severe expression. 'The fact is, Miss Carson, whatever you think of Charlotte, we are not in a position to let her stay on at school. We very badly need the money she would earn. Charlotte is nearly sixteen. She has already stayed on longer at school than she needed to. I could have taken her away at fourteen. She is quite old enough now to be earning her living. The same will be true of Bella when she turns fourteen. My husband has so far proved unfit to work and the burden falls on me. I work every hour God sends and frankly it is telling on me and my health.'

'Believe me, I do sympathize.' Miss Carson paused. 'But I think if you could last a little longer . . .'

'But it won't be a "little longer",' Ada protested, 'it will be *years*.'

'But in the long run you will benefit enormously, don't you realize that?'

'I realize that Charlotte will have to leave school,' Ada said, firmly rising from her seat. 'It is very good of you to be so concerned but I'm sorry, that is the position.' She paused for a moment. 'I wasn't born to this sort of life, you know, Miss Carson. My father had a good position and we lived in Karori. My parents were against my marriage, but I was very young, headstrong . . . Desmond then was a very attractive man . . . Well, look where it got me. Unable to see my children have a good education.' And with a shrug and a smile bleak enough to freeze the heart, she turned to go.

'Mrs O'Brien, wait a minute,' Miss Carson called after her just as she reached the door. Ada turned to see her coming towards her. 'I think I may be able to arrange some funds to help you out. We have contingency plans in the school for help when it is needed. It will not be a vast amount, but you might find it useful.'

'Well.' Ada turned back into the room and paused for a moment. 'Well, I don't quite know what to say.'

'If it works out, and I'm sure it will, I would much prefer Lottie wasn't told about this. It might make it very awkward for her with the other pupils if they got to hear about it. I do hope that might persuade you to change your mind, Mrs O'Brien.'

'It might,' Ada said grudgingly. 'I don't like charity, I'll tell you frankly, Miss Carson, so I'll have to think about it and discuss it with my husband. I'll let you know. Thank you, Miss Carson.'

As Miss Carson opened the door she saw Lottie sitting disconsolately outside, an expression of anxiety on her face, and gave her a fleeting, reassuring smile.

As the door shut behind her Lottie rose to greet her mother. 'What did she say?' she burst out when they were outside.

'She tried to persuade me that it might be in our interests as well as yours. I'm thinking about it. I'll talk to your father.' She looked at her daughter severely. 'Miss Carson seems to think very highly of you. I can't think what you've done to deserve it. She should see you at home.'

'Maybe I could take a weekend job and also work nights?'

'My, you do want it badly, don't you?' Ada said grudgingly. 'I'll see what your father says.'

As Lottie knew, what her father said went for very little in a household where Ada ruled and her word was law.

Desmond's approval, as usual, was not asked, but it could be taken for granted because he loved his bright, sparkling daughter Lottie. He loved Bella as well, but maybe he saw in Lottie more of himself – the young man full of hope, as he had once been. He also still loved his wife, remembering her when he first met her and he had by virtue of his Irish charm swept her off her feet, much to the disapproval of her parents.

How things had changed. Desmond O'Brien was a first-generation New Zealander born in Wellington. His parents were assisted immigrants from Protestant Belfast having been lured to a new land by promise of rewards and an enhanced way of life that had somehow not lived up to its promise. They had come from large families, had no relations in this country so far from home, and missed their parents. His father got a job as a carter and eventually Desmond, who left school at twelve, followed him, becoming a driver with the advent of the motor car. With the outbreak of war in 1914 he was more excited by the idea of adventure abroad than going to the defence of a country to which he owed no allegiance. Against Ada's wishes he eagerly enlisted and was among the first troops to leave the country with the New Zealand Expeditionary Force in October on the converted Union Company ship *The Limerick*.

But any hope Desmond also had of bettering himself vanished as he was absorbed into one of the infantry brigades that saw action first at Gallipoli, then on the Somme and finally at Passchendaele, where he inhaled the gas that so damaged his lungs. Battle-hardened, disillusioned and weary, he had returned home in 1918 with little to show for his misplaced patriotism other than a meagre pension and an inability to earn a living on his own, or frankly any desire to. By that time Ada, too, had changed from the vivacious, fun-loving girl he had loved and married to an embittered woman, resentful of having been left on her own with three young children for four years. Seeing the wreck her husband had become she had no sympathy for the ordeal – both physical and mental – he had been through, which was, anyway, beyond her imagination. Her attitude changed towards him, as it had towards the children she had had to bring up on her own, perpetually finding fault with them, especially with Desmond's favourite, Lottie, who she seemed to blame for all her ills. Her own parents had rejected her after her teenage elopement with a man with good looks but no prospects. In their opinion Ada had got what she deserved and she, in turn, was too proud to ask them for help.

Locked in depression, Desmond sat quietly for most of the day in his armchair, putting up with the jibes from Ada, grateful when she went off to her work and could no longer taunt him until she returned home and resumed with gusto, complaining about how hard she worked compared to what a lazy so and so he was. He spent most of his days lost in his own world and looked forward to the return of his children from school. Indeed, it was through them that he lived and had any enjoyment from life.

The subject of Lottie staying on at school was not mentioned for days after Ada's interview with Miss Carson, so in an agony of apprehension Lottie lived out the time wondering about her future. Miss Carson said nothing and neither did her parents. Finally, after school one day, having given her father a cup of tea and unable to contain herself any longer, Lottie perched on a stool next to him.

'Dad, did Mum say anything more about me staying on at school after she spoke to Miss Carson? She said she was going to talk to you.'

Her father's mystified look gave Lottie the answer she needed. 'You know your mother never asks for my opinion on anything, Lottie. It is as though I no longer exist for her.'

'Mum didn't say anything at all to you?'

Desmond shook his head. 'I don't suppose she would. You know who is boss here.'

'Could you ask her, Dad, for me? Say you think it's a good thing.'

'I wish I could help,' Desmond said then stopped, overtaken by a sudden spasm of coughing. Lottie watched him anxiously as he gasped for breath, then the door opened and Ada came in with Jack, who she had collected from school. She wore her usual harassed, bad-tempered expression, which became even more pronounced when she saw Lottie perched by the side of her husband.

'Can't you find anything to do, Lottie? Is tea not ready yet?'

Guiltily Lottie jumped to her feet as Ada took off her hat and coat. 'Put these in the hall for me, would you, Jack?' she said, handing them to the boy. 'And then go and change your clothes. Tea will be ready soon.'

'Yes, Mum,' Jack said with his customary docility and scampered out of the room.

Ada slumped into a chair by the side of the table and put a hand to her brow, wearily stroking it, her fingers pressing against it as if she had a headache. 'God knows, I'm tired having worked my fingers to the bone and no tea ready. Where's Bella?'

'She went to play with Gertie next door. Shall I get you a cup of tea now, Mum?'

'Well, that would be nice.' Ada looked mollified, her expression softened, the taut lines around her face eased. 'And then you can start on tea for us all.' She looked at her husband. 'Had another coughing fit, have you, Desmond?'

Desmond nodded and started wheezing again. 'Lottie was asking me about staying on at school.' Desmond gasped. 'I wish I could help and do some work, Ada. It's not that I don't want to. It is very good that Miss Carson wants her to stay on. She is a very clever girl.'

'You would think the army could find you some clerical job,' Ada said, ignoring his last remark. 'You nearly lose your life for a country you have never ever been to and then look how they treat you. You should never have gone to the war, Desmond. I told you at the time.'

This was a perpetual gripe of Ada, one she never ceased reminding him of. It had indeed made an enormous difference to their lives. Before the war things were reasonably harmonious between husband and wife and it was a much happier home. The experience had deeply soured Ada, exacerbated by the horrific number of casualties the ANZAC troops had suffered and the never-ending worry of daily expecting bad news. 'I'd have been better off dead,' Desmond said, not for the first time. 'Then you could have married again; someone who would look after you better than I can.'

Ada gave a derisive snort and looked up at Lottie, who had returned with a cup of tea. 'I could do with this,' she said, sipping it. Her mood seemed to have improved and she put the cup down and sighed deeply. 'I still think Lottie will be better off doing a job and helping us for a while.' She got up and handed her cup back to Lottie. 'I'm sorry, Lottie, but that really is the end of the matter.'

'I think you could have discussed it with Dad. He thinks it's a good idea,' Lottie insisted stubbornly.

Ada cast her husband a look of contempt. 'If your father got off his backside and did a job of work you could stay at school as long as you like,' she said, and with an air of finality went out to the kitchen.

Lottie lay in bed listening to the noise coming from her parents' room. As usual, they were shouting at each other again and she knew it was about her. Invariably her mother's voice was in the ascendant until the voices stopped abruptly and a violent spasm of coughing ensued, as was invariably the case with these rows between her parents, her father being too weak to argue with her for long. Lottie imagined him gasping for breath and feared, as she often did, that eventually one of these arguments would lead to his death. Sometimes she thought longingly of running away and starting a new life, but that would mean leaving her father and, besides, where would she go? How would she live?

In the bed next to her Bella stirred. The noise made by her parents had woken even a deep sleeper such as herself.

'It's about me,' Lottie said. 'I brought up today about staying on at school and Mum says I can't.'

'Dad always takes your side,' Bella said peevishly. As the younger sibling she always felt she fell between her sister who her father loved best and her mother who so clearly favoured Jack.

'And why shouldn't he?'

'I think it's very hard on Mum. I don't want to stay on at school for a moment longer than I need to. If I could leave now I would.'

'And what would you like to do?'

'Be a hairdresser, something like that.'

Lottie fell silent and there was no more noise from next door after the coughing subsided.

She put her hands behind her head and stared at the ceiling, listening to her sister's regular breathing as she fell once more into a deep sleep. It was all right for Bella, but she had far loftier ideas about her own future.

Returning home a few days later, earlier than usual, Ada found her husband not slumped in his chair half asleep but leaning forward to greet her with an expression on his face that was almost animated as he looked at her. 'What's up with you?' she asked, putting down a bag full of shopping and removing the pin from her hat.

'Look on the table,' Desmond said, eagerly pointing. 'There's a letter.'

Wearily, Ada picked up the single page lying next to its envelope and sat down on a chair. She had started work early, cleaned two large houses, done the shopping and felt deathly tired. Soon she would have to go out again and pick up Jack.

Dear Mr and Mrs O'Brien,

With reference to the talk we had recently, Mrs O'Brien, I have now had a chance to speak to the Head and she has kindly agreed to release funds to assist you during the time that Lottie resumes her education from next term onwards. The sum will amount to what Lottie might reasonably expect to earn, and in due course you will let me know approximately how much this is likely to be.

I explained to you that Lottie is a very able, keen pupil, an example to others with a bright future ahead of her, and I am sure she will benefit from further education, go on to advanced study, and that her future will be more rewarding and of benefit to you as a family.

As I explained it is important that this information is withheld from Lottie as we cannot extend it to other pupils in similar circumstances, however much we might like to. We are making an exception for Lottie.

I look forward to hearing that this offer is acceptable to you.

Yours sincerely,

Madeleine Carson

Two

For the rest of the school year Lottie worked hard to justify Miss Carson's faith in her. It ended at Christmas, which was the height of summer in New Zealand, and Lottie had turned sixteen in September. As expected she had come top in the Proficiency exam at the end of standard six, after which a lot of less able pupils would leave. The ones who decided to remain were, like Lottie, keen to progress into higher education and some were also aiming to be teachers, a profession on which Lottie had now set her heart. In time she hoped to attend the teachers' training college at Kelburn.

On Saturdays she did a menial job in the haberdashery department of Kirkcaldie and Stains, a large department store on Lambton Quay, and on Sundays she tried to catch up with her homework, but spent most of it helping her mother in the house. Although Ada had encouraged her to take a part-time job she never made any allowances for it and expected her to do as much housework as ever. She, too, had had a hard week, as she was never tired of emphasizing, so the bulk of the tasks fell on Lottie, including changing the beds when necessary for the whole family and doing all the washing. Often at weekends, Ada was called to work at Mrs Ellis's, who entertained a lot, so Lottie seldom had time to socialize with friends. Bella was supposed to help her but managed to contribute very little. Jack, of course, being a boy and so young, was never expected to do any work at all.

Lottie, however, didn't care. She felt buoyed up by the new outlook she had on life thanks to the opportunity provided by Miss Carson, who had somehow persuaded her mother to let her stay on at school. She continued to achieve brilliant results, was a model pupil and excelled at every subject in class, especially English literature. Lottie loved reading and whatever chance she got, whenever there was a respite from homework and household chores, she could be found curled up in a corner of the sitting room or on her bed with her nose in a book.

Miss Carson took Lottie's class for history and English literature and one day just before the Christmas holiday she asked Lottie to stay behind. 'Everything going well, Lottie?'

'Very well, thank you, Miss Carson.'

'I've thought recently that you look very tired, Lottie. I hope you're not doing too much?' Miss Carson stared at her with concern.

Lottie vigorously shook her head. 'I have to do a lot in the house and that's the way things are. Mum has to have help.' She didn't think she would tell her about the Saturday job.

Miss Carson nodded understandingly. 'Of course. Well, do take care and look after yourself. See that you get enough sleep.'

'Oh, I do, Miss Carson.'

'Lottie, I wondered if you would like to come to tea one day at my house? I'd like you to meet my sister, Violet. She is a little older than you, just nineteen, but she is training to be a teacher and I think you might get on well and have lots in common. Maybe after school. Do you think your mother would allow that?'

Lottie's expression managed to combine both excitement and anxiety. 'I'll ask her, Miss Carson.'

'Would next Wednesday be a good day for you? You can come home with me and I'll see you get back safely.'

Lottie's eyes shone. 'Oh, I would really like that, Miss Carson. I'm sure Mum will say yes.'

Ada had no option but to agree when Lottie asked her when she got home from school that day. She did a bit of grumbling about all the things she would have to do which would normally be Lottie's jobs, but she could hardly refuse a woman who had provided them with a welcome and unexpected source of extra income that arrived regularly by post in an envelope addressed to her.

Accordingly, on the appointed day, Lottie waited excitedly by the main gates to the school as she had been instructed. She had not been waiting long when a smart little car drove up with an open hood and at the wheel was Miss Carson, who waved and leaned over, throwing open the door to the passenger seat.

'Hop in!' she cried as Lottie contemplated the vehicle. She had never been inside a motor car and, feeling momentarily tongue-tied, clambered in nervously.

'Shut the door tight,' Miss Carson commanded. 'Don't look so frightened, Lottie.'

'I've never been in a motor car,' Lottie confessed.

'Well, sit back,' Miss Carson said gaily, 'and you'll be fine.'

'My father used to drive a van before the war and sometimes we went with him in that.'

'Was your mother all right about you coming to tea?'

Lottie nodded, still feeling awkward in this completely different environment, her eyes fixed nervously on the road in front of her as they made their way through the city towards the coast. She had never, in fact, known where Miss Carson lived or even that she possessed a motor car. For some reason she thought she lived near the school. Gradually the roads widened, the houses on either side grew more spacious and affluent and finally Miss Carson took a sharp turn up a slight hill and turned into a short drive which led to an attractive white colonial-style house flanked by a large garden. As she stopped the front door opened and a lady of ample proportions with a smiling, friendly face came down to greet them.

'This is my mother,' Miss Carson said, opening her door. 'Mummy, this is one of my star pupils, Lottie O'Brien, or I suppose I should say Charlotte O'Brien.' She went round to Lottie's side and helped her out of the car.

'What shall I call you?' Mrs Carson said, beaming in such a warm, kind way that completely captured Lottie.

'I'm always called Lottie, except when my mother's cross with me and then I'm Charlotte.'

Both women laughed and Mrs Carson preceded them up the steps and into the house. 'We're on the lawn,' Mrs Carson said. 'It's such a hot day. I expect you'd like a cool drink, Lottie?'

Lottie nodded. Despite Mrs Carson's obvious friendliness she still felt stupid and tongue-tied and regretted she had ever agreed to come. She had no idea that Miss Carson lived anywhere so splendid or that there would be other people for tea besides her. She didn't know what she had expected, but it certainly wasn't this.

As they came to the foot of a broad staircase Miss Carson said, 'I'm just popping up to change,' and ran up the stairs.

Lottie followed Mrs Carson through a long, cool hall with open doors at the far end, through which a welcome breeze blew. When they emerged she saw the broad sweep of a beautifully manicured lawn on which there were chairs arranged around a small pool. At the far side was a tennis court on which a man and a girl were engaged in a vigorous game.

Mrs Carson pointed to a chair on which Lottie sat, feeling clumsy and now awkward in her school uniform. Seeming to sense her unease Mrs Carson sat down next to her, leaning a little towards her, that warm, kind smile on her face. Lottie thought she was a very motherly type of woman, quite unlike her own brittle, hard-edged mother. In fact, everything about this place, the people as well as the location, was quite unlike anything she had ever known. She had rather imagined Mrs Ellis's house must be like this.

'My son and daughter are playing tennis,' Mrs Carson said, pointing to the attractive couple on the court. 'Do you play, Lottie?'

Lottie nodded. 'Not often, but I do when I get the chance.'

'They'll be finished in a minute when some tea appears. Ah, here it is.'

She smiled at the maid, who laid a tray on the table that had been drawn up in front of the pool, just as Miss Carson emerged in a swirling yellow dress that reached to her ankles. She helped the maid unload the tray and turned to Lottie. 'That feels better,' she said. 'Has Mummy been entertaining you?'

'I asked her if she played tennis.' Mrs Carson gestured towards the court. 'Hugh and Vi are hard at it.'

'Lottie is very good,' Miss Carson said as her mother got up and, going over to the court, clapped her hands.

'Tea!' Mrs Carson called loudly and the pair stopped playing.

'Tea or squash?' Miss Carson asked Lottie.

'Squash, I think, please,' Lottie said, her mouth by now so dry that the words emerged as a croak. She couldn't decide whether it was because of the heat or her nerves.

'I'm thirsty too.' Miss Carson poured the enticing-looking cool liquid from a large glass jug into two glasses, one of which she gave to Lottie. 'Cake?'

Lottie took a piece of sponge from the proffered plate. Despite her nerves and dry mouth she was feeling hungry. She wondered why Miss Carson had asked her. She had expected it would just be the two of them talking about books or something as they frequently did, when the situation was completely natural and there was no shyness or constraint between them. Here she felt awkward, out of place. Miss Carson appeared to be oblivious to this and sank into the chair beside her, just as the two tennis players arrived at the table with their mother, looking hot and eager for a drink.

Miss Carson jumped to her feet. 'Squash?' she asked and as they nodded in unison she began to pour. 'This is Lottie,' she continued, 'who I told you about. Lottie, my sister Violet and Hugh, my brother.'

Lottie struggled to her feet and the younger woman shook her warmly by the hand.

'Hello, Lottie,' Hugh said and held her hand with a firm, strong grasp.

There was a distinct family resemblance. They were all so beautiful, and Hugh, she thought, was one of the best-looking men she had ever seen. He was lean and forceful looking, towering over everyone, extremely tall with thick black wavy hair, knowing, slightly recessed dark brown eyes, a broad nose and a firm, determined chin. His smile, though, was warm, his manner confident and authoritative, a person one instinctively felt one could rely on and trust.

Violet was a smaller, more feminine version of Hugh, with dark curly hair and an open, friendly and engaging manner. Lottie liked her immediately and thought they would get on well.

She also saw Miss Carson in an altogether different light, her pretty summery dress contrasting with the sombre two-piece, usually in black or grey, that she wore as schoolmistress. She realized for the first time that Miss Carson was strikingly pretty. She had the family's dark curly hair, hers fashionably styled in a soft Amami wave, large limpid-brown eyes and a full, curved mouth. Lottie sat down and curled up in her chair, very conscious of being gauche and awkward in her school uniform among these glamorous, almost overpowering people she didn't know and in an environment strange to her. Instead of a pleasant afternoon tea with her teacher she felt completely out of her comfort zone and longed to go home.

'Hugh is at university,' Miss Carson said. 'He is hoping to be a doctor. Vi is training to be a teacher. She is at Kelburn, where we hope you will go one day, Lottie.'

'Madeleine says you love books,' Violet said, 'and are very good at English. Have you ever heard of Katherine Mansfield?'

Lottie shook her head.

'She is a writer and her family live in a very large house in Fitzherbert Terrace, just behind this road,' said Mrs Carson. 'She now lives in England where she is beginning to be well known, so a friend there tells me. Her father Harold Beauchamp is very wealthy and on the board of the Bank of New Zealand. We don't know them very well and they go away a lot. The family has suffered a lot of misfortune. I hear Kathleen, which is her real name, is very ill. Their only son, Leslie, was killed in the war and Mrs Beauchamp died a couple of years later, maybe from a broken heart. So, all in all . . .' Mrs Carson sighed and folded her hands in her lap in an attitude of dejection. 'We have a lot to be thankful for. What a terrible business that was. So many men killed or wounded and so far from home. They say the number of ANZAC troops killed was grossly out of proportion to the rest from other countries which fought in the war. My family came from England and naturally we support the mother country, but why when we have found a good life for ourselves here? You really ask yourself what it was all for . . .'

Mrs Carson's voice trailed off again as she didn't really know the answer and her children remained silent, thoughtful. Perhaps Hugh, who had been too young for the war, pondered that if he had been of age, he might also have gone.

'Happily I didn't have to make that decision,' Hugh said, voicing his thoughts aloud as if reading their minds.

His mother reached across for his hand. 'Thank goodness you didn't. You were too young and Daddy was too old. My husband is a surgeon,' Mrs Carson explained to Lottie. 'He's away at the moment at a conference.'

'My father was in the war.' Suddenly the vision of him sitting quietly in his chair all day in the corner, coughing away between gulps of cigarette smoke, seemed to make Lottie come alive. 'He was one of the first people to enlist in 1914 and he went all through the war, beginning with Gallipoli. He was wounded twice and gassed. I think my father was very brave, especially as he didn't have to go. Also his family was from Ireland not England, a country he's never been to in his life.' She looked around almost defiantly, as if expecting them to disagree.

'Oh, he was *very* brave,' Mrs Carson said admiringly. 'You must be very proud of him.'

'I am, but I'm sorry he went. He is a very sick man and it has a big effect on our family and our lives. Now my father doesn't think it was worth it and wishes he had never volunteered. He expected a better life and got nothing. They were not even fed properly in the trenches and nearly starved. When he came home he got no thanks either and he feels he has been left to rot. We were a lot happier before my father went away. After he came back everything changed . . .' Spurred on by waves of indignation she was aware that her voice had risen, and of their concerned, stricken faces staring at her. She stopped, suddenly conscious of her raised voice, thinking that maybe she had gone too far.

Mrs Carson, looking across at Madeleine, finally broke the silence. 'Did you know Lottie's daddy was in the war?

'Yes, I did,' Madeleine said quietly. 'And I do know what an effect it has had on the family. In fact . . .'

But before she was able to go any further Lottie suddenly wanted to deflate this nice, sympathetic but decidedly privileged group of people around her who had no idea what the war had been like for those involved or their families, and went on even more heatedly: 'As my father can't work my mother has to work very hard and she wanted me to leave school and help out. But Miss Carson persuaded Mother to let me stay on, so I think I owe them a big debt. In fact, sometimes I think I should leave and that is why I work very hard.' Aware that her cheeks were burning she stood up. 'I must go now. There is a lot to do at home.'

The atmosphere around her had changed, as if a cold gust of wind had somehow put a chill on the warm summer's day, reminding them all of the coldness and bleakness of the trenches and the mud in which men who were neither killed nor wounded sometimes drowned.

'Oh, but you've hardly been here any time at all. We haven't even begun tea. Don't think you must . . .'

'I must,' Lottie said firmly.

'Can't you stay a bit longer?'

'No, I can't and thank you very much for asking me and for the cake and lemonade. It was lovely.'

'I'll take you home.' Madeleine, visibly shaken by her protégée's outburst, also stood up.

'Please don't, Miss Carson. You have been very kind. I can walk or get a bus.'

'But it's a long way,' Madeleine protested. 'I'm taking you.'

'No, let me take her,' Hugh said to his sister. 'You look tired and you've been teaching all day.'

'That's very kind of you, Hugh.' Madeleine did look tired. 'I have a lot of end of term marking to do.'

'But I don't want to take your brother from his game. I feel I've been a nuisance.'

'Not at all,' Hugh said. 'I wanted to go into town anyway.'

'That's settled, then.' Madeleine smiled anxiously at Lottie. 'I'm sorry you have to go so soon. See you tomorrow. I hope you've enjoyed yourself.'

'Yes, I have.' Lottie turned towards the house, followed by a disconsolate group of people who suddenly seemed to feel that somehow they, too, had failed her.

The three women stood at the front door watching Hugh help Lottie into Madeleine's car, waving as he drove off.

'What a very sweet girl,' Mrs Carson said to her elder daughter. 'But I can't quite understand why you asked her. She was obviously very uncomfortable.'

'I didn't think it would be like this,' Madeleine, clearly shaken, said. 'I thought it would be nice for her to meet Violet and perhaps become more enthused with the idea of being a teacher. I think it was getting on to the war and her father. I just thought it would be a treat for her because I know she works so hard and has little time off. I realize now that it was a mistake.'

They wandered back to the garden and settled once more in their chairs. The maid appeared and asked if there was anything they wanted and Mrs Carson said tea might be nice. Being of English stock there was nothing quite like a cup of tea to calm the sense of agitation she felt after this curious and unsettling episode.

Violet poured herself more lemonade and sipped it thoughtfully. 'I thought she was interesting,' she said. 'I'm glad you asked her and I think you should ask her again. I liked her and I think she was shy. She'd get used to us.'

Madeleine looked at her gratefully. 'She *is* a very interesting and accomplished girl, old for her years – due, I think, to the circumstances at home. Her mother wanted her to leave school to help support the family. She is a worthy woman, but a real dragon. The father is an invalid. If you get the chance I would like you to talk to her about teaching. I think she'd be good at it. Anyway, it's good her mother allowed her to stay on at school.'

'Surprising in the circumstances,' her mother said.

'I helped in a way. I made an arrangement with her mother to make some funds available so that she would not have to leave.'

'From the school?' Mrs Carson looked with surprise at her daughter.

'No, from me. I can afford it, Mother. It is not very much because she would not be paid very much if she worked.'

'Does Lottie know this?'

'No. One of the conditions I made to her mother was she should not be told, but I did and do think that a big opportunity would be lost if she got into some mundane job that did not justify her talents.'

'Well, it was very generous of you,' Mrs Carson said. 'But I wonder if it was very wise?'

'Let's get on with your game,' Madeleine said, abruptly getting up. 'I feel in need of some vigorous exercise.' And she put out a hand and dragged her rather unwilling sister from her chair.

Lottie felt very awkward as Hugh maneuvered the car out of the short drive and into the road. She wished so much that he hadn't offered and that she had agreed to let Miss Carson take her home. She was nervous and lost for words in the dashing Hugh's company and curled up in her seat, eyes fixed firmly on the road, yet unnervingly aware of his masculinity so close to her. The whole afternoon had been a disaster and she was sorry it had ever happened. They had barely left the house before Hugh slowed and stopped the car outside a house smaller than the Carsons', but a pretty one with white walls set back from a sloping garden filled with flowers.

'That was where Katherine Mansfield was born,' Hugh said. 'I thought you might be interested. Her family now lives in a very large house in just at the back of our road.'

'Do they live there now?'

'Yes, but she is still in England, or so I believe. Her father remarried quite recently.'

Lottie nodded and stared thoughtfully at the house. 'I'd like to be a writer,' she said. 'I write stories for the school magazine.'

'Well, then that is all the more reason to stay on at school,' Hugh said.

Lottie stared hard at him.

'I'm sorry, did I say . . .?'

'Nothing.' Lottie vigorously shook her head and turned her eyes once more to the road.

Hugh put his foot down and drove on, aware of his passenger's discomfort and now feeling some of it himself. 'I would like to go to England and complete my training as a doctor.' He broke the awkward silence at last. 'And I hope, one day, that might be possible.'

Lottie didn't reply. Yes, it was a lifestyle a million miles away from hers. Even Katherine Mansfield had plenty of money, from the sound of things.

They drove through the town now in complete silence and eventually Hugh said, 'You must tell me where you live. Is it near the school?'

'Yes, quite near.'

Lottie was anxious for him not to see the rundown street where she lived, with its small, neglected-looking dingy houses, such a contrast to his own gracious home. So she misdirected him, finally telling him to stop in a street the other side of the school but not far from Broadway Terrace where she lived. 'This is it!' she cried, pointing to a neat house, part of a row with a well-kept garden.

'Oh, here?' Hugh said, braking. 'Which house?'

'This is fine.' Lottie prepared to get out of the car and opened the door.

'Thank you very much, Mr Carson. I hope you do well with your studies.'

Now Hugh seemed the awkward one. 'Please call me Hugh,' he said, 'and I hope I see you again.'

Lottie nodded and got out of the car, aware of those mesmerizing eyes watching her. She boldly opened the gate of this completely strange house, paused briefly to wave at him, and walked up the path, praying that the door would not open before he drove off. As soon as she heard the sound of the engine start she turned and, making sure he had disappeared, scampered down the path, shut the gate quietly and ran along the street until she was out of sight.

Quite breathless, she turned at last into Broadway Terrace and almost cannoned into her mother just a few paces in front of her. 'Mum!' she cried.

Her mother stopped and, looking back, stared at her. 'What on earth . . .' she exclaimed. 'You look as though you've been running a race.'

'Oh, Mum.' Lottie practically collapsed into her arms. 'Oh, Mum . . .'

'Lottie, whatever is the matter?' Ada, unused to such a display of emotion from her eldest daughter, put an arm round her. 'Are you all right?'

'Oh, Mum . . . I made such a fool of myself with the Carsons. It was a horrible afternoon.'

'What happened?' Ada, genuinely concerned, continued to walk slowly towards the house, one arm round Lottie.

'They are not like us, Mum. They live in a big house and have a maid to serve tea on the lawn and, oh . . . it was awful.' The tears started to trickle slowly down her face.

'But I thought you liked Miss Carson?'

'I do, and I thought it was just tea with her, but her mother was there and sister and brother and . . . Oh, Mum, they are not like us.'

'That is for sure,' her mother said, pausing in a rare moment of parental concern to produce a handkerchief and gently dab the tears away from Lottie's eyes. 'That is for sure. They are not like us. Maybe this afternoon has taught you a lesson, my girl.'

Half asleep as usual in his chair in the corner, Desmond looked up as Ada and Lottie came in. They presented such an unusual scene, with the mother's arm around that of her daughter, that he started up from his chair and went over to Lottie. 'What happened to you, dear? Are you hurt?'

As Lottie shook her head Ada let go of her arm and, taking the pin out of her hat, put it on the table and went towards the kitchen door. 'Nothing that a cup of tea won't cure,' she said and disappeared into the kitchen.

Desmond sat Lottie on the sofa and sat down next to her, peering anxiously at her tear-stained face. 'Did someone hurt you, darling? Did you fall over?'

Lottie shook her head, still finding it hard to speak. She felt ashamed of herself, not only for getting into this state but for letting her parents see it.

'Didn't you go to tea with Miss Carson?'

Lottie nodded and sniveled into her handkerchief.

'She found the Carsons were not people like us,' Ada said smugly, appearing with a tray which she set down on the table next to her hat. 'What else she expected I don't know, but what they actually did or said to her I don't know either as she was so flustered and upset when I met her outside in the street. Now, Lottie,' her mother said, firmly pouring the tea into a cup from a large brown pot, '*what* exactly happened at Miss Carson's?'

'Nothing.' Lottie screwed her handkerchief into her eyes. 'That's the trouble. Nothing actually happened. They were very nice but I never . . .' She paused, on the verge of sniveling again, 'I never felt *easy* there. I felt I didn't belong. Everything was different: the place, the house which is huge and has a tennis court on the lawn. Even

Miss Carson looked different. They were very *nice* to me. It's nothing they did and that is what I can't understand – why it all upset me so much. I had a feeling of panic, that I must get away, so I said I wanted to go home even before the tea had properly started and I know they couldn't understand it and neither could I.'

Faced with this logic, she felt her tears dry up and looked up at the faces of both her parents; father concerned, mother with that familiar expression on her face that was half sceptical and half critical, as if she regretted the impulse of putting a consoling arm around her daughter's waist in the street.

Lottie accepted the cup of tea from her mother and shook her head. 'I'm sorry, Mum. It was silly of me.'

'Well, you won't go there again.'

'I don't expect they'll ask me. I made a fool of myself. It was when they got on to the war . . .'

'They talked about the war?' her mother said, her face puzzled.

'About someone they knew who was killed in the war and as I hadn't said a word until then, I suddenly felt that I wanted to tell them about Dad and what he suffered and I thought how different Dad's situation now was from theirs. I felt very angry about the whole thing when I compared our lives with theirs. They seemed to me to be very self-satisfied despite being so nice. I was aware that I was almost shouting and they were looking at me as though they didn't know what had got into me. And that was it,' Lottie finished lamely. 'Then I just got up and said I had to go home and Miss Carson's brother drove me and stopped just past the school because I didn't want him to see where we lived.'

'And that's why you were so out of breath?' Ada gave a grim smile.

Lottie nodded. 'I went right up the path of a strange house and I was frightened someone would open the door.'

'No need to be ashamed of where you live, Lottie,' her father said gently, 'or of the sort of person you are, or who we are. I don't know Miss Carson, but you are every bit as good as her and her family.'

'They are just not like us,' Lottie said again, lamely.

'Then you should keep well away from them if it gets you in this state,' her mother said. 'I'm not sure it will do you much good to stay on at school. If it is in order to mix with people like them who get you into this sort of state I don't see the point.'

'It's education, Ada,' Desmond said patiently. 'It leads to all sorts of things we can never give Lottie. Things that will make her happier and improve the quality of her life.' His eyes shining in his tired weary face he looked defiantly at his wife. 'I'm quite sure of that.'

The following day Miss Carson asked Lottie to stay behind after class, ostensibly to go over one of her recent compositions. Fellow pupils sometimes talked among themselves of the favouritism Miss Carson seemed to show to Lottie and she was not unaware of this. She was popular and well-liked because, despite her abilities, she did not parade them, and fitted in well with the members of the class, many of whom came from the same background as herself and cherished the same ambitions to do well and better themselves. One had lost a father in the war and Lottie had proved extraordinarily comforting and helpful to her, perhaps out of fellow feeling because, although her father had not been killed, in many ways he was lost to them and had returned a very different man from the one who went away.

It was never a nice thing to be thought of as 'teacher's pet', so Lottie had not told anyone about the invitation to tea or the degree of intimacy she and Miss Carson shared.

However, as the girls filed out of the classroom, Miss Carson's attitude was very brisk and businesslike as she produced Lottie's essay from a pile of others, even before the door had closed behind the last pupil. 'This is very good, Lottie, one of your best,' she said. 'However, the one thing I want you to watch is letting yourself stray from the subject and going off at a tangent. You see, although Hardy's love of the land is an important background to the novel, the paramount story is about Henchard and his selling his wife and baby daughter in a drunken stupor. Now we may consider this a horrible thing to do, and it is. It is pivotal to the story, not the countryside surrounding Casterbridge, however beautiful and atmospheric it might be. Do you see?'

Lottie, standing beside the teacher's desk, bent her head, listening attentively to Miss Carson's words, and nodded. 'But the countryside is beautiful, Miss Carson. It is so vivid and Hardy makes me feel like I would really like to go there.'

'And one day perhaps you will if you progress with your education the way I feel you should. But Lottie, I do think you are looking very tired of late and I wonder if you are working too hard, helping your mother in the house or maybe doing all the housework yourself as I know she works very hard. You must have some enjoyment, which is why I asked you to tea. However, I felt it was not altogether successful. You were so anxious to leave and it worried me. I rather hoped that as you and Violet were so near each other in age you might become friends and Vi might help you towards becoming a teacher. Did something happen that upset you? Did anyone say anything?'

Lottie was aware of the colour mounting in her cheeks. 'It was nothing, Miss Carson. Everyone was very nice to me. I behaved badly and I felt ashamed, and I'd like to say that I am very sorry. It was just that,' she paused, 'somehow I felt out of place. Your life is so different from mine. I have never been to a house like that with a tennis court and a maid. You have never been to my house or met my father and, well, I just felt unprepared and overwhelmed by it all, by the contrast, that's all . . .' She faltered, feeling as awkward now and almost as tongue-tied as she had the previous day.

'I really am sorry about that, Lottie. It never occurred to me and the reason is that I believe all people are equal whatever their circumstances, and as far as I am concerned you and your family are no different from mine. The fact that we live in a large house . . . well . . .' Now it was her turn to falter, as if she was aware of the contradictions in what she was saying and what a great gulf did in fact divide them socially.

'By the way,' she said, taking some sheets of paper out of another folder. 'I have found some of the stories by Katherine Mansfield – you remember we talked about her – and I thought you might like to read them.'

'That's very kind of you, Miss Carson.'

'And write some of your own, perhaps? You write some nice little pieces for the school magazine. One day, when you've time, because I'm sure you have the ability, you could write something more substantial, but at the moment you must concentrate on your studies. I am very anxious for you to do well, Lottie, and justify the faith I have in you.'

'Yes, miss,' Lottie said as Miss Carson handed her the exercise book with her essay in it.

'Work a bit more on Hardy's characters next term and not so

much on the countryside around them, however beautiful it may be. Oh, and Happy Christmas, Lottie.'

'And to you, Miss Carson.'

'And don't work too hard. Try to have some fun and rest.'

And Miss Carson bent her head to the task in front of her as if in an attitude of dismissal.

Three

1922

Fun and rest were not exactly in Lottie's mind during the long Christmas holiday. She was offered full-time work at the department store to help them cope with the seasonal rush. It was a busy, popular, fashionable store in the heart of Wellington and she enjoyed her work there, although it was largely behind the scenes, fetching and carrying goods as they were required, to fulfill orders. Kirkcaldies attracted a good class of clientele, the wealthy folk from Wellington and its prosperous suburbs, and it had a noted tea room where people both liked to meet and, especially, be seen.

It was also a change from her drab daily existence, her fraught, mundane home life, and she made a point of getting there early and leaving late, which drew frequent praise from her superiors. As well as her time-keeping, Lottie found favour for her good looks, which attracted customers, appropriate dress sense, obedience, courtesy and generally obliging behaviour, always willing to please. At Christmas she was invited to choose a new dress at a large discount, which she was able to afford from the money she was earning.

However, the more time she spent at Kirkcaldies the less time she had for study, and success in her exams was essential if she were to fulfill the expectations Miss Carson had for her.

Early in the new year Lottie was coming down the stairs after her break to return to the haberdashery department when she heard a voice behind calling her and turned around. Close behind her was a stylish-looking young woman she couldn't immediately identify. She was dressed in a fashionably bright floral print frock; over one arm was a white handbag and she carried several shopping bags with the store's logo on them.

'You don't recognize me, do you, Lottie?' the young woman said with a smile. 'I'm Vi, Madeleine's sister.'

'Oh, dear, of course.' Lottie felt embarrassed and knew she looked it.

'It's the unfamiliar surroundings,' Violet said cheerfully. 'Last time I was in my tennis gear. How very nice to see you. Have you time for a cup of tea upstairs?'

'I'd love to,' Lottie said, rather overpowered by this dazzling, composed young woman she had last seen red-faced, hot and perspiring after a game of tennis. 'But I'm afraid I can't. You see, I've just had my break and I work here.'

'Oh,' Violet sounded surprised, 'do you?'

'Only for the holiday. But during term time I work here on Saturdays.'

'That must be so interesting. Look, we so enjoyed meeting you and I'm afraid we didn't give you a proper welcome – you left so early, and we'd love you to come to tea again. Madeleine wants me to enthuse you about teaching although I'm not sure I am very good at it, but she was very keen for me to try. What time do you leave work today?'

'*Today?*' Lottie faltered. 'Today I leave just after lunch. About two o'clock.'

'Look, come back with me. It's a gorgeous day. I'll hang around town and pick you up. I've lots to do. Oh, please say yes.'

Violet's enthusiasm was infectious. However, Lottie remembered her mother's warning – or was it a command? – not to go to tea again, but now it didn't seem to matter. She was seized by a mood of recklessness and her eyes glowed. The vision of that lovely house, the lawn with the pool and tennis court and those beautiful people was so compelling. She knew that she would love to live like them, to be more like the Carsons; that deep down it was an enviable way of life and one to which she aspired, leaving Broadway Terrace and its world far behind.

Sensing her change of mood, Violet said again, '*Go on.* It's such a lovely day.'

'All right,' Lottie said. 'Won't your mother mind?'

'Of course she won't mind. She'll be delighted. We all will. I'll pick you up outside. Two o'clock, say?'

'Two o'clock, then,' Lottie said, still rather bewildered and a little afraid about what she'd done. 'I really must dash or I'll get into trouble.'

The parcels she'd seen from Kirkcaldies were piled along with many others on the back seat of Violet's car when she arrived to pick Lottie up.

'I'm a compulsive shopper,' Violet said, glancing at her guiltily. 'Are you?'

'Not really,' Lottie replied. 'I don't have the money. But I bought this dress from the store before Christmas. They give staff a discount.' She looked down at the attractive gingham print she had changed into with a sense of pride and also gratitude that she happened to be wearing it on a day she was unexpectedly invited to tea with the Carsons. Maybe away from her school uniform she would have more confidence.

'It's very pretty,' Violet said.

The hood of the sporty little car was down as Vi headed away from the town towards the bay.

'Do you each have your own car?' Lottie asked.

'Yes,' Violet replied, glancing at her, and then, as if realizing it accentuated the gap between them, decided to keep her eyes firmly on the road. The wind blew in their faces anyway, making it difficult to talk, but they were soon slowing down as they approached the house and Violet turned into the drive where two other cars were parked. 'Oh, you might meet Madeleine's boyfriend,' Violet said suddenly. 'I think that's his car.'

Miss Carson had a boyfriend? The idea seemed both surprising and somehow a little shocking. Lottie began to feel nervous again and started to regret her rashness in accepting the invitation.

'He's very nice,' Violet said reassuringly. 'We think there may soon be an engagement.'

'What does he do?'

'He's in the army. I think he's on leave. His name's Andrew.'

Violet stopped the car and Lottie got out, scooped up some of the parcels and climbed the steps to the porch. Violet pushed open the door and called out when she got inside: 'Anyone at home?' When there was no reply she said, 'They must be in the garden. Andrew is keen on tennis.'

Lottie now felt very apprehensive about meeting Miss Carson's boyfriend. This was something entirely unexpected. It was as though she was seeing her teacher in a new and rather unwelcome light.

They put the parcels down in the hall and walked towards the open doors at the end. In front of them was the green expanse of lawn, but there were no players on the tennis courts, just two deck chairs by the pond with their backs to the house, linked by two arms, hands entwined.

'It's Andrew,' Violet whispered excitedly.

'Maybe we shouldn't disturb them. Perhaps I should go home?'

'Don't be silly. Madeleine would be furious if you went away. Hullo,' she called, and simultaneously two faces appeared around the sides of the chairs, their hands falling apart.

'Why,' Miss Carson got up from her chair, shielding her eyes from the bright sunlight, 'it's Lottie! *How nice*.'

As she came towards Lottie, a welcoming smile on her face, the man in the other chair slowly rose to his feet.

'Where did you find her, Vi?'

'At Kirkcaldies,' Violet said.

'And were you shopping there too, Lottie?'

'I work there, Miss Carson, during the holiday.'

'She also has a Saturday job. I think that's very enterprising,' Violet added tactfully, realizing she may have made a blunder.

'Ah.' The smile on Miss Carson's face was replaced by a slight frown, but she said nothing and turned to the man standing in the background. 'Lottie, this is a friend of mine, Captain Marsden. Andy, Lottie is one of my pupils from school, one of my *best* pupils, I should say.'

'How do you do, Lottie?' Captain Marsden said, coming forward and shaking her hand.

He was of medium height, dark-haired with a muscular frame and a firm handshake, not strictly good looking in the way Miss Carson's brother was. Like Madeleine, he was in whites and tennis racquets lay on the grass by the side of the chairs.

'How do you do, Captain?' Lottie said politely.

'You must call me Andy,' the captain said, smiling, and Lottie cast a doubtful look at Miss Carson, who nodded.

'And at home I'm Madeleine,' Miss Carson said, but Lottie didn't think she would ever get used to calling her by her Christian name. From now on she would probably not call her anything.

They strolled towards the pond and Andy put up two more deck chairs, indicating that Lottie should take one.

'Mummy's out playing bridge,' Miss Carson said. 'We were just relaxing. We had a very strenuous game.' On the table in front of them was a half-empty jug of squash and two glasses. 'Andy has to go back to camp this evening.'

'Then we should leave you alone,' Violet said.

Miss Carson shook her head firmly. 'Not at all. We've seen loads of each other, haven't we, Andy?' Miss Carson playfully took his hand and he held on to it while Lottie felt embarrassed as though, yet again, she was an intruder who had no place here.

'I wouldn't mind going on with the tennis,' Andy said. 'Do you play, Lottie?'

'She's very good,' Miss Carson said. 'She's good at everything.'

Violet jumped up. 'Let's do that. Let's knock a ball about and then have tea.'

'I'm not really dressed for tennis,' Lottie said awkwardly. Nor did she want to get her new, one good dress dirty.

'Neither am I. I've got a spare tennis dress you can wear – and shoes, if they fit.' Violet glanced at Lottie's feet. 'Come on.' She reached out for her hand. 'Let's race inside and change. It will be fun.'

Fun was something to which Lottie was unaccustomed. Suddenly it was as though her spirits had lifted, and the reluctance and awkwardness vanished as she ran across the lawn hand in hand with Violet. They flew up the stairs to her bedroom, which seemed almost as large as the whole house. It was flooded with sun and the windows overlooked the lawn. While Violet rummaged through her wardrobe for a suitable dress Lottie glanced out of the window. Miss Carson and Andy were locked in a deep embrace, their arms wrapped around each other, bodies close together, almost as one. Her eyes riveted; she felt like a peeping tom but was unable to look away.

Violet came up to Lottie, holding the dress against her as though measuring it for size, then following her gaze she saw the couple on the lawn.

'They are so in love.' She sighed. 'He's nice, don't you think?'

'He *seems* nice,' Lottie said guardedly. 'I can't really say, having known him for only a few minutes.'

Violet held the white dress against her. 'Try it on,' she said. 'Go on, I won't look.'

The dress fitted and so did the shoes and, feeling magically transformed by this change in apparel, Lottie flew down the stairs after Violet and through the hall to the lawn, where Andy was expertly swinging a racquet which he handed to Lottie. 'See if this is all right. It's one of Madeleine's.'

Lottie took the racquet and balanced it carefully between her hands, doing one or two imaginary shots.

'It's fine,' she said, smiling at him and, satisfied, the four trooped on to the court, Violet and Lottie versus Andy and Madeleine, and started knocking up. Lottie hadn't played for a while but the old feeling of self-assurance and confidence returned as she got into her stride. It was a lovely day with a soft breeze coming in from the sea, and she surprised herself by feeling so much at home in this company. What a contrast to her last visit when she was so gauche and awkward.

After winning the toss she elected to serve first, overcoming her nerves to knock the ball hard on to the base line of the opposite court. Andy, trying to retrieve the shot, sent it out of control high into the air and he and Madeleine only took one point, Lottie and Violet winning the first game with ease. They then went on to win the set and, hot and tired, left the court to refresh themselves with squash waiting for them on the table, brought out by the maid while they were playing.

'I really didn't know you were so good,' Andy said admiringly to Lottie. 'Otherwise I wouldn't have suggested a game.'

Sensitive to being patronized, Lottie retorted: 'I think you let us win.'

'You mean no one would deliberately play that badly.' He laughed and glanced at Madeleine. 'Not at all. We didn't let her win, did we, darling?'

'No,' she said, smiling approvingly at her protégée. 'I told you she was good.'

'Violet is very good,' Lottie said firmly. 'I enjoyed it. Another game?'

'Why not?'

They got up and played another set which the two girls won again, cementing Lottie's suspicions that the older couple were letting them win. Never mind – it was good fun.

Just as they finished, as if on cue, the maid emerged with tea, dainty cakes and sandwiches. Lottie, completely relaxed, wondered at the ease with which the family were now absorbing her into themselves, making her feel at home and one of them, and how she wished she was. It was a lifestyle that would have suited her and, as she drank squash and ate the delicious little cakes, she stretched back in her chair gazing around at the beautiful house – which had not only one indoor bathroom but two, the manicured lawn with its pool and tennis court, and decided that this indeed gave her a goal, something to aim for. But in order to achieve this she must better herself as Miss Carson had said by studying hard and moving into the professions. In a way, though she did not know it yet, it was one of the turning points in her life, a moment of illumination to which she would return in the years ahead.

Suddenly Madeleine interrupted her reverie, saying mysteriously, 'We have some news,' as she looked at the man beside her. 'Andy has asked me to marry him. We are engaged.'

'Oh, Maddy!' Violet jumped up and embraced first her sister and then Andy, while Lottie shyly hung back. Her first thought was how it might affect her life, losing perhaps her teacher, her champion. Besides, she had a poor opinion of marriage. The example provided by her parents was not a happy one.

As Madeleine looked over at her she said: 'I'm very happy for you. But I don't want to lose you, Miss Carson.'

'Oh, you won't *lose* me,' Madeleine said. 'We are not getting married at least for a year and then, well . . . we'll see what happens, but you will be very well looked after by the school, whatever happens to me.'

'Do Mum and Dad know?' Violet asked.

'No, you are the very first.'

'I just asked her,' Andy said, taking Madeleine's hand, 'and I can't believe my luck.'

'You have to ask Daddy,' Madeleine said teasingly. 'He might say "no".'

'Then what would you say?' Her new fiancé looked at her adoringly.

'I'd say, "Daddy, you are an idiot" and promptly leave home. But all this is academic. I know Daddy likes you and would approve of you as a son-in-law.'

'I should really get home.' Lottie had begun to feel uncomfortable.

This was an intimate part of their family life from which she now definitely felt excluded. She was no longer part of them – the dream had been broken. Time to retreat. 'It has been a wonderful day and thank you very much.'

'I'll take you home,' Madeleine said briskly. 'Mummy should be home soon and I must be here to tell her.'

'Then let me take her,' Andy suggested, but Madeleine shook her head.

'I want a word with Lottie. Run off and change, Lottie.'

Lottie ran up to the bedroom and was followed by Violet, who was still flushed with excitement. 'Isn't it *thrilling* about Madeleine and Andy? I told you they were in love. He must have proposed as they were kissing. Imagine that! We actually saw it happen. The very moment.'

Lottie smiled as she shrugged herself out of her whites and into her dress.

'Are you really worried about losing Madeleine?'

'Not really,' Lottie said, glancing at herself in the mirror and brushing back her hair.

'Nothing will change,' Violet said. 'You are our friend and will always be welcome here. Always. And look, one day I'm going to take you to the college and show you around. Really. Your enthusiasm might inspire me.'

'That would be nice,' Lottie said, 'but I thought you were the one who was supposed to inspire me!'

Both girls burst out laughing and Lottie at that moment felt closer to her new, slightly scatty, friend than ever.

'I must hurry,' she went on when the laughter had subsided, 'or Miss Carson will be cross.' She still couldn't call her Madeleine.

'Oh, she won't be cross, not today, not with anyone. She is too much in love. Look, you go on. I'm going to have a bath. I'll see you very soon,' and she gave Lottie a fleeting peck on the cheek. 'Tennis again, maybe next week?'

'We'll see,' Lottie said, and with a wave went downstairs to find Miss Carson and her fiancé standing together on the steps, hand in hand.

'Here I am,' she called. 'Violet is having a bath. I hate to take you away,' she said to Madeleine. 'I can easily get a bus.'

'Nonsense! Get into the car.'

With a smile to Andy, Lottie did as she was told and Madeleine got in beside her, putting the car into gear and smartly reversing, waving to Andy before they turned into the road.

'The captain is a very nice man,' Lottie said shyly, following Madeleine's gaze.

'I'm glad you like him.' Madeleine glanced at her. 'I haven't known him all that long, only since the winter. We met at a dance and it was, well, love at first sight, I suppose, for me anyway. He is lovely and generous and kind, and my parents like him and I love his parents, so I couldn't do better.'

Miss Carson slowed down the car and then stopped at the end of the next road and when she spoke the tone of her voice had changed from that of a woman in love to schoolmistressy again. 'However, Lottie, I did want to have a private word with you. I am very disappointed that you feel you have to work. I told you at the end of term that you were looking very tired and now I know why. When your mother and I talked about you staying on I never thought this would happen. I am very ambitious for you, you know, Lottie, and with good reason. But if you wear yourself out at the store and helping at home, as you know you do, you won't get the grades you need to go to college. I would like to have a word with your mother about it.'

'Oh, please, not now,' Lottie begged. 'I am already late home and Mum doesn't know where I've been. She will already be cross with me and, well . . . I have to work, Miss Carson. I feel I owe it to my mother to help as much as I can. You know my father can't work. Bella is better now at housework and Jack occasionally does errands. I promise I won't let it affect my work. I promise.'

'Well,' Miss Carson started the car and turned towards the town, 'I hope you're right because I see a brilliant future ahead of you. Maybe even university if you continue getting the grades you are now.'

Lottie remained silent, already nervous about the reception she might get at home. 'Do you mind stopping at the end of the road, Miss Carson? I don't want Mum to know where I've been.'

'But why not?'

'Just because I didn't tell her and she'll be angry. You don't know my mum when she's angry.'

'Oh, I think I can imagine it,' Miss Carson said with a grim smile. 'I do hope you won't get into trouble?'

'I'll think of something,' Lottie said as the car stopped by the side of the pavement. She looked at the anxious face turned to her and then impulsively kissed Miss Carson on the cheek. 'Thanks ever so much and really I am very, very happy for you, very happy. You and the captain are very well suited.'

'Why, thank you . . .' Miss Carson looked pleased and surprised by this unexpected and untypical gesture, and put a hand on her cheek. But Lottie, without another word or a backward glance, got out of the car, shut the door and sped along the street. She slowed down as she came to the house and apprehensively opened the front door.

Inside, as she expected, her mother greeted her with an ominous frown, taking an obvious and protracted glance at the clock on the mantelpiece. 'Do you know what the time is, Charlotte?' Lottie steeled herself. Her mother always called her by her full name when she was about to administer a reprimand. 'It's nearly seven. Where have you been? Wasn't it your half day? I expected you home hours ago. I had a lot of jobs lined up for you. I wouldn't have minded a little time off myself but, as usual, you are too selfish to think of me. Besides, I was very worried. Your father was worried.' Ada turned to the man sitting in his corner, who was looking at her with an uncharacteristically reproachful expression.

'Sorry, Mum. I met someone I know.'

'Who?'

'Someone.' Lottie faltered.

'You aren't meeting a *boy*, are you, Charlotte?'

'No, Mum, of course not.' Lottie coloured at the very idea.

'Who, then?'

'It was Miss Carson's sister, Violet. She came to the store and, well . . . she invited me to go home with her.'

'You went back to Miss Carson's *house*?' Ada's voice rose by an octave.

'Yes, Mum. I did.'

'And you never thought to say anything to me or think that I'd be worried? That your father would be worried?'

'I should have, but I didn't. I am sorry, Mum.'

'Sorry is not good enough, Charlotte.'

'No.' Lottie hung her head.

'You went back to a place you swore you never wanted to go to again because they made you feel inferior and you didn't fit in?'

'Yes, but I like Violet. She has offered to show me around the teacher's training college, where I may go one day. She's studying there which was why Miss Carson was anxious for me to meet her. Mum, I am sorry I upset you and it was selfish.'

'And was Miss Carson there?'

'Yes. She had just got engaged and her fiancé was there with her. A very nice man, a captain in the army.'

'And what did Miss Carson say when you just turned up?'

'She was very nice. So was the captain. We played tennis. It was nice. I really enjoyed myself.' A note of defiance entered Lottie's voice.

The idea seemed to enrage Ada more and she advanced towards her daughter, her expression even more forbidding. 'Charlotte, I thought we decided, *you* decided, that you would never go to Miss Carson's house again. You said you didn't fit in and your last visit made you very unhappy.'

'I know. But this time it was better. I felt happy there. They are very kind to me and it is a very nice, happy place. Much happier than here!' she burst out. 'Much, *much* happier.'

The blow across her face was as painful as it was unexpected and she reeled back, raising an arm to protect herself. But it was followed by another and she staggered against the wall.

'Much, much nicer!' she shouted between blows. 'Much nicer and happier. My, how I wished I lived there!'

With that she staggered out of the sitting room and ran upstairs to her bedroom, where she threw herself on the bed in a torrent of weeping.

Sometime later the door opened and Bella crept in and sat by her side, putting a hand on her shoulder and patting it.

Drying her eyes, Lottie sat up and put an arm round her sister, laying her head against her chest. 'I hate it here,' she said. 'I don't think I can go on living here.'

'Mum is very sorry. Dad actually told her off.'

'She has never hit me before. Never.'

'She said she didn't know what got into her. I never saw Dad so angry with Mum and it surprised her.'

Lottie continued dabbing at her eyes with a handkerchief and then blew her nose hard. 'I would leave here if it wasn't for you and Dad. I hate Mum and I know she hates me. I was silly today, but she's always picking on me and I can't stand much more of it.'

'Where would you go?'

'I don't know, but I'd find somewhere. I'd leave school and see if I could get a full-time job at the store. But I can't leave you and Dad and Jack with her.'

'I don't want you to leave either, Lottie.' Now it was Bella's turn to wail. But Bella was very good at wailing and did it a lot, whereas Lottie never cried and tried very hard to conceal her emotions.

'Don't worry, I won't.' She lay lengthways on the bed and pulled Bella down beside her. 'I will never leave you. Never. It is all a dream.'

Her arms tightly wrapped around her little sister, she closed her eyes and thought of the large, gracious house and the sunshine which seemed to sweep across the lawn dappling the pool, and the tennis court and how very, very different life could be – and would be, one day, she promised herself.

Ada, noticing the severity of her expression, faced Miss Carson across the table in the visitors' room. She had been summoned to a meeting a few days before the beginning of the Easter term and was asked once again not to say anything to Lottie. Ada had again donned her best hat for the occasion, though in a concession to the weather, which was still unbearably hot, she hadn't worn a coat. Despite the open windows no breeze disturbed the air in the stuffy little room.

'I'll come straight to the point, Mrs O'Brien,' Madeleine said. 'I'm very surprised and distressed to hear that Lottie has been working full time at Kirkcaldies, and also has a job there on a Saturday during the school term.'

'Well, what's wrong with that?' Gazing at her defiantly, Ada knew that Miss Carson didn't like her and the feeling was mutual.

'I thought last term that Lottie was looking extremely tired. Despite that she got excellent exam results, but it must take its toll on her. She didn't tell me she also had a job and I really feel let down, not by her but by you, Mrs O'Brien.'

'In what way do you feel let down, Miss Carson?' Ada asked, steely-voiced.

'The reason I arranged for you to have an allowance was so that Lottie would be able to concentrate on her studies. I know she helps out in the house – does the bulk of the housework, in fact – and with a full-time job or even a weekend job that will certainly eventually have an effect on her studies.'

'And what are you going to do about it?' Ada's tone grew noticeably more belligerent.

'I would like her to give up the job, which was the idea behind providing you with this subsidy.'

'It is only on a Saturday during term. She took the full-time job just for the holiday. I see no harm in that, nor does it give you any right to interfere. If you continue to object I will take Charlotte away before she goes on to the higher grade as she is now sixteen and fully capable of earning her own living. Anyway, I feel this is a matter for the school which gives me the allowance and in my opinion the headmistress should be talking to me, not you. What exactly is your interest in Lottie, Miss Carson?'

Miss Carson flushed and paused imperceptibly before replying, 'My *sole* interest in Lottie, Mrs O'Brien, is her welfare and helping to realize her academic potential.'

'Do you invite all your students to your house, Miss Carson, and play tennis with them?'

Miss Carson's flush deepened. 'I do invite the occasional student, yes, since you ask. But my younger sister Violet is at the Teacher Training College and I thought that she and Lottie might get on. They are close in age and, in fact, they do.'

'I really don't see any need for inviting her to your house. It is making her dissatisfied and discontented with her home and she has become much more difficult during this holiday. She told me, in fact, that she didn't fit in, didn't feel at home with you and that you were all very self-satisfied.' Ada adjusted the brim of her hat and got up. 'You see, it is doing Charlotte no good at all, Miss Carson. We are a very ordinary, working-class family who have difficulty making ends meet. My husband is an invalid as a result of the war and sits in a chair coughing his heart out all day, receiving a small pension and the occasional handouts from benevolent funds for ex-soldiers. I work all the hours God sends and the last thing I want is a daughter who is given false ideas about her expectations by people she has nothing in common with, will never be able to imitate and feels uncomfortable with. In other words, Miss Carson, I'll thank you to mind your own business and we will mind ours.'

Almost choking on her words, feeling perhaps that she had gone too far, Ada turned her back on the teacher and made for the door without saying goodbye, leaving a thoughtful, humiliated and much-chastened woman behind.

Four

In the course of the following term Miss Carson kept an eye on her protégée, but after the visit from Ada, and as much as she regretted it, she decided that any more intimate form of communication must stop and their relationship must be strictly that of pupil and teacher. No more home visits. She was afraid that if she ignored Ada's warning Lottie would be withdrawn from the school altogether.

Maybe Lottie appreciated it, too. If she regretted the end of visits to the magical house in Thorndon, the stimulation of thoughts of a better way of life, she understood the reason for it, having had a graphic account from her mother of her meeting with the teacher.

But not only did her relationship with Miss Carson change, the one with her mother changed too and deteriorated even further. It was as if Ada had cemented her hostility to her daughter, no longer trusted her and was suspicious of everything she did. She would cross-examine her constantly about the people she was seeing and asked her repeatedly if she had seen Miss Carson's sister, to which Lottie was truthfully able to reply that she had not. There was continual fault-picking all the time until Lottie dreaded going home each day, uncertain what she would encounter. Spurred on by that dream of a golden future, however, she was determined throughout all this time that her work would not suffer, sometimes working through the night to deliver an essay for the following day.

Towards the end of term Lottie and Bella got home one day to find that there was no familiar figure of their father sitting in his corner, eager to welcome them to relieve the boredom of his existence. This worried Lottie immediately, as of late his fits of coughing had repeatedly woken her during the night.

'Where's Dad?' Bella exclaimed.

Lottie shrugged, but she was worried. Their father seldom, if ever, went out and as time passed and their mother didn't turn up with Jack her anxiety increased.

She and Bella went up to change out of their school uniforms and when she came down she began to get tea, anxious not to have another rebuke when her mother returned.

She was still in the kitchen when she heard the front door open and she hurried out to find her mother, clearly out of breath, taking off her coat, Jack cowering by her side.

'Where's Dad, Mum?'

'Your father's in the hospital. He had a bad coughing attack just as I was leaving this morning, couldn't get his breath, so I had to run to the doctor who came and called the ambulance. I can't tell you what a bother this was and Mrs Ellis was at first angry with me for being late. Just like your father to be so inconsiderate. I went back to the hospital and all he had was an asthma attack. They will let him out tomorrow.'

She threw her hat angrily on the table, even shouted at her precious Jack, cuffing him lightly on the ear, and sent him up to change. All the indications were, Lottie knew, that they were all in for a very bad evening. 'Is the tea ready yet, Lottie?'

'Yes, Mum.'

'Well, that's something, I suppose.'

Ada sat down, her eyes fixed on the empty seat in the corner. 'I can't tell you what a worry your father is. It is no life for me. Sometimes I don't get any sleep. He does nothing to help himself, but sits slumped in that blasted chair all day while we wait on him hand and foot. The war is over now and he is lucky to be alive. No one asked him to go, so he has only himself to blame. I wish there was some home he could go to permanently and then we'd all have a bit of peace.'

'Oh, Mum!'

'Oh, I know you always defend your father.' Ada's resentment hardened. 'You never think about me, do you, Lottie? You take after him, selfish to the core. You defend him and he defends you. You deserve each other. Mrs Ellis doesn't know how I put up with it. After I explained today why I was late she was very kind to me. Made me sit down and gave me a cup of tea.'

And then to Lottie's dismay and astonishment Ada put her head in her hands and her shoulders shook in a violent spasm of weeping.

Lottie had never seen her mother cry and didn't know what to do. She stood gaping at her for a moment and then, stooping, very gently put a hand on her shoulder.

'There, Mum, please.'

Ada seized her hand and crushed it in hers, looking up at her daughter with tears still streaming down her face.

'You don't understand, do you, Lottie? You think I'm cruel. But you don't know how much I have suffered since your father went off to war. Fancy leaving me with three children, one scarcely a baby, and little means of support, reading daily about all the fatalities our forces were suffering and wondering if he would be killed. Then, when he came back, he had completely changed from the man I married. Oh, you should have seen him when he was young. He was so good looking, dashing and vital. Unlike anyone I had ever met before. My parents bitterly opposed me marrying him as he had a menial job as a driver, and my father had a good position as a store manager, a position of authority, but Desmond told me his prospects were good and he had a bright future, maybe one day owning a fleet of trucks like the people he worked for.' She paused and sighed wistfully. 'Those early days were so good and *happy*. I was only eighteen – seventeen when I met him so had no chance to make a career for myself. I was headstrong – a bit like you, Lottie, which is maybe where you get it from. I always thought I knew best. After I ran off with Des my parents would have nothing to do with me and when I tried to contact them during the war they sent me away and said I deserved all I got, even having no interest in their grandchildren. You didn't know that, did you, Lottie?'

'No, Mum.' Lottie, still holding her mother's hand, drew up a chair from the table and sat by her side.

'You see, I've protected you from all these things. I have been so lonely and alone.' Ada started weeping again and Lottie, still shocked and unprepared for this show of emotion, continued to make soothing noises and cling on to her mother's hand.

'Mum, I will do all I can.'

'What more can you do?'

'I could leave school and take a job. Make things easier for you.'

'Oh.' Ada appeared to consider this and then slowly shook her head. 'No, no. I will continue to make sacrifices for you. If you get a good education and a better job as Miss Carson said you will, we will all benefit. No.' She patted Lottie's hand and managed a bleak smile. 'You must go on at school and I will do my best to support the family and cope with your father. How, I don't know, but I will.'

Ada stood up and ran a hand over her face, smudging her tears. 'Now go and get those children who I suspect have been lurking upstairs listening to all this, and let's have our tea.' She looked apprais-ingly at her daughter. 'You're a good girl at times, Lottie, but a difficult one. Sometimes I feel I don't understand you and I do wonder what will happen to you. I only hope your life won't be like that of mine and your father's, full of disappointments and broken promises.'

Lottie dropped her mother's hand with the feeling that, despite this display of emotion, nothing would ever really change.

During the Easter holiday Lottie resumed her job with Kirkcaldies, who were beginning to value her as a potential permanent employee. She was eminently presentable, eager and quick to learn and the possibility was suggested that, if all went well, work on the serving counter with direct access to the public might be a possibility in the winter.

Lottie enjoyed getting out of the house, now even more so because it took her away from the situation at home which, if anything, had deteriorated since her father's return from hospital. Her mother kept on telling him what a burden he was and how suitable it would be if he could stay in hospital, or some similar institution, permanently. For a man of only thirty-seven, even the suggestion was like a life sentence.

Leaving the store early one Saturday afternoon and making her way along Lambton Quay, Lottie was hailed by a familiar voice and, stopping, saw coming along the street behind her Violet Carson with the usual collection of bags and parcels in both arms. She paused and smiled. 'Lottie, how lovely to bump into you again like this. How are you?'

'Very well,' Lottie said.

'What are you doing here?'

'Going home from work.'

'Back at Kirkcaldies?'

'Yes, for the holiday.'

Violet looked at her solemnly. 'I don't suppose I can persuade you to come home with me?'

'I'm afraid not. My mother . . .'

'Yes, Madeleine told me. I am sorry, but we still can be friends, can't we?'

'Of course.'

'Look, I've got my car. It's such a lovely day. Why don't we drive along to Petone Beach? We can just chat. That's all right, isn't it?'

'Well . . .' Lottie looked doubtful. 'I should get home.' Then, 'Just an hour, maybe.'

'Good. My car's just along there.' Violet pointed to Brandon Street that ran alongside Kirkcaldies, going towards the harbour. Feeling guilty that she was doing something she shouldn't, but nevertheless with a sense of excitement, Lottie climbed in beside Violet, who headed the car along the coast road in the direction of Petone Beach.

'We often go there to swim. Do you swim?' Violet shouted.

Lottie shook her head. It was difficult to hear with the roof of the car down and the sea breeze blowing strongly in their faces, so she didn't reply but remained immersed in her thoughts, which again were of envy at the disparity between her lifestyle and that of Violet, only too apparent. She never swam and could not recall a day out which was given to sheer enjoyment, so bogged down was she by the dreary routine of her daily life.

They came in sight of the beach where there were already swimmers in the water, and after Violet parked the car they sat for a few minutes looking at the scene, the long beach surrounded by hills overlooking the harbour. Violet reached into the back of the car for a sun hat and offered it to Lottie, who shook her head.

'No, thanks, I'm OK. I love the feel of the sun on my face.' She flung back her head and looked up at the clear blue sky. 'Thank you so much, Vi, for bringing me here. What luck we bumped into each other.'

Violet looked pleased. 'Shall we have a walk along the beach?' They got out of the car and started to stroll along the shore.

Impulsively Violet tucked her arm through Lottie's, who felt a warmth, a kinship emanating from the older girl and pressed her arm in response.

'How have you been, Lottie? We've really missed you. I haven't even had the chance to show you round the college, though I must say I prefer shopping to study, which makes my sister very cross. How is your father? Madeleine said you told her he had spent a few days in hospital. Very worrying for you.'

'It *was* very worrying. Dad has chronic problems with his lungs on account of his experiences in the war. He is frequently breathless.'

'I wonder if he would like to see my father? He's a chest specialist.'

Lottie stopped and looked at her. 'That would be wonderful, if it could be arranged.'

'I'll arrange it. Don't worry. Maybe it will bring your mother round to letting you visit us again.' She peered at her closely. 'Why doesn't your mother like you coming to see us? Is it because Madeleine is your teacher?'

'I think she feels I will get ideas above my station,' Lottie said with a wry smile. 'Especially since the war, life has been hard for us and it has made my mother very bitter. She thinks I should be doing a job to make money and support the family and, in many ways, she is right. Your way of life is quite different from ours. We're not of the same class. The first time I came to see you I felt out of my depth, quite upset, in fact, and told my mum in a moment of weakness that I had felt I didn't belong. She said I shouldn't visit you again and I said I wouldn't. But the second time, when you took me home, I enjoyed myself but she was very angry I'd gone. I think she has had one or two upsetting scenes with Miss Carson and I'm very sorry about that because I like Miss Carson and she is very good to me, but she and Mum do not get on. Mum is very proud and doesn't like being patronized.'

'Maybe if Daddy can help your father she will relent?'

'It is kind of you to suggest it. But, you see, there is the problem of money.'

'You mean paying Daddy?'

'Yes.'

'Oh, that will not come into it. I would never have suggested it if you had to pay.'

'Then that will hurt my mother's pride again.'

'But surely she cares about your father?'

Lottie looked doubtful. 'Yes, I suppose she does.'

Excited for once and optimistic, Lottie opened the door without her usual feeling of dread and apprehension. The house was very quiet and in the sitting room she found, for a change, her mother half asleep in a chair, her legs stretched out before her while in his corner Desmond snoozed over the paper. His loud breathing was the only sound to break the silence in the room.

Lottie crept into the kitchen without disturbing them and emerged a few minutes later with a pot of tea, milk, cups and saucers – sounds which disturbed Ada, who stirred, rubbed her eyes and said, 'My goodness, what is this? Whatever is the time?'

'Time for a cup of tea, Mum,' Lottie said brightly, pouring the tea and handing her mother a cup.

'This is very nice,' Ada said, gratified. 'You got off early today?'

'It's my half day, Mum, and guess what?' She poured herself tea and sat down by her mother's side. 'I bumped into Violet Carson as I was leaving the store.'

'Oh.' The pleasant expression immediately vanished from her mother's face and she visibly stiffened.

'I didn't go back to the house, Mum, but we did have a talk and she asked how Dad was and – what do you think? Her father is a chest specialist and she offered to arrange for him to see Dad.'

Almost on cue Desmond woke up, half taking in that the conversation was about him.

'And how much do you think that will cost?' Ada snorted.

'She said it won't cost anything.'

'There we go again.' Ada thumped her empty cup down on the table. 'Being patronized by the wealthy Carsons. I don't know what they've done to you, Lottie. Bewitched you, if you ask me. Have you no pride? If you haven't, I have. No thank you. We don't want handouts from them.'

'But Ada,' Desmond intervened in a weak voice. 'If it enabled me to go back to work . . .'

'Have you no pride either, Desmond O'Brien? If you got out of that chair and walked around a bit you would do yourself a world of good. Instead you are slumped there all day, nose in the paper while I slave all the hours God sends.' She stood up and shook her hand threateningly at him. 'I tell you I am heartily sick of it. Sick of you all. I'd like to leave you all to it and see how you get on then. Maybe then you'll get off your backside, Desmond, and start thinking about others.'

'Mum, I don't know how you can talk to Dad like that,'

Lottie said, outraged. 'You know he is a very sick man. The hospital said so.'

'And then what did the hospital do about it? Nothing. What did they do for an ex-serviceman? Nothing. Your father signed his own death warrant when he volunteered to go overseas and fight for a country he didn't know and which the majority of Irish people don't even *like*. Hate, in fact.'

'That was the Catholics.' Desmond gasped. 'We were Irish Protestants, part of England.'

'No, you were a *New Zealander*, Desmond O'Brien, born and bred. Your place was here, doing a good job as you had before the war when we were all happy and well looked after, when I didn't have to work my fingers to the bone and we all had enough to eat!'

And with that Ada stomped out of the room, banging the door behind her.

Desmond slumped back in his chair gasping, anxious and solicitous. Worried but also angry with her mother, Lottie poured him a cup of tea and brought it over to him.

'There, Dad. Don't get so upset. I wish I'd never mentioned it but it seemed such a wonderful opportunity to see a specialist privately. I might have known Mum would react like this. I told Violet Carson as much, but then she said that if Mum cared about you . . .'

'Your mother cares nothing about me, Lottie. You know that. I think she wishes I had been killed in the war and then it is true you would all be a lot better off.'

Bella, as usual, was waiting for Lottie as she emerged from the classroom after school during the first week of the Easter term. Lottie thought it was high time that Bella found her own way home and her sister's dependence grated on her. Sometimes she would have liked to stay on at school to work quietly in the library, away from the tensions and frustrations caused by the atmosphere at home. Ever since her mother's outburst and tirade against her father her parents had not been speaking to each other. She had thought rows and angry outbursts were bad enough, but somehow this eerie silence was even worse and extended to her parents' bedroom as well. She wondered how they could bear sharing a bed, but with only three small bedrooms they had no alternative.

A girl of mixed emotions, highs and lows, Bella was in an

unusually cheerful mood. She had been selected for the school basketball team. Lottie, too, was happy with the way the day had gone, so they chatted happily as they walked along and then, running up the path, flung open the front door.

As usual, their father was in his chair but unusually not half asleep with the paper on his lap. Instead he rose from his chair to greet them and then when he saw them and the bright smiles on their faces sank back in his chair and, to their astonishment, began to weep.

Lottie threw down her school bag and hurried to his side. 'Dad, *whatever* is the matter? Are you not well?'

For a moment her father didn't reply as his shoulders shook with sobs. It was an unnerving sight. Bella also stood anxiously by Lottie's side, finger in her mouth like a little girl, happiness gone.

'Should I get some tea?' she ventured.

Lottie nodded and as Bella left the room she repeated her question to her father, gently shaking his shoulder, both in an effort to comfort him and to try and elicit the reason for this outburst. 'Dad? Dad?'

Finally he attempted to stem his tears and dabbed at his eyes with a grubby handkerchief. 'Your mother's gone,' he said, looking at her bleakly. 'Left us.'

'Gone, gone where?'

'She didn't say.' He started to cry again as the enormity of what her father was saying gradually dawned on Lottie. 'She didn't go to work this morning, didn't take Jack to school and I wondered what she was up to as she spent most of the morning upstairs. She said nothing. As you know, for days she has not said a word to me, so that was nothing unusual. But then, around noon, she came down carrying two suitcases with Jack and he had one too, and they were both dressed for going out.' Desmond's chest heaved again. 'And she stood there . . .' He pointed in front of him with a finger that shook. 'She stood there and said "I'm leaving you, Desmond. I'm sick of the sight of you, *and* the girls, especially Lottie, who I have no time for at all. They can look after you". And then without another word, before I had the chance to open my mouth, she took up the suitcases and left, pushing little Jack, who had started to cry in front of her, never even giving him the chance to kiss me goodbye.'

Suddenly fresh sobs rent the air and, turning, Lottie saw Bella sink on to a chair and start weeping, having first carefully put a tea tray down on the table. 'Oh, Mum,' she started wailing. 'How could Mum do this to us?'

Lottie, her emotions ranging from shock, bewilderment to downright anger, could think of no suitable reply, but put her arm round her sister's shoulder and hugged her tightly.

'Perhaps if I'd have been here Mum would have taken me too,' Bella continued in her dirge-like voice.

Lottie turned on her wrathfully. 'Bella, how could you say a thing like that?'

'Well, maybe she would. I don't want Mum to go. Nor Jack.'

'I'll miss Jack, too.' Lottie suddenly realized just how much she would miss her little brother and thought, with a pang of pain, of him being pushed out of the house without even being allowed to kiss his father goodbye. How could anyone *do* that to a child – any child, never mind one as vulnerable as Jack?

'She'll be back,' Lottie said confidently, but her father shook his head.

'I don't think she will. There was something so final about the way she left. You look upstairs.'

'Let's have some tea first,' Lottie said practically, and poured him a cup while Bella went on sniveling in the chair beside her. 'Mum must have said where she'd gone?' Lottie said, handing him his cup.

'Didn't say a word. Just what I told you.'

'I still think she'll be back.'

Lottie poured herself a cup of tea, gave one to Bella and when she had finished hers ran swiftly upstairs and into her parents' room.

There was an air about it that justified her father's verdict. It all looked different, as if she'd swept it clean of her personal belongings. But for someone who had lived there such a long time, surely there would be more bits and pieces left lying around? But nothing. Her mother had really had very few possessions. She wore the same clothes day after day and none were left in the wardrobe or in the chest of drawers. It seemed to show Lottie just how destitute her parents were. In fact, how, as a family, they all were, and she thought of the Carsons and the wardrobe stuffed with clothes, even some spare like the tennis dresses in Violet's bedroom.

It then occurred to Lottie, as she slowly made her way down the stairs, that as it was unlikely to have been a sudden decision, maybe her mother had been planning this for some time and had been sneaking a few things to wherever it was she had planned to escape. Was that the right word, 'escape'? Yes, it was. Her mother had done what she for so long had wanted to do: escape to freedom. Now Lottie was chained, seemingly forever, to looking after her father and younger sister.

Once more she railed inwardly about their circumstances and resolved, in her heart, to make a better life for herself one day, however long it took.

The thing now was to continue to behave as normally as possible. To make things easy for her father and Bella to help them all get over the crisis. As for herself, combined with her anger and resentment over her mother's behaviour was, strangely, a sense of relief. Could it be that things in the O'Brien household might actually improve?

The week following her mother's departure was a difficult one. Even her father seemed to miss the perpetual abuse and nagging he got day after day from his wife and Bella moped about like a lost soul and spent a lot of time weeping once they got home after school.

Lottie herself, despite her good resolution, found herself struggling. Without her mother's wage what was there to live on except the small war pension her father got and the pitiful amount of money she got from Kirkcaldies? She did all the washing, cleaning and cooking as Bella was absolutely useless and her father had never lifted a hand anyway. Naturally her school work was suffering and so was her sleep, and she spent wakeful nights agonizing about the future, which seemed in reality to be a hopeless fantasy.

Daily, Lottie expected to hear from her mother or to see her when they got home from school, but all she found was her father even more dejected than he had been, unwashed, unshaven, morose and gradually sinking into a deep depression.

Towards the end of the week Lottie got home after a particularly difficult day. Her most recent essay had failed to get her usual high marks and Miss Carson had solemnly asked her if anything was amiss, commenting too on her appearance, her tired face and the bags under her eyes. Lottie had shook her head, assuring her that everything was all right, but instead of staying to chat had left as soon as she could, saying that Bella was waiting for her. She knew from her expression that Miss Carson was unconvinced.

As usual, Lottie found her father slumped in his chair half asleep, as if he didn't sleep enough. She sent Bella up to change while she tidied up and then her eyes alighted on a letter on the table addressed to her mother. 'What's this?' she asked, showing her father the envelope, and he jerked his head up and stared at it.

'That will be the money. You had better open it. We need it.'

'But it is addressed to Mum. What money?'

'Well . . .' Her father sank back in his chair. 'Well, it was to be kept a secret from you. I don't know why, but as usual I did everything your mother said. When your mother wanted you to leave school the school arranged for a sum of money to help out. It is very little. Only a few pounds a week. Your mother always kept it and put it in her pocket and that's all I know about it.'

'How long has that been going on for?'

'Oh, some time. It was when your mum saw Miss Carson about you leaving school. But the money came from the school, from some fund, or that's what I understood.'

'The money came from the school to support me and encourage Mum to let me stay on? I don't believe it.'

'But it's true.' Her father pointed to the envelope. 'You look inside it. You'll find some money there – five pounds, I think it is. You just put it in your pocket and spend it on getting some decent food for us, a piece of meat or something substantial. Not that I feel like food.' He sank back against his chair, then looked up and put out his hand. 'I do feel for you, Lottie. But I don't really know how we are going to go on coping. I really don't. I am useless. With the best will in the world I can't see what the future holds or how we can exist and go on paying the rent for this house.'

Lottie said nothing but stood studying the writing on the envelope, which was familiar from all the notes and remarks that had peppered her essays. Then she slit open the envelope and, sure enough, drew out five crisp pound notes and a handwritten note.

> *Dear Mrs O'Brien,* it said, in Miss Carson's familiar, precise handwriting, *please find enclosed, as usual, five pounds.*
>
> *Yours sincerely,*
>
> *Madeleine Carson*

The last lesson was English and after the class ended and the pupils began to file out Miss Carson remained perched on her stool behind her high desk, a stack of books to mark in front of her.

Lottie lingered until the last one had left and then came up to the teacher, who looked at her with a smile. 'May I talk to you, Miss Carson?'

'Of course, Lottie.'

She got up from her desk and went to the front row, where she took a seat inviting Lottie to sit beside her.

'What is it, Lottie?'

Feeling awkward, embarrassed and less confident now, despite her resolution to be firm and strong, Lottie drew the envelope from her pocket and placed it on the desk in front of Miss Carson who looked at it, then at Lottie and said, 'Oh?'

'I don't understand this, Miss Carson. The school has been paying my mother to keep me here?'

Trying to choose her words carefully, Miss Carson said, 'Not exactly, Lottie. It was when your mother wanted to take you away and I offered this as the sort of money you might expect to earn if you left. I thought you were such an exceptional student and I only had your best interests at heart.'

'Then why was I not to be told?'

Miss Carson, clearly ill at ease, shifted uncomfortably in her chair. 'Knowing you as a very proud girl, I thought you would consider it, well, patronizing.'

'I do,' Lottie said with a steely note in her voice and, taking back the envelope, she withdrew the pound notes still inside and spread them out in front of Miss Carson.

'It is kind of you and I am sure you had the best in intentions, but I don't want your charity or that of the school, thank you. Also, my mother has now left home so she doesn't need the money.'

'I heard that,' Miss Carson said quietly. 'Apparently Bella is very upset about it. I'm rather surprised you didn't say anything to me.'

'I shall have to leave school and take my mother's place, Miss Carson, to help support the family. There is no doubt about that now, no question of my staying on. So if you would make an appointment for me to see the Head I can tell her this and offer to repay all the money once I am earning my own.'

Miss Carson began to look visibly distressed. 'Really, that is not necessary, Lottie. Your whole future is in front of you . . .'

Lottie interrupted her. 'Miss Carson, we can't live on five pounds a week. Apart from a small war pension my father has there is nothing else for us to live on.'

'But where has your mother gone?'

'We don't know. When Bella and I came home last week my father, very distressed, told me she just left with my young brother Jack and did not say where she was going. We have no idea where she is and have no means of contacting her.'

Miss Carson looked even more shocked. 'How can a person behave like that?'

'Ask my mother. If you knew her well you might not be so surprised. I think Kirkcaldies might give me a job. They told me during the holiday they were very pleased with my work and that during other school holidays there might be an opportunity for me to work in the store instead of the stockroom.'

Moved by Miss Carson's obvious distress, Lottie's expression softened. 'Believe me, I am grateful for your concern, Miss Carson. I might not seem to be, but I am. However, although life with my mother was difficult, we were used to it and somehow we got by. My father, however, is a very sick man and he needs all the help he can get.'

'I think Violet suggested he might see our father. That offer is still open, Lottie. My father is very eminent in his field. I know you might consider this charity, but it is not. It is sincerely meant to help a brave ex-serviceman and I hope for your father's sake you will consider it.'

To her anger and embarrassment, Lottie felt tears prick the back of her eyes and momentarily she struggled for words.

Miss Carson leaned forward and put a hand on her shoulder. 'Believe me, Lottie, I don't mean to be patronizing. That was never my intention and I know my actions have been misinterpreted.'

Lottie burst out, 'It's just, how can you possibly know what it's like, living the way you do? How can you *possibly* know, Miss Carson?'

'I do know, Lottie. I am very aware of how hard things are for much of the population. You know what empathy means? Well, I feel for people in a very acute way. We have many pupils at the school who are in a situation not unlike yours. You may not be aware of it but they are in other classes. By inviting you to our house I didn't mean to patronize you or emphasize the difference between your life and ours. It never occurred to me. I simply wanted you to meet Violet and perhaps be encouraged by her to train as a teacher. I thought you would get on, and you do.'

'Yes, I do like Violet. I like all your family, Miss Carson. I can't explain my attitude, except that I think I was overwhelmed. When you first invited me for tea I imagined you lived in a house a bit better than ours maybe, but somewhere quite small and I would meet your sister and we would all have tea together and chat. I never imagined a house as big as yours with a tennis court and a maid. I was envious, but if my mother taught me anything it was to have pride and she worked so hard while my father was away. And then when he came back he was a different man, not young and strong and cheerful as he had been. My father is only thirty-seven. He's a young man and he looks about sixty. So I felt angry and jealous and . . .' She pushed the notes even further towards Miss Carson. 'I just want to see the Head and arrange to repay the money. There is no question but that I have to leave school and that I'm going to do so straight away.' She paused and examined Miss Carson's face closely. 'Do the other pupils you talked about get money from the school?'

Miss Carson's expression went blank. 'I . . . er . . .'

'The money is from you, isn't it, Miss Carson? I know a lot of girls who are hard up like us and I never heard of anything like this. So my mother said I could stay on after she came to see you. I never thought anything of it at the time, but now . . .'

'It is from me, Lottie. You will now feel more angry and patronized than ever, but I beg you not to be. You may want to leave school and now I think you will and nothing I can say will change your mind. But despite this terrible setback I am still optimistic for your future. You have got such character as well as talent that I think you will succeed in whatever you do. But I want you to know that everything I have done has been with the best intentions and I will always be here for you, Lottie, if you need me.' Miss Carson gently pushed the notes back in Lottie's direction. 'Lottie, please keep this for the time being until you are on your feet and independent, which I am sure will be soon.'

'No,' Lottie said stubbornly.

'Regard it as a loan and then when it suits you, you can pay it back.'

Lottie hesitated. 'All of it?'

'All. I promise.'

Lottie slowly put a hand on the notes and edged them back towards her.

'But there is one thing I do beg of you,' Miss Carson went on, 'and that is to go home and think about our suggestion of medical help, to give your poor father the chance of better health. At the very least, think of him.'

Five

Lottie stared out of the window of the waiting room in Dr Carson's consultancy rooms in central Wellington, gazing down at the people passing in the street outside and wondering if she'd done the right thing. She felt tense and nervous but, above all she had, as Miss Carson had urged her, thought about her father, under forty and already an old man.

Even the prospect of coming to see the doctor had bucked him up. He had shaved, dressed carefully and neatly, though in a thread-bare suit, and there was the suspicion of a spring in his step as he ventured outside and walked to the tram stop at the corner of the street. It was the longest journey he had made for some time. He had looked with interest out of the window of the tram, as though seeing things for the first time, and commented on how much the city had changed since he had last been there.

Yet she felt that once again they had put themselves in a position of dependency on the Carsons. After her interview with Miss Carson she had gone back to the school to take leave of other staff and her friends, an emotional time, and told Miss Carson that she would accept her offer to see her father and they were grateful for it. She also said that she would continue to accept money from her for the time being so long as it was understood that when she was in a position to do so she would pay it all back.

Soon after that had come the letter from Dr Carson, inviting her father for a consultation.

Her father had been in the consulting room for a long time and she was beginning to feel anxious when the door opened and the doctor's receptionist beckoned to her, inviting Lottie to follow her, which she did down a long corridor and then into a large, sunlit room. Her father was sitting in front of his desk as Dr Carson got up to greet her, shaking hands politely and inviting her to sit down.

Then he returned to his chair and, joining his hands in front of him, looked first at her, then at her father. Dr Carson was a tall, pleasant, kindly-looking, grey-haired man of about fifty-five or so, not stern-faced and formidable as she had somehow expected from her limited knowledge of the medical profession. His daughters resembled him, but his son took after his mother.

'Now, Miss O'Brien, thank you for bringing your father to see me. I am very glad you did.'

He looked kindly at Desmond who, appearing very relaxed, smiled back.

'I have given him a very thorough examination and want him to have further tests at the hospital, but as far as I can ascertain there is nothing seriously amiss with Mr O'Brien – physically, that is.'

Dr Carson rose from his desk and began to pace about the room, one hand in his trouser pocket, another resting on his brow as if in thought, so that he could choose his words carefully. 'During the war which, as we know, was a terrible one, the casualties were not only physical resulting in death and injury but mental, too. A lot of men suffered from what we came to know as neurasthenia or shell shock. That is the effect their experiences had on their minds.' Now Dr Carson looked up as if he had resolved a problem and then sat down again. 'From what your father has told me with some emotion, I hope he won't mind me saying, I know that the war did have a very profound effect on him and he has been haunted by many of the dreadful sights he saw which he hasn't been able to get out of his mind. Isn't that right, Mr O'Brien?'

Desmond nodded vigorously. 'Indeed, sir, it is.'

'He experienced many terrible things and remembers that he went all through the war with very little respite. I consider his behaviour, along with that of all his comrades, quite heroic. In fact, there are many men here in New Zealand who are similarly afflicted and what bears on their minds has an effect on their physical health, as it undoubtedly has on your father. But now we know that this can be treated by procedures which have been adopted in hospitals all over the world as well as here in New Zealand, and I am sure that when this is taken care of your father's physical condition will improve enormously and he will be partly, if not fully, restored to health. Believe me, I am very familiar with this syndrome. I have been over to England and America to study it, where a lot of work has been done, and there are steps we can put in place immediately.'

He concluded with such a beaming and reassuring smile as he stood up that Lottie, noting how her father smiled back, felt she could have almost wept with relief, such was the great burden being lifted from her.

It felt strange to be returning to the school and yet no longer part of it. Strange and sad. But Lottie was nothing if not practical, and had become even more so since she had been in charge of running the house. Her decision had been inevitable and she knew she had no choice, but it was still a wrench as she waited outside her old classroom, hoping to catch Miss Carson before she picked up Bella, who now normally had to make her own way home from school.

Finally the school bell rang and a few minutes later the classroom door opened and the pupils poured out, many of them not noticing her in the scrum, some of them stopping to stare and a few to greet her warmly and ask if she was coming back.

'No,' she said, at last pushing past them and tentatively popping her head inside the classroom where Miss Carson sat in her usual place behind her high desk, a pile of exercise books in front of her.

'Lottie!' Miss Carson cried as she saw her and, stepping down from her chair, hurried towards her as she came into the room.

'Hello,' Lottie said shyly, not quite knowing how to greet her – a handshake, a kiss on the cheek now that their relationship had changed? Instead she did neither but went on: 'I do hope you don't mind me popping in. I just came to pick up Bella.'

'Of course I don't mind,' Miss Carson said, drawing her to a chair in the usual place behind a desk in the front row and sitting alongside her. 'I'm delighted to see you. I miss you. We all do.' She leaned forward eagerly. 'Now, tell me, how have you been?'

'Fine.' Lottie smiled reassuringly. 'But the reason I am here is to thank you for asking your father to see Dad. I should have thanked you before, but it has been a busy time and I now have a job.'

'Back at Kirkcaldies?'

'Yes, still in the stockroom, but things may improve later on. If they don't I'll look for something else. The money you send is a big help.' She looked at her gratefully but Miss Carson waved a hand dismissively.

'And tell me, how is your father?'

'The improvement to Dad in such a short time has been quite remarkable. He has been making his own way to hospital for these tests and the sessions he has with a psychiatrist which are shared by other ex-soldiers. He didn't know they existed and he is beginning to make friends. They go to a club for veterans: the RSA, the Returned Veterans' Association. At first it was not easy, but recently there has been more progress and he feels more confident. He used to sit in the same chair day after day, but is now more active and even does some shopping.'

'That is very good news.' Miss Carson studied her face searchingly for a few moments. 'And you, Lottie? Are you happy?'

'I am quite happy,' Lottie said, not entirely truthfully. 'I miss school, of course, but it was something I had to do so I don't have any regrets.'

'And you can keep on with your reading.'

'I do when I have time. Not much, I'm afraid, but I like Katherine Mansfield.'

Miss Carson smiled with satisfaction. 'I thought you would. Violet was going to come and see you, but she has been busy too with exams. I'm afraid she might not be cut out as a teacher, but she perseveres with lots of encouragement from me. Look, Lottie, now that your mother is no longer with you, wouldn't it be all right for you to come and see us again? Violet especially would like it so much, and I think you are a good influence on her.'

'Me?' Lottie looked at her with astonishment.

'Yes, in many ways. Your dedication to hard work. Your commitment and maturity. Violet is too fond of shopping and having a good time.' Miss Carson shook her head regretfully.

For a moment Lottie looked thoughtful. Then, as if realizing that she was now free to do what she liked, said, 'I don't know about my influence on Violet, but I do like her and would like that very much.'

'How about next Sunday? Would that be a good day for you?'

'I think that would be lovely.'

'One of us will come and get you.'

'Don't worry, I can find my own way. I can take a tram if need be.'

Reminded of Lottie's defiantly independent streak, Miss Carson concurred.

'About three?'

Lottie stood gazing out of Violet's bedroom window at the bare-looking lawn without its deckchairs and the deserted tennis court, the net rolled up for the winter. Behind her Violet was riffling through her wardrobe and kept turning to Lottie and showing her various dresses which she wanted her to have. Lottie, though not ungrateful, felt rather apathetic about the whole thing. However well-intentioned she felt that the Carsons somehow couldn't help demeaning her. They didn't mean to, she was sure, but there it was and it jarred. She had avoided taking the tram and walked all the way to the house on a chilly winter's day with, unusually, a light dusting of snow topping the distant hills, and when she had arrived an hour earlier a warm welcome had awaited her. The door was opened by a smiling Miss Carson, who gave her a quick embrace and then led her along the wide hall to the lounge where Mrs Carson hurried towards her and kissed her on the cheek and Violet hugged her.

Suddenly and unexpectedly, her apprehension had vanished and she felt that it was nice to be back, almost as one of the family.

This, after all, was the house and the family of the miracle man who had put her father on the road to recovery.

They had had tea round the fire, just the four of them. Hugh, Mrs Carson explained, was away continuing his studies at the medical school in Dunedin. The atmosphere was cosy and relaxed and the chat was normal and everyday about the weather and the fact that broadcasting had recently started in New Zealand. The Carsons were hoping to be among the few people to acquire a wireless set, still a rarity. Her husband, Mrs Carson said, needed one for his work. Lottie then told them how grateful she was to Dr Carson for doing so much for her father and what an improvement there had already been in his health.

After tea Violet invited her to come upstairs, saying rather mysteriously that she had something to show her and when they were in her bedroom explained how she had too many clothes and wondered if Lottie would be interested? 'Not cast-offs,' Violet added quickly. 'Some of them I've hardly worn.'

Lottie smiled, thinking of the times she had seen Violet leaving the store laden with parcels, and recalled her one good dress, which was still all she had. But, with it, the doubt returned, the suspicion that once again she was being patronized, and she had gone to the window and gazed broodingly out over the lawn, the scene of so much in the summer. She mentally visualized the vigorous activity on the tennis court, but more importantly, something that lingered in her mind: Miss Carson and the captain kissing so passionately by the pool, which had introduced her in an immediate and unexpected way to the meaning of carnal love that, in the hostility of her parents' marriage, she had not witnessed before.

Violet turned from the wardrobe, a dress in her hand and, crossing the room, held it against Lottie. 'This will suit you very well.'

It was the latest fashion: mid-calf, dropped waist with short sleeves and a round neckline in a soft, floral-patterned fabric.

Lottie gasped. 'Me? Wherever would I wear it?'

'Oh, you know, to a party. Try it on. We're all having our hair cut now.' She patted her neat bob.

'I never go to parties,' Lottie said, but to be polite she tried the dress on and, indeed, it suited her perfectly as she turned and swirled in front of the mirror.

'It's you,' Violet said firmly. 'And the first party to wear it to might well be Madeleine and Andy's wedding. They're sure to invite you.'

Lottie looked surprised. 'Is it soon?'

'Maybe. Date not quite decided but Andy might be posted abroad and she would like to go with him.'

Lottie took off the dress and put it on the bed. 'Well, if you're sure, yes, I'd like it very much.'

Violet perched on the bed. 'How are things with you, Lottie? I mean, really? Madeleine did tell us that your mother left home. Has it been very difficult for you, or is that a silly thing to ask?'

Lottie sat on the bed beside her. 'It has been difficult, of course. Everything for a time was upside down. We always relied on Mum. I hadn't realized how much. So I had to leave school and find work. Kirkcaldies have let me stay on at my old job which is fine for the time being. They say economically things are very difficult.'

'We're protected from it all,' Violet said, sighing. 'Sometimes I feel unduly privileged, Daddy having a good job and not threatened with unemployment like so many people. I am not madly keen on teaching, to be honest. I'm afraid Madeleine is worried that I might be an idler and is insisting I take my exams.'

'I think she's right,' Lottie said. 'Then whatever happens you'll be set up in a profession. I should go. With only Bella and Dad at home I have to look after them.' She glanced down at the dress. 'If you're sure?'

'Sure.' Violet also stood. 'I'll take you home.'

'There's no need, thanks.'

'Please,' Violet began, but suddenly Lottie snapped, weary of so many well-meaning attempts by the Carsons to improve her life: inviting her to their affluent home, offering her clothes, the help of their father. Unable to stop herself – and to her subsequent regret – she sprang up from the bed on which they were sitting and turned on an astonished Violet.

'Don't patronize me, please, Violet. I got here by myself and I can get home by myself. I know you don't mean to but you do, you all do, and by the way,' she looked down at the garment still lying on the bed, 'I don't really want that dress. I shall never wear it and, frankly, I don't think it is me. I think it's you.'

She crossed the room and, opening the door, went swiftly down the stairs, bumping into Mrs Carson, who had just come out of the sitting room.

'Oh, there you are, Lottie. Did you girls have a nice chat?'

'Very nice, thank you, Mrs Carson,' Lottie said, reaching for her coat lying on a chair. 'But I really must go now. Dad and Bella are waiting for their tea.'

'But Lottie, we've hardly seen you.'

'I've enjoyed it, I really have.' There was an air of urgency about her, as if she feared someone would try and stop her leaving the house, and she edged towards the front door, still speaking. 'But really, I must go now. Thank Miss Carson for me.'

And just as Madeleine appeared at the door of the sitting room Lottie, ignoring her, let herself out and ran down the steps towards the gate.

Madeleine looked with astonishment at her mother. 'What on earth has happened?'

Mrs Carson was too surprised to speak as they both looked towards the stairs and at Violet, slowly descending.

'Violet,' her mother said sharply, 'did something happen upstairs to upset Lottie?'

Violet, still shaken, shook her head as they walked back into the warmth of the sitting room. 'I offered her one of my dresses. I said it wasn't a cast-off and that I never wore it. She tried it on and it looked great on her. At first she said she'd take it and then suddenly she changed her mind and became quite agitated.' Violet sank dejectedly into a chair. 'She said she had to go and get tea for the family and I offered to drive her home. Suddenly she turned on me and said she didn't want a lift, didn't want the dress and felt patronized by us. It was quite an outburst, which shocked me. Then she ran to the door and that was that. She really is a very odd girl, interesting but odd. Difficult to fathom, really.'

For a moment there was silence as the other women digested what had happened. After a moment Madeleine walked to the window and stood looking out the way Lottie had gone. 'Perhaps she's right.' She turned and faced her mother and sister with an air of resignation. 'Perhaps we *have* patronized her. Perhaps the gulf separating us was too big and we didn't realize just how big and how it affected Lottie, who is essentially a very proud and independent person, much older than her years. I don't expect now that we shall ever see her again.'

'I told you that you should be careful with her,' Mrs Carson said a little primly, 'long ago, and that you might regret it. Lottie is a dear, don't misunderstand me, but after all, people like that aren't *quite* like us, are they, dear, however much we might wish it?'

Lottie knew she had behaved badly, irrationally and that she had probably destroyed a friendship with Miss Carson and her family, who surely had only the best intentions? But the fact was that, with all chances of higher education abandoned, she was less like them than ever, regardless of what had happened since her last visit in the summer. There was a degree of familiarity that should have been there, but was still not. In fact, in a way it made it worse. It was when Violet sat down on the bed and asked her how things were that she realized that of course they knew all about her – how her mother had deserted them and she had had to leave school and go to work. Why, after all, did they want to be so nice to her? Why, for instance, had Miss Carson even singled her out from her other less well off pupils? She was grateful, but uncomfortable about feeling like an object of charity rather than an equal, one to whom they did good maybe to ease their conscience about their own very different circumstances. They had a big house, each had a motor car which still was very rare in Wellington, and Violet had so many dresses that she felt she had to give some away – to the deserving poor, perhaps? To her? Once again she had wished she hadn't gone, and with it had come a violent need to flee. So she'd fled out of the house and down the steps and walked very quickly all the way home.

She didn't imagine she would hear from the Carsons ever again after a display of such ingratitude, considering all that Dr Carson had done for her father.

After all, she had few friends. Her family had been her life and she had never liked to ask people to her home to see her depressed father, bad-tempered mother and the general state of poverty they lived in. She had withdrawn from most forms of social intercourse and the Carsons, who had offered her friendship, who had tried to envelope her in their life, had been rudely and severely rebuffed.

But what was done was done and, being a practical girl, Lottie tried to put all speculation about the Carsons and their inevitable reaction to her behaviour to one side. She had briefly toyed with the idea of writing to Miss Carson to apologize, but that would mean, she knew, they would make every effort to see her and the whole process would begin all over yet again.

To Miss Carson's credit, the weekly envelope still continued to come through the letterbox with Lottie vowing even more to repay it as soon as she could.

So life settled down to a routine that was not unpleasant, that had for Lottie few highs but none of the terrible lows they had had with their mother. Gradually the memory of her as a person almost faded and they still had no idea where she and Jack had gone. Even Jack wasn't missed as much as she had thought he would be. He was a dear boy, and she would always love him, but being so much younger he was peripheral to her life.

One day her father came home, appearing if anything even more cheerful and pleased with himself than he had been. There had been such a change in him in a relatively short time that the household was really much happier and a more pleasant place to be. In the evening when she got home after work her father was not slumped in his corner, having gone to his veterans' club where he seemed to spend most of the day after the hospital.

Bella, too, had settled down, having seemingly abandoned the idea of leaving school early, and applied herself to her studies. Now that the atmosphere at home was much calmer and more conducive to work she was making rapid strides and had moved from near the bottom to the middle of the class, with the prospect of proceeding even further upwards.

Lottie was putting the tea on the table as her father appeared, shutting the door and standing there for a moment, looking at her. 'Hello, Dad,' she said cheerfully, 'you look pleased with yourself. Had a good day?'

'Very good,' her father said, taking off his coat and hat, rubbing his hands and blowing on them. 'I'll be glad when this winter is over, but Lottie, I have some very good news to banish the winter blues.'

'Oh?' Lottie sat down opposite him, elbow on the table.

'I saw Doctor Carson today,' her father went on, 'and he had all my medical reports and told me how pleased he was with my progress. My chest is almost clear now that I don't smoke – they have forbidden it – and the psychiatrist thinks I am much improved, too, and I am.'

'You are. That's splendid news, Dad.' Impulsively Lottie got up from her chair and kissed him on the cheek. For a moment he held her tightly against his chest, and she could feel the steady beat of his heart.

'I do love you, Lottie,' her father said, his voice cracking with emotion. 'You have done so much for me and I have a lot to thank you and your friends the Carsons for. I hope you will tell them how grateful I am.'

Lottie didn't reply as she returned to her chair. She had not told her father about her last visit, now some weeks ago, or mentioned them again. Nor would she if she could help it. 'How about some tea?'

'There is better news. Doctor Carson thinks he has a job for me. A friend of his, a supreme court judge, wants a chauffeur and, knowing about my past experience, Doctor Carson has suggested me. Isn't that great? I am to see this eminent gentleman, Sir Eustace Frobisher, tomorrow. Have you heard of Sir Eustace, Lottie? Did your friends ever mention him?'

'No, Dad. But that is really good news.'

'What's more,' her father went on eagerly, 'I'll be able to help out financially, provide for my family as a father should. Regain my self-respect. That means a lot to me.' Lottie went over and, eyes shining, embraced her father, who held her tightly in his arms.

'I love you, Lottie.'

'And I you, Dad. And I have never, ever lost my respect for you.' Momentarily they clung to each other. Then, freeing herself, fearful of breaking down, she said briskly, 'Let's have tea,' and went to the bottom of the stairs to call Bella. 'Now we have even more to celebrate.'

Yet despite her overwhelming pleasure at the news, mainly for the effect it would have on her father if it happened, there was a sneaking regret that now there was yet another reason to be grateful to the Carsons. She knew how her mother would have reacted and for once she experienced a moment of sympathy for her. Somehow this family seemed to possess hers and she wondered if they would ever be free of their influence, however benign and well meant?

Six

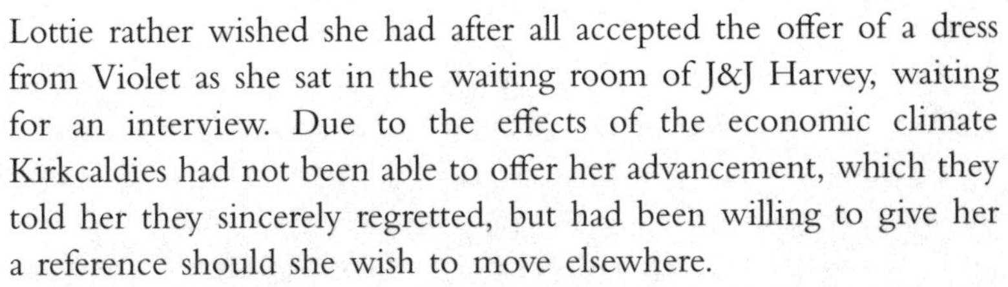

Lottie rather wished she had after all accepted the offer of a dress from Violet as she sat in the waiting room of J&J Harvey, waiting for an interview. Due to the effects of the economic climate Kirkcaldies had not been able to offer her advancement, which they told her they sincerely regretted, but had been willing to give her a reference should she wish to move elsewhere.

After a few unsuccessful applications Lottie had seen the

advertisement for a sales assistant in the local paper and this was her first interview.

J&J Harvey was a smaller store than Kirkcaldies, situated in Manners Street and judged to be rather exclusive with a good reputation. She wanted to be, and look, her best. She had dipped into her meagre savings to buy another dress, less fashionable than the one offered by Violet, more demure and perhaps, in the circumstances, rather more suitable.

She looked up as the door opened and a man beckoned to her. 'Would you come in, please, Miss O'Brien?'

He led her into a small office overlooking the street and asked her to take a seat, then he sat at a desk opposite her and for a moment studied the papers in front of him which included her application, school reports and the reference from Kirkcaldies.

After a few moments he looked at her and gave a pleasant smile. He was about forty, of medium height with a moustache, large brown eyes, dark, sleeked-back hair neatly parted and a smart pinstriped business suit, white shirt with a stiff collar and a restrained club or possibly service tie.

'I am Mr John Harvey, Miss O'Brien, son of the founder of the store, also called John.' He paused and looked at her keenly.

'You are rather young, Miss O'Brien. Just seventeen, I see. What makes you think you would be suitable for a post for which you obviously have little or no experience, although it is a junior one of sales assistant, and you will be well supervised?'

'I hope I would,' Lottie replied, careful to measure her words. 'I occasionally did help at Kirkcaldies in the store, but mostly my job was in the stockroom.'

'That could be to our advantage,' Mr Harvey murmured. 'Stock control is vital to a successful business.' He looked at her again, as if trying to get under her skin, and perhaps also calculating that her striking good looks would be an additional advantage to her sales expertise.

'You know that we have a reputation for exclusiveness, with a mainly affluent clientele? Do you think you would fit in?'

'I cannot promise but I would do my best,' Lottie said, with a sinking feeling that the job was slipping away from her.

'I'm sure you would,' Mr Harvey said pleasantly. 'I like your honesty.'

He studied the papers before him again. 'I see that you have an excellent school record. Why did you leave?'

'I had to help support my family. My father was an invalid from his war experiences. He went all through the war in Europe.'

'Have you no mother?'

'She left home. I also have a younger sister, still at school.'

'I see.'

Mr Harvey tapped his lip thoughtfully and his expression changed, as if he had come to a decision.

'I see you are a very resourceful young lady and you have an excellent record. There is something I like about you, Miss O'Brien, despite your youth. Your experiences in life have obviously made you older than your years and I like that. I can well imagine what you have been through and I like your spirit. Therefore I am prepared to take you on a temporary basis to see how we get on.' He stood up abruptly and, coming round the desk, extended his hand. 'Welcome to Harveys, Miss O'Brien. May you have a long and successful career with us. How soon can you start?'

1923

The next six months passed relatively peacefully in the O'Brien household. Lottie enjoyed her work at Harveys. Her colleagues were pleasant, helpful and gradually she was given more responsibility. Her father was also well looked after as chauffeur to Sir Eustace, who proved a kind, even indulgent employer. It transpired that he had a son who had been wounded in the war and so did a lot to help ex-servicemen, which was why he had been glad to employ Desmond O'Brien.

Lottie's social life also slowly improved as she made one or two friends at Harveys, particularly a girl called Mavis Pearce who was a senior sales assistant in a different department to Lottie, slightly older and whose background was not dissimilar.

Lottie gradually became more accustomed to her independence and to having a little money of her own, and slowly the memory of the past and the fears associated with it began to fade away. There was more money with her wage and her father's and Bella had become more responsible and helped with the household chores.

This had enabled Lottie to begin to repay Miss Carson in monthly installments, always accompanied by a little note which Miss Carson punctiliously acknowledged, though they did not meet. Memories of school had begun to recede in the same way that her old life had faded into the background.

Consequently it was a surprise when, arriving home one day, Lottie found an envelope addressed to her in familiar handwriting and, opening it, withdrew a printed card inviting her to be a guest at the wedding of Miss Madeleine Carson to Captain Andrew Marsden. It was to be a late spring wedding in November with a reception in the garden afterwards.

The following day she and Mavis sat studying the embossed invitation during their lunch break, sitting on a bench on the waterfront. Mavis was impressed. 'It looks very smart,' she said.

'It is smart. They are smart and I can't decide whether or not to go.'

'Why ever not? I'd go like a shot.'

So Lottie told her all about the Carsons and her relationship with them. But she didn't tell her about the money because that was something she felt inherently ashamed about and wanted to keep to herself. Although she and Mavis came from the same social class she was sure they had never experienced the poverty she had and it was something she wished to forget. Mavis was also the member of a large and apparently happy family, with devoted parents, quite unlike Lottie.

All this took such a long time that their lunch break was nearly over and as they rose to go a young man waved to them and, coming over, greeted Mavis.

'Hello, George,' Mavis said and turned to Lottie. 'This is my brother, George. He works on the wharves with my father. This is Lottie. I think I told you about her.'

'Hello,' George replied and was about to say something but Mavis told him they must hurry back or they'd be in trouble.

'He looks nice,' Lottie said as they walked quickly up the street.

'He is nice.' Mavis turned to her as they were about to part. 'I'd go to that wedding. It sounds as though the Carsons are good people and think a lot of you.'

'But what can I wear?' It was the eternal question.

'Ask Mr Harvey if you can borrow a very smart dress from the store. I'm sure he'll say yes. Everyone knows he likes you.'

* * *

Birthdays in the past had not been much celebrated in the O'Brien home, at least as far as Lottie was concerned. In fact, it wasn't she who suggested celebrating her eighteenth but Mavis, whose birthday happened be on the same date, though she was a year older. A few days before the event she asked Lottie if she would like to make up a foursome with her brother and her boyfriend, who Lottie had not known existed.

They met at Mavis's house, which was not far from Lottie's in a similar street, quite small and also with an outside lavatory. Mavis's mother and father were both large, jovial people and Lottie felt immediately at home when she arrived, though she was rather nervous as it was her first visit.

Mavis's brother George was there plus the boyfriend called Josh, who also worked on the wharves. It was a nice, normal, happy family, one she wished she had grown up in. The table was laden with sandwiches and cakes and a special birthday cake with nineteen candles on it. First Mavis was asked to blow them out and when one was removed they were re-lit and Lottie did the same while everyone sang *Happy Birthday to You*, which made her feel happy and special.

'I wish Dad and Bella had been here,' she said wistfully while they were cutting the cake.

'You should have asked them, dear,' Mavis's mother said. 'Where do you live?'

'Broadway Terrace.'

'Well, that's not far away. We'll think of it next time. I'll ask them round for tea one Sunday. Is your mum . . .' She paused.

'No, Mum doesn't live with us,' Lottie replied without further explanation, and Mrs Pearce nodded as if she understood.

'Well, one day we'll arrange it – your dad and sister must come to tea.' She put a hand on Lottie's arm and looked at her fondly. 'I'm so glad Mavis has a nice new friend like you. You must consider yourself one of the family, dear. You're always welcome in our house,' and spontaneously she gave Lottie a hug and a whacking kiss on the cheek which, in this emotional and highly-charged atmosphere, almost brought tears to her eyes.

'Mum,' Mavis said as they were helping clear the dishes, 'we just thought we'd go to Jerry's for a while. Is that all right? I promise we won't be late.'

Jerry's was one of the jazz clubs that had sprung up since the fashion had swept the world from America.

Her mother pulled a face. 'Well . . .'

Her husband put his arm around her. 'Come on, Betty. They are old enough to look after themselves.'

'I promise we won't be late,' Mavis repeated.

'Would your father mind?' Mrs Pearce looked doubtfully at Lottie, who seemed surprised by the question.

'Oh, my father never minds what I do. Besides, I hardly ever go out.'

She tried to suppress the keen feeling of excitement that gripped her. A jazz club would be an entirely new experience.

'Besides, Mum,' Mavis said teasingly, 'we've got these two strong men to look after us.'

'That's what worries me,' her mother said, but she was smiling.

The four got a tram to the centre of town and then walked along Manners Street, into Willis Street and then Lambton Quay, past Kirkcaldies and through a side street where the steady thump of music led them down some steep steps into a basement and a dark, small, overcrowded room. The stifling atmosphere was thick with cigarette smoke, while an enthusiastic band pounded out the music from a small raised platform at the back. In the centre of the floor several couples jived energetically, while others crowded round a bar, manned by a sweating barman with a cigarette dangling from his mouth, waiting to be served.

'Do you want a beer?' George shouted to Lottie above the din. Almost drunk with excitement, Lottie nodded and found her feet irresistibly tapping in tune with the beat of the music.

Mavis and Josh had eschewed drinking and were enthusiastically dancing in a manner that showed they had done it often before. For a time Lottie watched them in admiration, then a beer was thrust into her hand and she shouted her thanks. George held up his glass and she toasted him back, nearly spilling the contents as her arm was knocked by a man squashed beside her.

George by now was wiping the perspiration from his face, his eyes, too, alight with excitement. Any conversation was impossible and the two just stood pressed together by the crowd, drinking and watching the throng on the floor. Even if they had wanted to join them it seemed impossible. Eventually there was a welcome rush of air from a door that had opened on to a backyard and George tugged at her arm and shouted in her ear: 'Let's go outside,' which to Lottie was a welcome relief.

She leaned against a wall, aware that her clothes were clinging to her body, and took several deep breaths. 'My,' she gasped.

'Have you ever been here before?' George perched beside her, a half-empty glass in his hand.

'Never.'

'We like it and come quite often. There are other places but this is one of the best. Believe it or not the others are even noisier and more crowded.'

'I really should go home,' Lottie said. 'My father may be worried. I am not usually out so late.'

'Just one more dance?' George said and she nodded. Feeling a little refreshed they returned to the dance floor, which by now was less crowded as other couples had drifted outside in search of fresh air.

The pace of the jazz music allowed little close contact and, though entirely new to it, Lottie, feeling a natural aptitude for dance, quickly and easily got into the steps. Finally the band decided to take a break and Lottie looked round for Mavis, feeling that she really must go. However, there was no sign of her or her partner. She looked at George in some alarm. 'They seem to have gone.'

'Maybe when we were outside.' He appeared unconcerned.

'I didn't notice them when we came back, did you?'

'I never looked. Don't worry.'

George caught her by the hand and drew her towards the exit. 'I'll see you home.'

Once out in the night air Lottie felt rather chilled and rubbed her arms.

'Let's walk quickly,' she said. 'Look, there is no need to take me all the way home.'

'It's not so far from us.' He put an arm round her shoulder and then, sensing her lack of response, quickly withdrew it. 'Just trying to warm you,' he said.

'That's all right,' Lottie replied, but she was embarrassed. She had never been out with a man before and realized what a cloistered life she had led. She was gauche and awkward and she felt that there was something about her that put men off.

They walked for some time in silence.

'Would Mavis have gone home?' she asked eventually.

'Perhaps,' George replied, and she decided not to question him further. She rather suspected from his cagey reply that Mavis had not gone home and she didn't really want to know the answer.

Finally they reached Broadway Terrace and stopped outside the house. She didn't mind George knowing where she lived because his street and house were similar to hers. They were from the same background, the same kind of people, so it didn't matter, which was a relief.

'Thank you,' she said, smiling at him. 'I enjoyed the evening.'

Even though the lights were on she didn't ask him in.

'I enjoyed it, too,' George replied. There followed a long pause, during which they both stood looking at each other as though unsure of the next move. 'Maybe we can see each other again?' He made a sudden, jerky gesture towards her, but she quickly stepped back.

'All right,' she said.

'I'll arrange something with Mavis.'

'That would be nice.'

'Happy birthday, anyway.'

Without replying, Lottie walked towards the door and then impulsively turned before she opened it, feeling she had perhaps been a little graceless, but it was too late and George was already sauntering up the street, hands in his pockets.

She looked after him, feeling inadequate and helpless. George was very nice. He was good looking, a bit quiet, reserved like she was but, given the chance, could have been good company. The nature of the evening, the noise of the jazz club and the long, practically silent walk home had meant there had been no chance for any kind of development. She longed for intimacy, but didn't know how to go about it and George had not helped her. Perhaps he didn't know either, but she doubted it.

She had made a fool of herself. She was naïve and had messed up her first date. Her birthday, no less.

Eighteen and never been kissed.

Seven

Lottie felt very nervous as she walked up the path to the church. Not for the first time, as far as the Carsons were concerned, she wished she had not come, but it was too late to turn back. Besides, she had made such an effort. Mr Harvey had agreed she could borrow a dress of her choice and she had selected a pretty frock of pale blue organza with a dropped waist, a round neck, ruched sleeves and a long, dipping hemline. She had had her hair cut shorter but not bobbed in line with the fashion, because she didn't think it suited her. Also, unlike most of the women walking up the path with her, she wore no hat, which she now feared was a mistake. The trouble with her, Lottie knew, was that, despite appearances, she lacked confidence. Fortunately she also knew that it didn't show, or was disguised by her carefree, almost nonchalant air as she reached the church steps and stood in the porch which was crowded with people waiting to be shown their seats.

'I said I hoped to see you again,' a voice murmured in her ear and, startled, she gazed into the eyes of a man who she immediately recognized. 'But it was a long time ago. It is Lottie, isn't it?'

'It is,' she said.

'Hugh. Hugh Carson. I drove you home a while ago.'

'I know you did – of course I remember.'

'Madeleine told me to look out for you.'

'That was very kind of her. How is she?'

'She is very well, nervous, excited.' Hugh looked at his watch. 'Look, I'm an usher. Let me show you to your seat and afterwards I'll take you back to the house.'

The church was already packed. The organ played softly, scarcely audible above the murmurs of the crowd, men in morning dress and women in all kinds of fashions which, since the end of the war, had been changing so quickly. Some wore the latest dresses, a few couture or bought from smart boutiques or maybe even Harveys. Lottie thought she might well recognize customers. Almost everyone wore hats, some broad-brimmed, others close to the head. She didn't care. She felt transformed by his presence, even mildly elated as this handsome man escorted her down the aisle, as if she were a person of some importance, and seated her halfway down the nave from which she had a very good view of the ceremony.

'I'll be back,' he whispered and as he walked away she followed him with her eyes, watching him walk to the front to talk to Andy the bridegroom, who was already in place, dressed, she could see, in uniform. As Hugh came back up the aisle he smiled at her and she smiled back. She knew it was a special smile, which made her more at ease with herself and everybody else, even the Carsons. No longer a schoolgirl but a woman, singled out now by the dashing, accomplished Hugh.

He looked very attractive in morning dress, like most of the men present, but even more attractive than she remembered before. She recalled how she had thought he was one of the best-looking men she had ever seen, and had no reason now to change her mind. She settled back, the feeling of confidence increasing as she accepted the fact that she was being looked after and admired, and then the music changed and the congregation rose. Turning, she saw Miss Carson walk slowly down the aisle on the arm of her father, followed by six bridesmaids in cream dresses. One of them was Violet, who smiled at her as she passed. Miss Carson's dress was of white satin with a high neck and long sleeves tapering at the wrist, intricately embroidered at the bust and with a long train carried by the smaller bridesmaids. It was impossible to see her expression under the veil which concealed her face, but Lottie had no doubt it was a happy one.

As the bride reached the altar and the groom stepped out and took his place beside her, Lottie vividly recalled that scene on the lawn, that moment of intimacy and promise when they had first kissed and she herself had had inkling, an unexpected foretaste, of carnal desire.

There was a huge marquee on the lawn which was approached by a red carpet from the house, at the end of which stood the bridal pair and their respective parents, greeting the guests. True to his promise Hugh had again escorted her to the car and was still by her side as, once more overtaken by shyness, she approached the bride, no longer Miss Carson but now a married woman.

She saw how truly beautiful the bride looked. Her veil, thrown back to reveal her face, was held in place by a diamond circlet. There was something quite awesome and splendid about her in her new role, but her eyes were welcoming and her smile genuine as she leaned forward to kiss Lottie on both cheeks.

'I am *so* glad you came.'

'As if I'd miss it,' Lottie said, feeling quite emotional as the bride turned to her husband.

'This is Lottie, darling – you remember her?'

'Of course I do, and how she beat us at tennis.' He, too, shook Lottie warmly by the hand. And then she was greeted warmly by Dr and Mrs Carson, with whom she exchanged a few words, and then the captain's mother, who apparently was a widow.

Still at her side, Hugh led her on to the lawn where waiters circulated with trays of champagne and canapés.

'I shouldn't keep you from your friends,' Lottie said. 'You've been very kind.'

'Let me introduce you to some people.' Hugh steered her towards a group of younger men and women. 'These are some of my friends from medical school.' He introduced them one by one and she stood chatting quite naturally or listening to them, when Violet came up and kissed her.

'Really lovely to see you again, Lottie. Is Hugh looking after you?'

'Very much so,' Lottie said. 'I feel quite guilty.'

She smiled gratefully at Hugh, who lightly touched her arm and said, 'I've just seen someone I must talk to,' before moving away.

'You look really lovely, Lottie,' Violet said admiringly. 'That's a beautiful dress.'

'Thank you.' Lottie suddenly remembered the scene in Violet's room when she had thrown the dress on the bed and stormed out. With these recollections stuck in her head, she wondered why they had invited her.

'There are so many people here and I don't know anyone. In fact,' Lottie looked at Violet, 'I don't really know why Miss Carson invited me. I behaved so badly when I was last here.'

Violet put a hand on her arm. 'Please don't talk about it. It's all in the past. This is such a happy day. Madeleine is very fond of you. We all are. Tell me, what have you been doing?'

'I work at Harveys. I'm a senior sales assistant. I've been there over a year.'

'That is fantastic. Do you like it?'

'Very much so.'

'I must come and see you.'

'I wonder I haven't seen you there already!'

Violet took her by the arm. 'Come and meet more people,' and they strolled among the crowd, Violet occasionally stopping to talk and introducing her to people she would possibly never meet again and certainly never remember. However, her experience in the store had taught her how to deal with all sorts of people in all kinds of situations. She was no longer the shy young girl who the Carsons had known, so she joined in the small talk quite easily until a bell sounded and guests were invited to take their seats in the marquee, where the wedding breakfast was to be served.

'I don't think you're with us,' Violet said, 'as we all have to sit on the top table, but I know you have been put with nice people and will be looked after.'

In the melee there was now no sign of Hugh and Violet took her into the marquee, found her table and said: 'Here you are. These are some of my friends, mostly from college. This is Ethel and her brother Jeremy. You will get on well. I'll see you afterwards.'

Feeling quite calm, relaxed and fortified by the two glasses of champagne she had drunk, Lottie looked round the table at her fellow guests, who all seemed to know one another. For a while she was happy to watch the proceedings at the high table until Ethel started to engage her in small talk and the meal was served.

Ethel was pleasant and so was her brother on the other side of her, the food was excellent, the speeches entertaining and some quite amusing, and it wasn't until the end as people started to rise that Lottie began to think about getting home.

Next but one to Ethel had been an older man who'd occasionally glanced at her and now said something to Ethel, who brought him over just as she was getting up from her chair. 'This is Edward. We all call him Ed. He's keen to meet you.'

'How do you do?' he said. He was not more than thirty or so, but leaned quite heavily on a stick. 'I am a friend of Andy's. We were in the army together, only I was in the war.' Edward tapped his leg.

Lottie smiled sympathetically and shook his hand, thinking it was not quite the occasion to tell him about her father.

'Have you known Madeleine long or are you a friend of Violet's?'

'Both . . .' Lottie began when Hugh came up to them and smiled at Edward. 'The bride and groom are just about to leave. Do you want to see . . .?'

'Oh, yes!' Lottie cried. 'I didn't even see them leave the table.' She smiled uncertainly at Edward.

'I'll skip that, I think,' Edward said, 'and get myself another drink. I never really got your name, but nice meeting you.'

'And you,' Lottie said and moved away with Hugh. 'He seemed nice.'

'He is very nice. Ed Frobisher. He was very badly injured in the war. Nearly lost his leg.'

'Did you say Frobisher?'

'Yes.'

'Is he related to Sir Eustace?'

'His son. Do you know him?'

'My father is his chauffeur. Your father got him the job.'

'Well, what a coincidence. It's a small world.'

'Isn't it? Is Sir Eustace here?'

'No, he was invited but I think he's got some important court case. Lady F is but I can't see her. Do you want me to find her?'

'Not particularly, but I would like to see Madeleine leave.'

As they reached the porch the bridal pair were already in the drive. Tin cans were tied to the back of the car together with a large placard saying JUST MARRIED.

Madeleine and Andy were standing in the drive taking leave of their parents and Lottie edged her way past the throng of people to get a good view. At that moment Madeleine turned, waved at the crowd, and suddenly and impulsively seemed to aim her bouquet straight at her which, although others reached out for it, Lottie somehow managed to catch. She held it aloft and waved back enthusiastically, aware that there were tears in her eyes.

'Goodbye!' Madeleine cried and blew kisses as they got into the car. Andy took the wheel and with a loud blast of the horn drove away.

'I must go, too,' Lottie said to Hugh, who was standing behind her.

'I can take you.'

'No, I can't take you away from the party.'

'Madeleine told me to. I can't disobey orders. I'll soon be back. Are you sure you want to go? There's dancing.'

'Sure.' Lottie clutched the bouquet to her nose, inhaling the fragrance. 'I think she wanted me to have it.'

'I think she did,' Hugh said.

The wedding seemed to mark another important turning point in Lottie's life, though at the time she was not aware of it as such. But things were never quite the same afterwards. In many ways it intensified her dissatisfaction with her lot after mingling with the sort of people she would so like to be, the kind of life she aspired to. It dawned on her more forcibly when she had to hand back the dress she had borrowed and appeared once again in her neat uniform of a black two-piece and white blouse, standing on the shop floor looking pleasant and assisting the wealthy in their choice of dress or, if they were undecided, advising them what to wear.

Indeed, after the wedding she felt like Cinderella, back from the ball before the prince had come to find her.

But, in fact, her prince did appear quite soon after and it came about through Violet who, characteristically and true to her promise, turned up one day, looked round on the pretence of buying and as an aside invited Lottie to lunch.

Just for fun they had it at Kirkcaldies, where Lottie had not returned since she had left. It was nice to ascend to the top floor as a customer, to sit in the restaurant and be able to order delicious food for which Violet insisted on paying.

'I'm not being patronizing,' she said with her disarming smile. 'I invited you.'

'That was silly. I apologize now and I should have before. I was rude to you and your family.' Lottie leaned back in her chair and pulled a face. 'I am more grown up now. I have turned eighteen.'

'Oh, when?'

'September.'

'And what did you do?'

'I went to a jazz club.' Lottie smiled. 'Quite an adventure for me.'

'Was it Jerry's?'

'Yes. Do you go there?

'Sometimes. It is very popular, but it is always so hot and crowded. Who did you go with?'

'A friend of mine who also works at Harveys and her brother.'

They paused while the waitress laid their food before them and for a while they ate in silence. Then Lottie said, 'Have you heard from Madeleine?'

'No, not yet. They went to England and the Continent for their honeymoon. I imagine they'll be having a very good time.'

Violet put down her knife and fork. 'Hugh and I wondered if you'd like to come out on our boat?'

'Oh, you have a boat?'

'A small sailing dinghy. If the weather is good, how about Sunday?'

'Sunday sounds fine but,' Lottie looked doubtful, 'I've never been sailing.'

'Don't worry about that. Hugh is an expert.'

'And what do I wear?'

'Something you feel comfortable in. We'll pick you up at Lambton Quay by Kirkcaldies and take you to the boat. About ten o'clock?'

Sunday was hot and sunny. Lottie settled on a cotton frock and took a cardigan in case it was cold. She got to Lambton Quay early and perched on the balustrade, looking at the water. Already there were a few yachts about in the bay. Very soon the car appeared with Hugh at the wheel, apparently alone. He jumped out and came over to Lottie.

'Sorry, am I late?'

'I was early,' Lottie said, looking past him into the car. 'No Violet?'

'Violet sends her apologies. She isn't well. She suffers from migraine and the sea and bright sunlight would have been too much for her. Having suggested it we didn't want to disappoint you. I go sailing anyway most Sundays. I hope you don't mind it being just me?'

'I don't mind. But I won't be any use to you as crew. I don't know a thing about sailing.'

'You don't need to.' Hugh opened the door of the passenger seat. 'Hop in. We keep the boat at Oriental Bay. I thought we'd just sail round the coast. Mother made us up a picnic.'

'That was very kind of her.' Lottie felt slightly uneasy and puzzled, quite glad to be alone with Hugh but nervous, too. However, the drive to Oriental Bay in the open car, with the wind blowing through her hair and the sun beating down on her face, relaxed her and by the time they got to the boat harbour and she saw the anchored yachts her nerves had disappeared and she jumped out of the car and helped Hugh carry his gear to the yacht, which was bigger than she had expected. It had a small cabin with plenty of space and after she had helped Hugh store the equipment he had brought and the food for the picnic she sat in the stern, one arm dangling over the side, admiring the expert way he prepared the boat for sailing, unfurling and then hoisting the sails. Finally he started the small engine above the propeller and they were off across Wellington Harbour.

It really was, she thought, the most beautiful place in the world, with the Rimutaka and Tararua Ranges far away in the north, the lush green native bush on the surrounding hills in the east and west, and stretching before them the calm blue water of the harbour.

When they were well out into the harbour he switched off the engine and, sitting beside her, took the tiller. 'I thought we'd make for Eastbourne and have our picnic. Maybe walk up through the bush to the top. Have you been there?'

Lottie shook her head.

'There are some marvellous places to explore. That's where the boat is so useful.'

They sailed past the Somes and the smaller Ward islands and soon the long, beautiful sandy beach of Eastbourne overlooked by hills came into sight.

'Here we are.' Hugh steered the boat alongside a small jetty, jumped out with a rope in his hands and secured it. 'Hungry?'

'Very.'

'Let's picnic on the beach then take a walk up the hill.'

He carried the picnic basket to the beach, spread out a rug and laid out the food, which was quite basic but nourishing: chicken and ham sandwiches, cake and squash to drink.

They ate largely in silence, but it was a companionable rather than an awkward silence, like a couple who had known each other a long time, occasionally looking up and exchanging glances. Lottie felt quietly, calmly, perfectly happy.

When they finished Hugh took the basket back to the boat and stored it in the cabin, while Lottie shook the sand out of the rug and folded it away.

Then they took the path leading away from the beach towards the bush and started the steepish climb up the walking track to the top of the hill, from which there was a spectacular view all round across to Wellington. They sat on a hillock slightly out of breath, shading their eyes.

'I'd love to travel,' Lottie said. 'You know, abroad.'

'Really?' He looked at her with interest. 'I hope to go to England. Maybe next year. I take my finals soon in Dunedin and after that, as a qualified doctor, I can transfer to the hospital in Wellington. I want to look after children and there is a famous children's hospital in London called Great Ormond Street where I would like to do further study.'

'That sounds very exciting.'

'Nothing is fixed, but it's my ambition.' He turned and studied her face closely.

'And you, Lottie, what is your ambition?'

'I would like to do well in my job. Mr Harvey allows me to think I have a future in the store. It is doing well. One day, perhaps, I may even be a buyer. That might give me the chance to travel to England and the Continent, too. But it's still a long way off.'

She returned his gaze, aware, as he undoubtedly was, of the growing feeling of intimacy and attraction between them. Everything so far had been so natural, as if they were not virtual strangers but had known each other for years.

'Madeleine said that you might be a teacher.'

'That dream vanished long ago when I had to leave school. But now I'm happy where I am.'

'And marriage and family?'

'Oh, that's a long way off. One day, perhaps, but I'm not ready for it yet.' Lottie turned her gaze once again towards the city.

'You seem a contented sort of person, Lottie. Completely natural and unaffected.'

'But you don't know me, do you?'

'No, I don't.'

'I might be completely different from what you think.'

'You might.' He looked puzzled. 'Lottie, exactly where is this getting us?'

She returned his gaze. 'Hugh, you must know an awful lot of girls. Do you take them all out on your boat?'

'Sometimes.' He seemed taken aback by the question. 'Not often. You're rather special. I remember when I first met you, you were a schoolgirl. I haven't forgotten that day and how you went up to a house that wasn't yours and then when you thought I was out of sight ran all the way back and along the road to, I suppose, where you really lived.'

Lottie turned scarlet. 'You saw all that?'

'Through the mirror of the car.'

'I was silly and naïve,' she said defensively. 'I would never do that now. The thing is I always think your family patronizes me.'

'They don't. They like you, so get that out of your head once and for all.' He reached for her hand and held it tightly. 'Don't underrate yourself. No need. Besides, you're very pretty. Don't tell me you don't know that and use it.'

'I think that *is* patronizing,' she said angrily, wrenching her hand away.

For a moment they glared at each other. Then he rose and, reaching for her hand, pulled her up and, drawing her towards him, kissed her hard on the lips until, feeling her respond, he put both arms around her, holding her very tight, and they stayed like that for a long time.

Finally they drew apart and Hugh rather prosaically but with a catch in his voice said, 'I think we should get back. It is later than I thought.'

And then, hands joined they partly walked, partly ran, down the hill back to the shore.

It was almost evening when he sailed into the mooring at Oriental Bay. Lottie sat in the stern in a state of bemusement, trailing a hand in the water, not quite believing what had happened. She remembered watching Miss Carson and Andrew from the window the day they became engaged – that kiss, and had wondered what it would be like. Now she knew.

Hugh was different, too, and they said little but kept on exchanging glances because they knew things had changed. Or did he do that with every girl he took out in his boat? That was the puzzle.

Once anchored at the jetty he began the business of taking down the sails, securing the boat and leaving it ready for its next outing. Lottie made herself useful, tidying the cabin, repacking the picnic basket and throwing uneaten cake and sandwiches to the gulls which hovered expectantly.

When they had finished he straightened up and said, 'I'll take you home. Home to where you live.'

She nodded, aware that some kind of boundary between them had been crossed and there was no going back.

When he stopped outside the house Lottie said, 'Come and meet my dad and sister.'

'I'd like that,' Hugh said and helped her out of the car.

Her father was sat reading the paper. He looked up as they came in, rather startled to see Lottie's companion, and rose from his chair.

'Dad, this is Hugh Carson. We've been sailing.'

Hugh went over and shook his hand. 'Very pleased to meet you, Mr O'Brien. Please don't get up.'

'Where's Bella?'Lottie asked.

'She's out. Not sure where. I never know where she gets to these days.'

Lottie frowned. 'She should let you know where she's going.'

'She's seeing some friend. I expect she's all right.' He looked again at Hugh as he slumped back in his chair. 'I'm very grateful for what your father did for me, Mr Carson.' He tapped his chest. 'Made a new man of me.'

'I'm very glad to hear it.'

'Hugh is a doctor, too, or nearly.'

'Well, I hope you're as fine a doctor as your father. Did Miss Carson not go with you?' He looked over at Lottie. 'I thought you said . . .'

Hugh answered for her. 'Unfortunately my sister didn't feel well, so Lottie agreed to come out with me. We had a very nice day, didn't we, Lottie?'

'Lovely,' she said. 'Eastbourne, Dad. Wonderful views from the hill.'

'Eastbourne is very nice,' Desmond agreed. 'Days Bay, Mahina Bay, all around that side of the harbour is lovely. Haven't been since before the war.' He sighed deeply. 'You were lucky you escaped the war. No one escaped unharmed and many never came back. Far too many,' he shook his head, 'with no known grave. Buried in the mud, some of them, forever.' He shook his head mournfully.

'I know,' Hugh said. 'I was very fortunate, but you were very brave. You must be proud.'

Desmond waved a hand as if denying any such thing and shook his head again. 'Made me lose my wife and son. I was never the same man.' He gazed sadly across at his daughter. 'Luckily I have my Lottie. She looks after me.'

'Mr O'Brien, it is very nice to have met you,' Hugh said. 'Unfortunately I have to get back. I have to do so many hours study every day to pass my exams.'

'I'll see you out,' Lottie said, quite relieved to put an end to this conversation which, if she knew her father, would become more and more maudlin and probably end in tears.

Hugh again shook hands with Desmond and then he and Lottie walked to the car where they stopped and looked at each other.

'It's been a lovely day,' Lottie said. 'Thank you. I hope you find that Violet feels better when you get back.'

'Will you come out with me again? I go back to Dunedin tomorrow for my exams, but I'll see you as soon as I get back.'

Not waiting for her reply he leaned towards her and kissed her again, full on the mouth.

When he stepped back she said banteringly, 'Do you do that with all the girls you take out in your boat?'

'Only some,' he said. 'The special ones. You're one.' And she couldn't tell if he was joking or not.

'Write,' she called after him as he hurried away, but she didn't think he heard.

Lottie stood watching the car until it was out of sight and then she turned and went slowly back into the house.

'He seems a nice man,' her father said.

'He is, very nice.'

'I thought you didn't like the Carsons very much?'

'That was a long time ago, Dad. Things change.'

She sat down opposite her father, trying desperately to put Hugh out of her mind.

'Dad, I am concerned about Bella and the fact that you don't know where she goes. You know now that I work all day I can't keep an eye on her. She is only fifteen.'

'Well, I can't keep an eye on her either,' her father said grumpily. 'I work, too. I think she's old enough to look after herself.' He looked at her querulously. 'Lottie, are we going to have any tea, or is your mind too full of Mr Carson?'

Eight

Lottie's mind was indeed full of Mr Carson and remained so for some time after the trip to Eastbourne. She had hoped he might at least have written, even a note, in reply to hers, but there was no word and she imagined him busy with his exams, completely oblivious of her. As the days passed she thought eventually that maybe she had read too much into the sailing trip, the tightly clasped hands while they scrambled down the hill; that kiss, the glances, the very real sense of intimacy they had shared. She lingered on each word he'd said to her, finding each time a new meaning.

Was she in love? How could one tell?'

After all, he was a very attractive man, a professional man destined perhaps to be a distinguished surgeon like his father. He came from a different world, a moneyed world, a world of motor cars, yachts and wirelesses, a world of plenty. From the guests at the wedding you could see not only how many people they knew but what sort of people they were. People like them, not like her. And how *did* he behave towards all the women he took out on his boat? Why should she think she was so special? The longer the break the more she thought she was not so special to him really, just a whim. She should not deceive herself that she had any future with Hugh Carson.

'What are you doing for Christmas?' Mavis asked as they were having their customary lunch break by the harbour wall.

'So far no plans. We never do much anyway,' Lottie replied. 'You?'

'I wondered if you'd like to come and have a bite with us on Christmas Eve and maybe go to a club or somewhere. I know George would like to see you again.'

'I'd like that,' Lottie replied, 'providing it's all right with Dad and Bella. I can't see them minding, though. Besides, I think Dad is working and Bella probably has her own plans. She is a bit of a worry to me, my little sister. She used to cling to me but since Mum left she's become fiercely independent. However, I can't be forever protecting her. She is very clever and we hoped she would go on to make something of her life, but now she's talking again about leaving school and getting a job and mine isn't too good an example to stop her. Besides, I have done quite well and can't say now that I regret it.'

'Then can we say yes?'

'Yes. That's really kind of you.'

'I'll tell George. He'll be pleased.' Mavis studied her friend's face closely for a minute. 'Did you like him, Lottie?'

'Yes, I did. I liked him a lot.'

But not as much as Hugh, she thought in the course of the afternoon. She had not told Mavis about Hugh and the day at Eastbourne, and she was rather glad she hadn't. Because occasionally she wondered if she had read too much into the whole thing and would never see him again.

It was true that she enjoyed her work. She got on well with her immediate boss, Mrs Morgan, who was in charge of the department. She was given quite a lot of responsibility because Mrs Morgan admired her judgement, her dress sense and above all the patience she had with customers, many of whom were capricious and hard to please. Her sales record was also impressive. Everyone liked Lottie.

Gradually she grew in confidence and this was reflected in her demeanor and also in her attitude to life. She did indeed look and seem much older than her years. Since the war the position of women had advanced significantly. They had had the vote since the previous century, New Zealand being one of the few democracies in the world to lead the way in women's suffrage. With her undoubted flair and interest in fashion she could imagine herself achieving success in the fashion business, not just in Harveys but maybe elsewhere? It compensated a lot for having to leave school early and she valued her independence and her ability to earn her own living. The family finances now were on a much firmer scale and she was well into repaying her debt to Madeleine.

A few days after her talk with Mavis she arrived home to find a familiar car parked outside which made her quicken her step, and when she opened the door there was Hugh sitting in her father's chair, obviously at ease, chatting away to Bella, who appeared to have just brought him a cup of tea.

The mutual delight as Lottie and Hugh looked at each other was obvious.

'Hugh!' Lottie cried. 'What a lovely surprise.'

'Your sister has been entertaining me.' Hugh went up to her and kissed her lightly on the forehead, holding her tightly but briefly by the arm before reluctantly letting go of her.

'When did you get back?'

'Last night.'

'I got him a cup of tea,' Bella said smugly.

'She's been telling me about her wish to be a hairdresser.'

'Yes. I only recently heard about it. I'm not too happy about it as she is doing well, but she now insists on leaving school.'

'*You* did,' Bella said accusingly.

'The circumstances were a little different,' Lottie replied tartly. She then asked Bella, 'Could you get me a cup of tea too, please?'

As Bella went off to the kitchen Hugh said, 'Did you think I'd forgotten you?'

'No,' she lied, feeling so happy to see him again, not mentioning the unanswered letters. 'You said you were busy with your exams. All finished now?'

'I have one or two vivas after Christmas. Lottie, I have tickets for a dinner dance on Christmas Eve for us. Is that all right?'

Lottie frowned. 'Well I'd like to, but I have just accepted another invitation. Mavis, my friend who works at Harveys, has invited me to eat with her and her family.'

'I'm sure she'll understand if you cry off.'

'I hope she will. I'll try. Yes, I'll try.'

'Would you mind very much if I didn't join you on Christmas Eve?' Lottie looked anxiously at Mavis, who paused in the act of taking a bite from her sandwich. The two women were having their usual lunch break by the harbour wall.

'Why, did your father mind?'

'Not exactly.' Lottie paused. 'You see, and I do feel rather bad about this, but Hugh Carson has invited me to a dinner dance and . . .'

'Oh, I *see*.' Mavis finished her sandwich and brushed the crumbs from her hands. 'Something better has turned up?'

'It's not like that. It's just that, well, I really like Hugh.'

'But you said you really liked George.'

'I did like George. I do.'

'I suppose Hugh is from a better class and has got more money. Why, you hardly know him.'

Lottie began to feel uncomfortable. 'It's not at all like that, Mavis. I do know Hugh, better than you think. I didn't tell you but a few weeks ago we spent a very nice day together. He took me over to Eastbourne in his yacht and we struck a sort of relationship.'

'Oh!' Mavis exclaimed. 'Did you kiss?'

'Yes.'

'Oh, just a kiss? That's all?

'Yes.'

'And you think that constitutes a relationship, do you?' Mavis sniggered unpleasantly.

'No, but there was an atmosphere, a feeling between us that I can't exactly explain. I didn't tell you because I didn't quite know what to make of it. He had to go to Dunedin where the medical school is to do his exams and I didn't see him again until last night – he was waiting for me to come home. I did say I had accepted another invitation.'

'Not quite the same thing, though, is it? A ball? A bloke with a yacht, rich friends?'

'Please don't be like that, Mavis,' Lottie pleaded. 'You know I'm not like that at all.'

'I'm beginning to wonder what sort of person you are, Lottie.' Mavis got up from her seat and shook the crumbs from her lap. 'Sometimes I think you're not really like us at all.'

'How *can* you say that?'

'Well, that's what I think, but of course you must go ahead and I hope you enjoy yourself. I'll have to tell George he should get a yacht if he wants to be in the running.'

And with that Mavis stalked off ahead, leaving Lottie sitting on the bench by the wall, looking thoughtfully out across the harbour towards Eastbourne. She didn't hurry after her. Perhaps in many ways Mavis was right. George didn't have a yacht and she thought he never would. To look into the future and envisage life with someone like George would be to remain where she was, and she wanted so desperately to move on.

They glided across the dance floor, Hugh's arm tightly clasping Lottie's waist, bodies almost touching. For a moment he let his mouth brush against her cheek and then moved to her ear. 'You look ravishing,' he whispered. 'Really beautiful.'

She smiled at him, doubting that he could possibly know how much trouble she had taken with her appearance, ably assisted by Mrs Morgan, who had selected for her a sleeveless evening dress in *eau de nil* silk shantung with a dropped hem reaching just above her ankles and a deep V-shaped neckline. There was beading at the waist and around the neckline. Her hair was cut in a fashionable bob which tapered at the back of her neck and her natural curls, which shone almost bright gold in the light of the many chandeliers suspended from the ceiling of the ballroom, were restrained by soft finger waves done by the best hairdresser in Wellington. She looked elegant, stylish, fashionable but, important in this context, because of her obvious youth, not overdressed as many of the women in the room were in their efforts to keep up with the latest rampant fashions of the twenties. Her use of make-up, too, was careful: a touch of bright red lipstick and the merest shimmer of face powder. Hugh led her expertly round the dance floor and, despite being completely inexperienced, her natural sense of rhythm enabled her instinctively to follow his lead.

The dance ended and as they walked back to their table hand in hand she was aware of the many eyes of her fellow revellers, seated at other tables, following her. They shared their table with a number of medical students, mainly men, also celebrating the end of finals with their partners. There had been an almost endless supply of champagne, but Lottie was careful to restrict herself to a couple of glasses. She didn't want to risk ruining such a perfect evening by losing control. She recognized some of the students from Madeleine's wedding.

'Cigarette?' The man on her left proffered his case, but she shook her head.

'I don't smoke, thank you.'

'Not yet?' he said jovially as he tucked one into his mouth.

She didn't want to say she hoped not ever, but she knew what a protective life she had led and that things might change. Hugh also puffed away, one arm casually draped round the back of her chair, a finger occasionally lightly caressing her bare back.

Suddenly the band broke into a jive and, extinguishing his cigarette, he seized her by the hand. The last time she had jived she had been with George, and she felt a momentary sense of guilt which soon vanished in tune with the music.

It was well after midnight when the party broke up and they wandered out into the moonlit night with the waters of the harbour sparkling in the distance, stopping while Hugh exchanged farewells with his friends. They then walked to the car park and got into the Daimler he had borrowed from his father for the evening.

As they drove away from the hotel Lottie sank back in her seat and sighed deeply, wishing that the night would never end. 'That was perfect,' she said. 'A really lovely evening and I liked your friends.'

'You looked stunning – all eyes were on you, Lottie. Where did you get that marvellous dress?'

'From the store,' she said. 'It's only on loan. Like Cinderella, I will have to take it back after the ball.'

'But, Cinderella, I didn't know you could dance so well.' Hugh glanced at her. 'You told me you had never been to a ball.'

'It's true. I have never been to a ball like that, only a jazz club.'

'You've been to a jazz club?' Hugh looked startled.

'Oh, for my birthday. With my friend, Mavis, her brother and another man.'

Hugh remained silent, then slowed down and diverted down a side road, stopping by the harbour. 'Is there anyone you're seeing Lottie? You know, anyone special? You were going out with Mavis again tonight, weren't you?'

'No, there isn't anyone, no one special.'

'Sure?'

'Sure.'

He leaned towards her, looked into her eyes and then, gently cupping her face between his hands, he kissed her lightly, at first just brushing her lips and then more firmly, his mouth pressed against hers.

Entwined in each other's arms they embraced for a long time and when eventually he released her she sat back, breathless, afraid to speak and spoil the magic, the enchantment of that moment.

At last, she felt she was not just a whim. She was special, after all.

1924

For the next six months Lottie was transported to the kind of world she had always dreamed of. She was courted, feted, loved and admired.

Without neglecting her own she became almost part of the Carson family; all unease around them had evaporated. Her life changed dramatically and it was reflected in her work. The volume of sales increased with her self-confidence and despite her youth there was a rumour she might even be promoted with a view to taking over the department when Mrs Morgan was promoted. Mrs Morgan began taking her to fashion shows with mannequins modelling the latest designs from abroad.

Not only did she learn to sail, but also to ride and, for the first time, wore breeches and looked as elegant in them as she did in the clothes she wore both for work and for pleasure.

And what pleasure! Hugh, now attached to the hospital in Wellington, often picked her up after work and they drove to the sailing club if the weather was fine before winter set in or to the stables where the Carsons kept their horses. Sometimes they were joined by Violet or even Madeleine and Andy if he was home on leave. But, best of all for Lottie and Hugh was to be alone enjoying each other's company, conscious of the extent to which they were falling deeply in love.

It was a chilly autumn day and they had been for a brisk canter in the hills above Thorndon where the Carsons stabled their horses. Lottie, in a short time, had become a proficient if not yet an accomplished horsewoman. She had a good seat on a horse and rode well. Because she was sporty and liked the outdoor life she had the gift of picking up things easily.

As they dismounted the stable groom came up to lead their horses away.

'Do you know when you will be out again, Doctor Carson?' the groom, who had already been rubbing down the horse, asked.

'I'm not too sure. I may be going away. I'll be in touch. Anything you need?'

'No sir, the horses are in good form. Mrs Marsden takes them out regularly with the captain. They will be well looked after.'

Hugh gave his horse a pat on the flank and, putting his arm through Lottie's, led her back to the car and settled her in her seat.

She waited until Hugh was settled and about to drive off. 'Going away?' she said. 'For long?'

He turned to her, an apologetic expression on his face. 'I should have told you before the ride but I only had the letter a few days ago and I was leaving it until we had the chance to talk.'

'Then let's talk,' Lottie said, hating the air of mystery, the flicker of fear that had made her flesh go cold, and the apprehension that finally, this perfect lifestyle that she had taken so long to achieve might be under threat.

'Look,' Hugh said briskly, starting the car. 'Mum and Dad are away and Violet is out. Let's go to my place and I'll explain everything.'

'I should go home and get tea ready for Dad and Bella.' Lottie looked doubtful.

Hugh glanced impatiently at his watch. 'Do that later. I want to talk to you.' And without waiting for a reply he drove in the direction of Thorndon while Lottie, still perplexed and rather anxious, sat in silence by his side.

The Carsons' house was no longer a strange place; it was almost as familiar to her as her own home and Lottie threw her coat carelessly on the chair in the hall as they came in and then went into the lounge and waited for Hugh to join her. She had finished work at lunchtime that Saturday and Hugh had picked her up and taken her to the stables where she changed. There had been nothing amiss during the short drive, no hint of anything untoward, and she looked forward to spending the rest of the day with him with her usual air of eager anticipation. Indeed, Hugh had seemed unusually relaxed and happy.

Still in his riding clothes he came into the lounge and sat beside her on the sofa, putting his arm round her shoulder and pressing her close. 'I've had a letter offering me a job in England for a year. The Great Ormond Street Hospital I told you about. One of the best children's hospitals in the world will give me an internship for a year and if I take it I have to go soon.'

'I see.' Lottie managed a wry smile. 'Well, if you must, you must. I understand that, Hugh. It is your career, after all. However, you didn't even tell me you'd applied to the hospital. I find that a bit hurtful.'

He squeezed her hand and kissed her lightly on the cheek. 'I was so sure the answer would be negative and I thought there was no point as it might worry you. And a year isn't a very long time,' he added.

'Oh, I know. I'll miss you, that's all.'

'And I shall miss you. Very much, Lottie . . .' Hugh paused, his face solemn. 'I don't know quite how to say this but I don't want you to think I'm leaving you or not thinking about you and how much we have come to mean to each other. That's true, isn't it?'

Lottie nodded. 'But . . .' she said, fearful of his answer.

'But I want to marry you and for us to get engaged now so that you know I'm serious and you will be here for me when I get back.'

For several moments Lottie was speechless. Then, 'Are you quite sure about this?'

'Quite sure. I know you are very young, but I can't imagine not wanting to spend the rest of my life with you. Do you feel the same about me, Lottie?'

He searched her eyes anxiously and she gazed steadily, lovingly, back at him.

'I think you know I do. But have you spoken to your family?'

'About us? No need. They know. Well, they know how I feel about you and I am sure they will be delighted if we get engaged. I assure you I don't need their permission.'

'I am a very ordinary girl.'

'You are a very exceptional girl. All my family love you. You know that.' Then he folded her in his arms and they were still locked in a deep embrace when the door opened and Violet stood on the threshold, gazing at the scene before her in astonishment.

'Sorry,' she said and was about to back out of the room.

'Don't go,' Hugh called, releasing Lottie who sank back flushed and breathless on the sofa. 'I want you to meet the girl I'm going to marry.'

'Oh, *Lottie*.' Violet ran towards her. 'How wonderful. Really wonderful.' She stooped as if to kiss her and then paused, looking at her brother.

'Yes, she knows,' he said. 'About England? I just told her and she has still said yes. She'll wait for me.'

'It will fly by.' Violet now bent and completed her kiss. 'It will be so exciting preparing for the wedding. We'll have a big one like Madeleine's.'

'I can't believe it,' Lottie said, still slightly shaken. 'It's all so sudden.'

'I'd have got round to it.' Hugh sat by her side again, his arm encircling her waist. 'Maybe not quite so soon, but I couldn't risk you getting away.' He stood up. 'Now, if you want I'll take you home and ask formal permission from your father. Then we must go out and celebrate. Champagne, I think, for dinner.'

It seemed only a short time later, but it was a matter of a few weeks when Lottie stood on the wharf waving as the ship gradually pulled away until Hugh's figure could be seen no more. Even then she wanted to stay and watch until the ship rounded Point Jerningham out of sight on its way to Pencarrow Head and out to sea, but it was a grim, cold day and Violet gently touched her arm and led her away.

The tears that Lottie had so far managed to restrain for Hugh's sake now coursed freely down her cheeks.

Violet put her arms right round her and held her close. Then she stood back and, producing a handkerchief, gently dabbed at the tear-stained cheeks. 'He'll be back soon,' she promised. 'The time will fly by. You'll see.'

'A year is a long time,' Lottie murmured, now dry-eyed. 'More if you count the journey.'

It took six weeks to get from New Zealand to England. A three-month round trip.

'Come back to the house,' Violet said. 'Madeleine may be back.' Madeleine and her husband had been visiting friends in the South Island, but Lottie shook her head.

'I feel I must go back to work. I have had so much time off lately and they are very good to me. I don't want them to get sick of me.'

'I'm sure they won't do that, but when you are married you'll leave anyway, won't you?'

Lottie looked at her. 'Do you know, I never thought of that. It seems such a long way off.'

'Oh, I'm sure Hugh won't want you to work and anyway,' Violet looked at her slyly, 'perhaps you'll be planning a family?'

'Perhaps.' Lottie smiled. 'Who knows?'

Planning a family. This kind of thing had been far from her mind in the few hectic weeks that had elapsed since Hugh told her his dramatic news and they had become engaged. Needless to say, her father's permission had not been withheld, even if he was somewhat overwhelmed by the thought of his daughter marrying into the Carson family. It seemed to mark a new stage in all their lives.

Back at work, Mrs Morgan greeted her kindly and took her into the little room she used as an office. 'You will miss your fiancé, Lottie.'

'Very much,' Lottie said. 'But it is important for his work and they all say the time will fly.'

'Have you any plans for after you're married?' Mrs Morgan sat back in her chair and studied her face. 'Mr Harvey saw the announcement of your engagement in the paper and at first he couldn't believe it was you. I had to laugh, but I told him it was and he was slightly disappointed because we had great hopes for your advancement in the firm and he imagined you would be leaving. I told him the wedding wasn't for eighteen months at least and that seemed to reassure him. Of course, we all realized one day you would marry – you're such a pretty girl it was inevitable – but marrying into the Carson family surprised us all, I must say. Still, anything can happen, can't it?'

'How do you mean?' Lottie looked at her in bewilderment.

'Well, anything can happen to any of us. That's all I'm saying.'

'I suppose there is nothing that says I must leave when I'm married,' Lottie said. 'You're married yourself, aren't you, Mrs Morgan?'

'Yes, I am, but I have never had children, much to my sorrow, because I did want to.'

'Then maybe the same thing will happen to me,' Lottie said, rather annoyed at the tone of Mrs Morgan's remarks, the implication that Hugh Carson was marrying beneath him. 'As you say, anything can happen and I think it is far too early to look into the future. I am happy where I am and certainly want to stay.'

'And we're happy for you.' Mrs Morgan stood up. 'You are a most accomplished saleswoman and your effect on the department's sales has been quite dramatic.' She put a hand on Lottie's shoulder. 'We should miss you terribly if you left.'

Lottie felt very bleak when she got home that night. The last six months had so transformed her life that it was an existence she had become used to. She had also become used to Hugh, seeing him regularly, being with him and she knew, without any doubt, that she was in love with him. Being older and in many ways wiser than her years she had also realized that she was still very young and the turn events had taken so suddenly and unexpectedly had astonished her. Preparing for a wedding that seemed so far off was a daunting and somehow unreal task, and she wished now that they had got married in a simple ceremony before he left and she was now on the boat with him. It could have been their honeymoon.

For once, her father was home. He often worked late for Sir Eustace or dropped in at his veterans' club where he was now a familiar face and had made many friends, a changed man indeed from the past.

Yes, how the Carsons had changed both their lives, she thought as she started preparing tea.

'Isn't it time Bella did more to help you now that she's left school?' Her father, seated in his usual corner chair, put down his paper and watched her laying the table. Bella had left school at the end of the year despite family opposition and also to the concern of her teachers. However, her looks and charm had secured her an apprenticeship at a good city hairdresser.

'In time Bella will have to.' Lottie smiled as she turned to go back into the kitchen. 'Just for now I'm used to it, and faster.'

Desmond resumed reading his paper. Now that he was in employment it never occurred to him that he should do anything to help her himself. In fact, her father never lifted a finger except to make himself a cup of tea and perhaps a sandwich when he was home early from work or Sir Eustace was away. Nor did he ever make his own bed, but left that and other domestic chores to his daughters, but mainly to Lottie as Bella somehow regarded herself as exempt from domestic routine as well.

Bella, although to all appearances docile and pretty, was at heart selfish and self-absorbed, believing that the world owed her a lot for depriving her of a mother. She had taken full advantage of the change in fortune which had happened to the family in the past two years, mainly her father's and Lottie's ability to raise themselves from the ranks of poverty and give them a reasonable, even comfortable standard of living.

As soon as Bella came home they sat round the table for tea and Bella, noticing her sister's forlorn face, asked her about seeing Hugh off. Sometimes she had seemed rather envious about Lottie's engagement and was deliberately offhand with Hugh, even to the extent of seeming to appear rude.

'Violet was there,' Lottie said. 'That helped a bit.'

'Soon to be your sister-in-law,' her father said with some pride.

'Not just yet, Dad. Hugh only left today.'

'The time will fly by, you'll see,' her father said. 'But you'll feel very sad this evening, Lottie.'

'Very sad,' she said. 'Sad but glad for him that he's doing something he wants so badly.'

'Mr Barker said he can't believe you're marrying into the Carson family,' Bella said, Mr Barker being the proprietor of the salon.

'Oh, why not?' Lottie bridled. 'Too good for me? Did he say that?'

'Just said,' Bella mumbled. 'He says he sometimes does Mrs Carson's hair, but I wouldn't know because I don't know what she looks like.'

'In fact, that's the second time I've heard that today,' Lottie said. 'Mrs Morgan said Mr Harvey couldn't believe it was me when he read the announcement in the paper.'

'Well, no offence meant but you can't really blame them.' Replete, Desmond leaned back in his chair. 'Sir Eustace said the same to me. Asked me if it was really my daughter. He said I'd be too proud to be his chauffeur – joking, of course.'

Lottie got up angrily and took the dishes back into the kitchen, putting them with such force into the sink that she broke a plate. She knew then that she was very near to tears of rage and frustration at the unfairness of it all. There were people who would constantly try to drag her down, remind her of her origins and how different they were from the family into which she was marrying. Once again she was reminded that she was not like them, and coupled with this was the realization that she was now alone, because Hugh was no longer there to comfort and support her.

Later that night, Bella, who now had Jack's old room, crept into her sister's room and snuggled close to her in bed.

'Sorry,' she said in a small voice.

'About what?' Lottie's arm closed round her.

'What I said at tea. Dad also felt bad. No reason why you shouldn't marry Hugh Carson, is there, Lottie?'

'None that I can see. Obviously he doesn't think so either.'

'Pity you didn't get married before he left.'

'That's exactly what I thought today. We could have been honeymooning at sea.' Lottie's arm tightened around Bella's waist. 'Think how romantic that would have been.'

'Funny Hugh didn't suggest it.'

'There was no time. It is only three weeks since he got the letter from the hospital. Besides, he wants a big wedding and I'm not sure now that I do.'

'Why not?'

'Because of the nasty, catty remarks people will make as you heard today – that I'm not good enough for Hugh Carson. We are supposed to be a modern, democratic country and yet there is still a lot of class prejudice about. It's suddenly hit me now that Hugh has gone.'

'There's something I should tell you,' Bella whispered as though anyone else might be within earshot. 'I saw Mum today. I bumped into her in the town during my lunch break.'

'Mum?' In the dark Lottie turned to face her sister.

'I'm afraid you won't like it very much, but I have to tell you. She said Mrs Ellis had showed her the paper about your engagement and she couldn't believe it was you. I didn't like to mention it at tea because I haven't told Dad.' Bella sighed deeply. 'Mum was very nice. She hugged me and said she had missed me. She was glad to hear about my job and that I wasn't wasting my time getting educated.'

'Well, it has taken her long enough to tell you.'

'She wants to get divorced from Dad as she is seeing someone and wants to marry again.'

'And you didn't tell Dad that?'

'Didn't mention it. Didn't dare.'

'Did she say how Jack was?'

'She said he misses Dad and us, but otherwise he is fine. He's doing well at school, but she doesn't mind that because he's a man.'

'And where does Mum live?'

'In Island Bay. She works for a very rich family, friends of Mrs Ellis. She has her own little house in the grounds and says she is very happy. Her gentleman friend works for them as well as a gardener.'

'Did she send you any message for me?'

'No,' Bella said after a pause. 'Well, not really. She didn't mention you again after telling me about Mrs Ellis seeing your engagement in the paper. That was what surprised her. Astonished her, really.' Bella paused again. 'She said she didn't know what Hugh saw in you, but you and Mum never got on, did you, Lottie?'

'Never,' Lottie said firmly. 'Never, and I wouldn't care after the way she has behaved if I never saw *her* again.'

Once more Bella sighed deeply. 'You know, I miss Mum. I really do. We had a great big hug and she said she would see me again soon. Maybe take me to where she lives and introduce me to her gentleman friend.'

Mavis said, 'I hardly ever see you these days, Lottie. I expect you are busy with your fiancé.'

There was a strange tone in Mavis's voice that made Lottie feel guilty.

It was true they met rarely; the lunches had lapsed and daily encounters were in the past. The fact was that her whole life had changed and continued to change even after Hugh left. Mavis was no longer a confidante. That role had been taken over by Violet, with whom she spent a lot of time, and her social life had been greatly enhanced. Had she changed? Yes, she supposed she had, not intentionally but inevitably.

Mavis had popped into Lottie's department during a lull.

'Hugh's gone to England,' Lottie said. 'For a year.'

'You must miss him?'

'I do. Yes.'

'It's nearly your birthday. I wondered if you'd like to come out again in a foursome. Your fiancé wouldn't mind?'

'No, of course not. Only I can't; not this time.'

'Something else on?'

'Yes. Hugh's family has invited me over to their house. I hope you don't mind, Mavis.'

'Of course I don't,' Mavis replied. She looked solemnly at her friend for a moment. 'I just hope you don't get spoiled, Lottie. You are different.'

'I am not different,' Lottie said defensively. 'Things have changed. Circumstances have changed. But I'm still me. And I'd love to come out another time, so please ask me again.'

'It's just that everyone is amazed that someone like you is marrying into the Carson family. It's bound to change you. I just think it's a pity, that's all.'

And with that Mavis turned on her heels and left.

The next six months were difficult ones for Lottie. Difficult but exciting, too. She became more involved with the Carson family.

They gave her a nineteenth birthday party, just a small one at home, and she spent most of Christmas with them. They invited Bella and her father, too, for Christmas lunch, and any slight awkwardness was mitigated by their warmth and genuine friendliness. She went to a big New Year's Eve dance with Violet, Madeleine, Andy and two of Andy's army friends as escorts so that by the autumn she felt perfectly at home with them and their lifestyle. It was as though they were grooming her to be completely absorbed into the family, to become, in effect, a Carson. And meanwhile there were frequent letters from Hugh and she wrote to him constantly. There were even vague wedding plans for the winter after Hugh had returned home.

And then, one day there was a letter. A special letter, one that completely took her breath away.

> *My own darling,* Hugh wrote, *it seems ages since I heard from you, about you, what you are doing and how much you are missing me. I miss you so much, my Lottie, and I'm so afraid of losing you that I wondered if you could bear to come over here for a time. I would pay your fare and, although I would be busy, you would have lots of free time to explore London, which is a marvellous city.*
>
> *I know it means you giving up your job for a while, but I'm sure if you explained they would have you back until I am able to return to New Zealand, which may be a little longer than we thought. They are very pleased with my progress and my chief has asked me to extend my period here. I'm not quite sure for how long, but if you could stay for a while it would make it so much easier. Please reply by wire and I'll put everything in motion.*
>
> *Love you, my darling. Hugh*

Nine

England, 1925

Lottie could see him on the dockside, one face among many, but he stood out because he was tall and handsome and, above all, because she loved him. She was excited, almost mesmerized by the sight of him and started to wave frantically until, at last, he seemed to see her and waved back.

She couldn't believe it was happening after such a long journey. Here she was: the home of Shakespeare and Thomas Hardy, the place where fellow New Zealander Katherine Mansfield sought and found not only refuge but fame. A new world was opening indeed.

As the gangplank was lowered and passengers started to descend, Lottie ran excitedly along the deck and then walked more sedately down the gangplank past the crowds thronging the quay to where Hugh stood waiting for her. He removed his hat and stooped to kiss her perfunctorily on both cheeks as one might a friend or relative, not a lover.

Then he stepped back and looked at her as though searching her face for signs of change. 'I can't believe it's you,' he said. 'It's been so long.'

His voice was strange and she had a sense of disappointment at his lack of warmth, as though she was a stranger. No sense of '*my own darling, how I've longed to see you*,' as his impassioned letters suggested, here. Had something happened since?

She put her hand to his cheek and stroked it tenderly, gazing into his eyes. 'Everything all right?' she asked.

'Everything is fine. Where's your luggage?' Hugh said briskly.

Lottie looked around. 'Being unloaded, I hope.'

'The car is just outside the dock. I'll go and find out what's happening.'

Soon the luggage arrived and was stowed in the back of the car. Hugh saw her into her seat and got into his. 'Good trip?'

'Wonderful. Long, though, but we saw some amazing places. People were very nice.'

'You'll love London – it's an amazing place, too.' Briefly he touched her hand. 'Excited?'

'Very. It was difficult getting away, as I told you. You got my letters?'

'I think so. Not sure if I got them all, but I remember reading that Harveys weren't pleased about releasing you.'

'Not at all. They said I should have given them more time. I think I skewered my chances of going back.'

'Oh, they'll probably change their minds. You know how they value you.'

'When do you think you'll be returning?'

'That, I don't know. I am learning a lot and they like me. It is too good an opportunity here to think of going back yet.' He patted her hand again in that vaguely unsettling, avuncular fashion. 'We've plenty of time.'

'I thought perhaps I might look for a job in London.'

'A job?'

'In one of the big stores. It would add to my experience of the retail and fashion business if I ever go back to Harveys or anywhere else. Doesn't have to be Harveys.'

'We'll see.'

'Where are we going now?'

'To my digs. I've got you a room on the floor above mine. I think you'll like it. It's in a nice district, not far from the hospital, and very central.'

It was a nice room looking on to a small backyard, quite large with a bed, washstand, wardrobe, chest of drawers and a table with two chairs. Functional rather than personal, like what she imagined a hotel room might be. Lottie didn't know quite what she had expected but she hadn't expected this. This was not like a reunion with a fiancé and there was a detachment in Hugh's manner that unnerved her.

She began to unpack her things and stow them away, wondering as she did how long she would be there for.

After a while there was a knock on the door and Hugh put his head round. 'Everything OK?'

'Everything is fine.'

Hands in his pockets, Hugh wandered over to the window. 'This is Lamb's Conduit Street. The hospital's just round the corner. I have to go back this afternoon and then I thought we might go out for supper and I'll show you around. Perhaps you'd like a little rest?'

'I think I'm too excited to rest. I'd rather stretch my legs. Maybe I'll just wander around. If you show me where the bathroom is I could spruce up a bit.'

'It's just along the hall at the end on the right.'

He kissed her on the cheek again. 'I must go as I have a ward round. I'll see you this evening.'

* * *

The restaurant was round the corner from the boarding house, newly opened, Hugh told her, as they strolled towards it. After he left in the afternoon she had felt restless and wandered round the area, finding without any difficulty the hospital where Hugh worked. It was a huge place, the most famous children's hospital in the world. She enjoyed exploring the area round the hospital: the maze of tiny interlocking streets and then, feeling suddenly exhausted, went back to her room and lay on her bed, thinking about the day's events. She was visited then by a sense of despair, comparing the almost unbearable excitement and anticipation with the disappointment and apprehension at Hugh's strangely stiff and formal welcome.

It was a small, intimate restaurant specializing in French food and they were given a place in the corner and presented with the menus.

Lottie opened the conversation while Hugh was studying the menu. 'Did you have a good day? I had a little walk round and saw your hospital. It is very big.'

'It is amazing and wonderful to work in.' Hugh paused while the waiter came to take their orders and ordered a bottle of wine. 'Yes, I had a busy day. I was in the operating theatre assisting, though it will be a long time before I qualify as a surgeon.' Hugh gazed fixedly at Lottie. 'And that is the difficulty. I may extend my time here. In fact, I want to get experience here I would never get in New Zealand.' He leaned across the table and put a hand on hers, the first gesture of any intimacy or affection since she had arrived. 'I'm afraid that will make a difference to us, Lottie.'

'How do you mean?'

'I won't be going back next year and that will affect our marriage plans.'

'We could get married here.' Lottie returned his gaze. 'I wouldn't mind. In fact, I rather wished we'd got married at home and I could have come over with you.'

Hugh withdrew his hand and there was a pause while their meal was served. At his suggestion they had started with escargots, which Lottie had never eaten before and to Hugh's amusement she looked at them with dismay as they were put before her, complete with implements. So he showed her how to tackle them using the special tongs and tiny fork provided and this provided some light relief in a rather tense situation. 'But the family are so looking forward to a big wedding,' Hugh said as he resumed his meal.

'But we aren't, are we? We don't need a big wedding, do we?'

'We'll have to think about it.' Hugh kept his eyes on his plate. But Lottie persisted.

'Well, what is there to think about? I don't understand.' Lottie put down her tongs. 'I don't actually like these very much. May I leave them?'

'Of course.' Hugh reached across the table. 'I'll finish them for you.'

She watched him as he attacked and finished the rest of his course. 'Hugh, is there something you don't want to tell me?'

'What?' Hugh looked up, startled.

'Do you still want to get married?'

Hugh finished his last snail and wiped the plate with a piece of bread. 'Of course I do. I just mean it will take some time. But we are still very young. Besides, Lottie, I am not in a position to get married at the moment. I couldn't afford to support a wife and family without the help of my father and I don't want that. When we got engaged I didn't realize the full extent of my ambitions. I thought I'd just become a physician with a local practice, but since I've been here my horizons have changed. I hope you understand and it won't spoil your visit. We'll still have a good time and there is plenty to do and see. When you go back I'm sure Harveys will re-engage you. You enjoy your career, don't you?'

'Yes, but that isn't the point, is it?'

'What do you mean?'

'I asked you if you still wanted to get married and your reply doesn't convince me. How long do we wait? Years? We have already been engaged nearly a year. And when I go back to Wellington how can we sustain that love so far away from each other? I'd hoped we would go back together and start planning for the wedding. That's all. But if not I am prepared and willing to stay here with you.' She looked apathetically at the dish that had been set before her. 'I really don't know why you wrote so urgently to me, Hugh, asking me to join you. I don't understand it at all.'

* * *

Despite being totally exhausted with the dramas and disappointments of the day – she had been up well before dawn, standing on deck as the ship approached Tilbury, anticipating a blissful encounter with her fiancé – Lottie felt unable to sleep. She was too tired to sleep and too shattered to cry. She only wished she had never come all this way to be greeted by someone who was almost a stranger. She was overwhelmed by a wave of homesickness and longed to be back.

Sleep eventually overtook her; she supposed it was about dawn, but she still only slept for a couple of hours and when she awoke she was hungry, having eaten so little the night before. She knew that Hugh had to leave early, but he'd told her that breakfast was available downstairs and after a quick wash in cold water she threw on some clothes and went downstairs to the small dining room at the back of the house. There was only one other person in the room, sitting at a table by the window, and she smiled at her uncertainly.

'Do sit down,' the girl, who was about her own age, said as the landlady bustled in and gave Lottie a welcoming smile.

'I know it's awfully late,' Lottie said apologetically, 'but I overslept.'

'That's all right, dear. The doctor said you would be tired after your long journey. He had his breakfast at seven and asked me to look after you. It is a bit late but I'll make an exception. I can do you bacon and eggs and a cup of tea.'

'That would be wonderful,' Lottie said gratefully and smiled at the girl opposite her.

'Have you come far?' the girl asked.

'From New Zealand. I only arrived yesterday.'

'New Zealand!' The girl was impressed. 'My name is Flora Anderson. I'm an art student.'

Lottie reached over the table and shook the proffered hand. 'I'm Lottie O'Brien, Hugh Carson's fiancée.'

'Oh *that* doctor. I wasn't sure who Mrs Smith meant. I didn't know he was engaged.'

'Then you don't know Hugh very well?'

'Not at all well. We hardly see him. He keeps himself to himself and scarcely ever eats here. Occasionally I see him at breakfast, but I'm down late too. I must say he is very good looking.' Flora's expression was a little envious, Lottie thought.

'How long have you been here?'

'A year. Have you heard of the Slade?'

Lottie shook her head.

'It's an art school, not far from here. What do you do?'

'I work in the retail trade in Wellington, in a department store. I'm a senior sales assistant.'

'And are you here for a holiday or for good?'

'Ah, that's the question. I thought Hugh was here for a year, but he told me last night he might stay on indefinitely. He's studying to be a surgeon at Great Ormond Street.'

Flora was striking to look at rather than pretty. She had a mane of untidy long, wavy black hair and a classical sculpted face, haunting dark eyes that were almost black and a firm, determined chin. There was something of the gypsy about her and Lottie liked her instinctively. Mrs Smith appeared with the plate of bacon and eggs and also a sausage and tomato which she put before a grateful Lottie.

'That will fill the empty space, dear.'

'Thank you very much,' Lottie said. 'I promise I won't be late again.'

'Oh, don't worry about that. Flora is always late, aren't you, Flora?'

Flora nodded guiltily.

'Do you know if you and the doctor will be eating in tonight?'

'I don't know,' Lottie said.

'Didn't he say?'

'No.'

'Will you be seeing him during the day?'

'I don't think so. Sorry, I don't know his plans.'

'Well, I'll have something ready just in case. I do a very nice stew with mashed potatoes.'

Mrs Smith went off and Flora sat looking with curiosity at her new friend.

'Didn't you see him before he left?'

Lottie shook her head.

'Don't share a room then?'

'Oh, no.'

'Oh, is it like that?'

'Like what?'

'Well, if you don't share a room . . . Sorry, I'm being nosey.'

'No, we don't share a room.'

Lottie felt very naïve. Of course, Flora was a sophisticated person living in London, an artist and everyone knew artists were different, with loose morals. But she then felt rather silly at the admission that they didn't share a room or obviously sleep together. Not only that, but never had, and perhaps that was at the root of her feelings of disappointment and rejection which his greeting yesterday had left her with. She had hoped to go beyond all the kissing and cuddling, the steamy sessions they had indulged in during their courtship in Wellington. Wasn't that, after all, the purpose of getting married to someone you loved?

'What are you going to do today? Or didn't you discuss that either with Hugh?'

'I'm just going to look round. I've never been to London. I've hardly ever been out of Wellington.'

'The British Museum is quite near or do you prefer the shops?'

'No, I'd like to see the British Museum and Buckingham Palace and the Tower of London.'

Lottie laughed and poured herself a fresh cup of tea. 'If you like I'll walk you to the museum or point you in the right direction as it's not far from the Slade.'

In fact, Flora walked Lottie almost to the entrance of the British Museum, pausing at various places on the way like a tour guide to point out places of interest. She was a good and entertaining companion and Lottie liked her more and more, grateful to have found a new friend so early in her visit. It took away some of the anguish she felt about Hugh.

'This area is called Bloomsbury,' Flora explained. 'It is quite an artistic part of London. I suppose you've heard of it?'

Lottie shook her head. 'I really am very ignorant, but I'll soon find out.'

'Maybe Hugh will take you round at the weekend?'

'Oh, I'm sure he will.'

'Do you have any idea when you'll be getting married?'

'Not really. Those plans are delayed by his decision to stay on longer. The idea was that we would return to New Zealand together. Now . . . Well, I don't know.'

Flora unexpectedly tucked an arm companionably through Lottie's. 'You sound disappointed.'

'Not disappointed,' Lottie said defensively, 'just a bit uncertain about our plans. But we do love each other very much and will definitely be getting married, only maybe not just yet.'

'Will you go back to New Zealand alone?'

'Maybe or I may try and get a job in a store in London. It is very early days and I still have to have a talk with Hugh to see what he wants.'

She was anxious to draw Flora's attention away from herself. 'Where do you live? I mean, where do your parents live?'

'Did you hear of a place called Dorchester?'

'Of course – Thomas Hardy. I love his novels. I studied him at school. I read several of them again on the voyage over.'

'Well, we live quite near him. He has a house called Max Gate and we are quite near.'

'Oh, do you know him? I'd love to meet him.'

'No, he is a very old man now, very important and not often, if ever, seen about the town, though my father has seen him.'

'I would really love to go to Dorset and see Hardy country. Maybe Hugh will want to go.'

Flora paused in their walk. 'Well, if he doesn't, I will. In fact, I am going home in a week or two and you can certainly stay with us. That is, unless Hugh wants to take you there.'

'That's very kind of you, Flora.' Lottie began to feel quite excited. 'I'll have to ask Hugh. Maybe he can take a short break.'

'Here we are.' Stopping, Flora pointed to the imposing building behind them. 'The British Museum. Enjoy your day. Oh, and Lottie,' Flora took a step back and studied her face, 'I hope you don't think I am too personal but you have a very interesting face, full of character. You are a beautiful girl and I wonder if I may perhaps be allowed to do some sketches and paint you?'

Lottie stared back, dumbfounded, and uncharacteristically could think of nothing to say.

'Think about it,' Flora said and, with a wave and a smile, walked away.

The British Museum was almost overwhelming and Lottie did not really know where to begin or what she was looking for. In the end she bought herself a guide and decided to take it back and study it before venturing to such an imposing place again. Perhaps the shops would have suited her better.

She left the British Museum clutching her guide and began wandering around the adjacent streets trying to find the shops. The truth was she had really no idea where she was or where she was going or how on earth to get to the shops. She had a moment of panic as she realized she was lost, wondered how she was going to get back and eventually had to ask a passer-by for directions to Lamb's Conduit Street. In fact, she had to ask several times and was exhausted by the time she finally reached the boarding house. It was about four and she had had nothing to eat, so she simply collapsed on her bed and went to sleep. She was awakened by a knock on the door and, thinking it must be Hugh, jumped up, ran across the room and flung it open to find the landlady standing on the other side.

'Oh, Mrs Smith. Do come in.' Hiding her disappointment, Lottie stood back and Mrs Smith entered, looked at the crumpled bed and then at Lottie.

'I was just having a little lie down,' Lottie said apologetically. 'I went to the British Museum and got lost.'

'It's just that Doctor Carson came back.'

'Oh, dear, and I missed him.'

'No, he couldn't stay, dear. He just wanted me to tell you he won't be in this evening for a meal and asked if you'd mind eating on your own?'

'Of course not,' Lottie said. 'Did he say anything else?'

Mrs Smith shook her head. 'Is that stew I told you about all right for you, dear?'

'It'd be lovely,' Lottie said, not telling her how hungry she was – hungry, exhausted and by now very dejected.

After a brief tap on the door Hugh put his head round, surprising Lottie, who lay on her bed reading the guide book to the British Museum. She had eaten alone in the dining room but it was not yet quite time for bed.

'Sorry, did I startle you?' Hugh came over, gave her a peck on the cheek and perched on the bed beside her. Lottie put her book down and gazed at him, overcome by her love for him, by that feeling of longing that had seemed to enrapture them both during the enchanting days of their courtship in Wellington and that now seemed part of a distant past. She reached for his hand and clasped it. Unresponsive, he took up the book and read the title. '*Guide to the British Museum.* Did you go there?'

'Yes, but I didn't understand much, it is so vast.'

'It is huge. Lottie, I am terribly sorry about tonight, but I have been in the operating theatre all day. We have some very interesting, very difficult cases. I am learning a lot.'

'That's all right,' Lottie said. 'I quite understand. You have to work, Hugh. What I don't quite understand is why you were so eager to have me over here if you are so busy?'

'I missed you. Really. I am truly sorry, but I'll make up for it.'

'Hugh, we still do love each other, don't we?'

'Of course we do,' he said. 'Why wouldn't we?'

'I just thought yesterday . . . Well, your welcome was a bit cold.'

'Darling, you've scarcely been here twenty-four hours. We've been apart a year, you know.'

'But I still feel the same about you.'

'And I feel the same about you. Honestly. Give it time.'

She clasped his hand again and leaned eagerly towards him. 'I thought maybe if you have a few days off we could go to Dorset.'

'Dorset? Why Dorset?'

'I loved Thomas Hardy at school. Your sister used to tell me off for concentrating too much on the countryside rather than the plot of his novels, particularly *The Mayor of Casterbridge*, which is supposed to be Dorchester. I'd love to go there.'

'Well . . .' Hugh looked doubtful.

'No time off at all, Hugh?'

'Oh, yes, but I'm not sure exactly when.'

'Because if you can't go Flora has asked me to go and stay with her. She lives there, which is a happy coincidence.'

'Flora?' He sounded mystified.

'One of the residents here, a pretty girl with black wavy hair. Surely you must know her?'

'Oh, *her*. Now, Lottie, you don't want to have too much to do with her. How on earth did you come across her?'

Lottie tried to hide her surprise. 'She was at breakfast. I thought she was rather nice.'

'She is not the sort of person you should get yourself involved with.'

'Why not, for goodness' sake? Hugh, you are being so mysterious.'

Hugh rose from the bed and, both hands thrust in his pockets, walked around the room, head bowed as if deep in thought. 'Without being too specific, and I don't know any details, she does have men in her room.' He looked across at her. 'You know what I mean?'

'Not really.' Lottie bridled, knowing exactly what he meant.

'Her morals aren't all they should be.'

'How do you know?' Lottie said, anxious to defend a person who had shown her such kindness. 'They might just be friends visiting. She's an artist.'

'I think there's more to it than that.'

'I rather liked her. She walked me all the way to the British Museum. Oh, and . . .' Lottie paused, '. . . and she wants to draw, perhaps paint me. She says I have a very interesting face. What do you think of that?'

Taking her by surprise, Hugh sat down on the bed and took her face between his hands, gazing into her eyes with that loving expression she remembered so well.

'I think she's right. You do have a very interesting face and a lovely one . . .'

Leaning towards her, his lips brushed hers and he then folded his arms round her and they embraced as they had not embraced since those heady days of their courtship in Wellington. Lottie lay back on bed and he lay next to her, bodies touching. Slowly he pulled away, his eyes remaining fastened on hers.

'I don't mind,' she said, 'you know . . .'

Hugh crept away at dawn, Lottie half asleep, half awake, her mind befuddled and confused at the events of the night. But above all she felt deliriously happy that it had happened at last, the thing that joined men and women, every bit as good as she thought it would be. She thought that now they really belonged to each other. Hugh, loving, tender and kind, so understanding about her shyness, the inevitable moments of awkwardness, the strangeness of it all. He had gone back to his room and returned prepared, explaining to her that they didn't want any babies, yet.

At breakfast she wanted to tell Flora all about it, that it had happened, but Flora wasn't there so she ate alone and then wandered out into the London sunshine thinking things had never been so good. She found her way to Regent Street, walking all the way because she liked exploring and, despite an almost sleepless night, seemed to have a profusion of energy, fuelled by the exhilaration of her first complete sexual experience.

She found Piccadilly Circus with its statue of Eros and walked past the store Swan and Edgar and then along Regent Street, finally pausing at another store, Dickins and Jones, whose reputation was famous even in Wellington. She went inside and climbed the stairs to the various departments, looking for a gift for her beloved. Finally she chose a rather smart but discreet tie and then went back into Regent Street and along Oxford Street, exploring the streets around until she began to feel very tired. So once again, lost, she had to ask directions to find her way to Lamb's Conduit Street and, not realizing how far she had come, eventually got back. Flinging herself on her bed she went to sleep, hoping that when she woke Hugh would be beside her again and they could resume where they had left off in the early hours of the morning.

When the knock on the door came it was not the person she had hoped for or expected. Answering the invitation to enter Flora popped her head round the door and looked concerned when she found Lottie lying down.

'Are you all right?' she asked anxiously.

'Just tired,' Lottie replied. 'I had a long walk exploring the city. Got lost, as usual.' She swung her feet off the bed. Her euphoria was still there, but somehow reality had set in and she had lost the desire to tell Flora about it. 'What time is it?' she asked.

'Just after seven. Look,' Flora perched on the bed beside her, 'I am going up to Dorset next week for a few days and I wondered if you would like to come with me and use the chance to explore Hardy country.'

'That would be very nice, but I did mention it to Hugh and I think we'll go when he has a few days off. It is very kind of you but I hope you understand.'

'Of course I understand,' Flora said. 'I can give you advice about where to stay and so on when you do decide to go. Just thought I'd ask. Are you eating downstairs tonight?'

'I think Hugh will be back soon. I'll wait for him. I may see you there.'

'Fine,' Flora said, and with a wave left the room.

By eight there was no sign of Hugh and, beside herself with hunger, Lottie descended the stairs to the dining room, which was in darkness. However, there were lights on in the kitchen at the end of the corridor and making her way there she stood hesitantly at the entrance and peered in. Mrs Smith and another woman were washing up and looked up when they saw her.

'Hello, dear. Is there anything you want?'

'I wondered if Hugh had been in touch or left a message? I've been out all day.'

'No, dear. I haven't seen him since he left this morning after hurrying through his breakfast.'

'Oh, well.' Lottie was about to turn back.

'Have you had anything to eat, Miss O'Brien?'

'No. I was waiting for Hugh.'

'We can't let you starve, can we?' Mrs Smith said jovially. 'I have a bit of pie left I served for supper. Steak and kidney. You go and sit in the dining room and I'll bring it to you.'

'That is very kind of you,' Lottie said and, going back to the dining room, switched on the lights and took her seat at a table by the window.

'The doctor is a very busy man,' Mrs Smith said, setting down a well-filled plate in front of Lottie. 'In fact, he hardly ever eats here in the evening. I think he must eat at the hospital.' She looked at her thoughtfully for a moment. 'Do you have any other friends in London, dear? Otherwise you will spend an awful lot of time on your own.'

'I expect I'll be all right,' Lottie said firmly. 'We will probably have a holiday quite soon and I may look for a job.'

'Any idea when you're getting married?' Mrs Smith looked meaningfully at the ring on her finger.

'Our plans have changed a bit because Hugh is going to continue his studies here. So, no – not at the moment. Thank you very much, Mrs Smith,' she said, taking up her knife and fork in an effort to bring an end to this unproductive conversation. 'You are very, very kind.'

Once again Lottie did not sleep very well, not because she was making love this time but because there had been no sign of Hugh.

At midnight she even crept to his bedroom but there was no answer to her timid knock on the door. In the morning there was no Hugh either and she began to worry if something had happened to him, but didn't dare voice her fears to Mrs Smith in case genuine concern turned to pity – the last thing she wanted. Flora, also, was not at breakfast; perhaps she had already eaten and, Lottie coming down late as usual, it was to solitary silence. Even Mrs Smith seemed disinclined to chat and Hugh wasn't even mentioned.

Lottie even considered going to the hospital to enquire about her fiancé, but knew in her heart that it would make him angry and she didn't want to exacerbate an already tense situation.

She spent the morning once more wandering around and visited the British Museum again, being much surer now of the route than to the shops in the West End, but feeling very uninspired by the few exhibits she saw and didn't stay long. She felt this showed up her complete ignorance and emphasized the fact that she was an uneducated colonial, hopelessly out of place in this great city which was the mother of the Empire. By now desperately tired again, she had a bite to eat at a café near the museum and went back to the digs to try and catch up on her sleep.

As she entered a smiling Mrs Smith greeted her with the good news that 'the doctor' was in and, thanking her, Lottie flew upstairs and knocked at his door.

'Oh, Hugh!' she cried as he opened it. 'Here you are. I was worried about you.'

She was about to fling herself in his arms longing for his consoling, comforting, above all loving embrace, and the words she so desired and expected, but there were no open arms and he stepped back and looked at her coldly. 'Lottie, what on earth is the matter? Making such a fuss to Mrs Smith won't help, you know, and it embarrasses me.'

'Making a *fuss*!' Lottie retorted. 'I did not make a *fuss*. I merely asked if she had heard from you. That's hardly making a fuss.'

'She said you seemed very upset.'

'Well, what do you expect?' Lottie sank on to a chair by the side of his bed.

'It does seem odd that I don't hear from you or know where you are. I don't want to be a nuisance Hugh but . . .' Once again she felt close to tears of despair and put her head in her hands.

She felt a touch on her head and looked up to see him gazing fondly down at her. 'Lottie, Lottie. Don't be so upset. Look . . .' He went back to his bed and sat on it. 'Truthfully, I'm extremely tired. I've had twenty-four hours on duty with no, or very little, sleep. You know they work us junior doctors to death, but we have a lot to learn and I am in a privileged position. They only took me on because of my father's influence. He pulled strings for me and I can't let him down. It has been a particularly stressful time trying to prove my worth to the hospital and keeping up with the workload, and I realize I may seem to have neglected you.'

He leaned forward, his hands loosely joined in front of him. 'Look, let me get a few hours' sleep and then why don't we go out for a nice meal this evening and I'll make it up to you? Dress up a bit and we'll have a good time.'

They danced close together, cheeks almost touching as they had in Wellington that Christmas Eve which had marked the beginning of such good times – six months of bliss, heavy with expectation which was realized when he asked her to marry him. Lottie wore the one dress she had packed for such an occasion and Hugh wore a dinner jacket. She had never been in such a glamorous place in her life: Ciros off Trafalgar Square, whose large main room where they were dancing was flanked by vast ornate pillars in green and gold reaching to the ceiling, and a gallery with couples leaning over watching the dancing on the floor. They had bopped and jived and now the tempo had changed and there was a slow, smoochy foxtrot. When the music finished Hugh led her back to the table in the corner by one of the pillars and they resumed their leisurely meal.

'It reminded me of Wellington,' Lottie said, gazing at him across the table.

He looked puzzled. 'Wellington?'

'The night you took me to the Christmas Eve Dance.'

'Oh, yes. Yes.'

She wondered then why it seemed such a distant memory to him, but she felt too overwhelmed by happiness to give it more than a moment's thought. She stretched her hand across the table and put it on his, displaying the ring he had given her. 'Did you have any more thoughts about Dorset?'

'Ah, Dorset. Yes, I was going to talk to you about that. For the moment it is not possible for me to get away. In fact, Lottie, I have been giving it some thought and I wondered if you should be thinking about going home. Just make this a brief holiday and then later perhaps . . .' He paused and looked at her placatingly. 'Harveys may take you back if you haven't been away long.'

She stared at him in utter shock. 'Go back to Wellington? I've only just arrived.'

'I don't mean immediately, but maybe we should have a change of plan. You see, to qualify I may be here for some time. Years, maybe.'

'*Years?*' Suddenly the euphoria of the evening vanished. 'And you don't want me to stay with you?'

'It's not that, of course I do, but as I told you I'm not in a position to keep you. That worries me. I never realized the potential I would have here and I want to make the most of it.'

'Hugh, I am perfectly happy to marry you without any ceremony and live as we are. I can get a job. I was in Dickins and Jones the other day and they have a large dress department. If they or someone like them took me on I could improve my experience, too, but I want to be with you, not thousands of miles away.'

His hand clasped hers and held it tight. 'Well, it is something we can certainly think about, but not just yet. I think you should go home. Bella and your father must miss you and Harveys won't wait long to replace you. Anyway, let's enjoy ourselves while we are here.' As the music resumed he stood up, reaching for her hand, and they spent the rest of the evening dancing close together like two people in love.

And it continued when, very late or rather early morning, they got back to the digs and walked up the stairs, hand in hand, pausing outside his room where they stood gazing at each other.

'It's very late,' he said, nuzzling her ear. 'I'll just see you to your room,' and they continued up the stairs and stood outside her door while she turned the key in the lock. She felt his arm encircle her waist and he pressed her against the wall and kissed her passionately, only releasing her reluctantly.

'Come in,' she whispered, but he shook his head.

'I'm on duty at midday. I'm desperate to get some sleep.' Then he kissed her again, only lightly on the forehead, and she watched him go down the stairs before she went slowly, a little unsteadily, into her room and shut the door. She sat for a long time on the bed gazing at the floor, slightly befuddled, she knew, with tiredness and drink that she was unaccustomed to, but clear enough to know in her heart that all was not as it should be between herself and Hugh.

Ten

Dorset

From the road Lottie could see the top of the turreted, red brick house but nothing else as it was hidden by a high wall and surrounded by trees. The gate was securely closed. Little hope of seeing the great man as they said he hardly ever went out. Once he was a familiar figure in the streets of Dorchester, but no longer. Lottie lingered as long as she could in the hope Mr Hardy just might emerge, but time passed. She could imagine that Flora, strolling about some distance away as if she sensed that Lottie wanted to be alone, was getting restless. Still, she could say that she had seen Hardy's house and that would be something to tell Madeleine. It felt like a pilgrimage.

Finally, after a last look Lottie turned away and returned to the car where she was joined by Flora, who got in and sat next to her.

'Well, I've seen it,' Lottie said, sighing deeply. 'I'll be able to tell Madeleine when I get home.' Seeing Flora's puzzled expression she continued: 'Madeleine was my school teacher – Miss Carson, the sister of Hugh. She knew that I loved Hardy and encouraged me to read, but told me off for paying more attention to the descriptions of the countryside than the plot!' She smiled at the memory. 'Of course, the Mayor of Casterbridge, Henchard, sold his wife and daughter and Casterbridge was based on the town of Dorchester. Sometimes I can't believe I'm actually here. It's like living history.' She turned to her new friend and lightly touched her arm. 'I owe all this to you. Thanks, Flora.'

'It's been a real pleasure,' Flora replied. 'Would you like to go to the coast and see more Hardy country?'

They said little during the drive through the beautiful countryside, miles of heathland and areas covered by gorse or woodland, undulating fields with grazing cattle, and Flora indicating points of interest on the way. It was all seen at its best on an almost perfect English summer's day. In New Zealand it would be midwinter.

'Egdon Heath, of course, is a name invented by Hardy and could refer to any part round here, but I want to take you to the nicest part where you can see the sea and we can have our picnic. It is called the Isle of Purbeck and Purbeck marble is very famous. Hungry?'

'A bit,' Lottie confessed and was not sorry when, after a lengthy drive through spectacular scenery, Flora finally drove into a place by the side of the road from which there was indeed a wonderfully panoramic view of the sea.

'It's almost as beautiful as New Zealand,' she gasped as Flora, with sweeping gestures, indicated the scale and scope of the view.

'And down there,' she pointed, 'though you can't see it from here – hardly see it at all, in fact – is a tiny, tiny, very old village called Tyneham and beyond that, over there,' another sweeping gesture, 'is Warborrow Bay where we used to go and swim when we were children. It is very warm.'

They returned to the car and from the boot Flora produced a large picnic basket and some rugs which Lottie carried through the gate leading into the field and, after spreading it out, flopped on it as Flora examined the contents of the basket. Shading her eyes against the sun, Lottie looked out to sea and thought how far away it was from home. This filled her with sadness as well as nostalgia, and Flora commented on her expression as she sat down beside her.

'Penny for them?' she asked and indicated the pile of tempting-looking sandwiches arranged on plates she'd set before them. 'Help yourself.'

Lottie made her choice. 'These look lovely,' she said hungrily, taking a bite. 'The sea made me think of New Zealand and how far I am from home. But,' she ate a bit more of her sandwich, 'I think I may be returning sooner than I planned.'

'Oh?' Shocked, Flora paused in the act of eating. But Lottie took her time in replying and finished what was in her mouth.

'I don't think Hugh loves me any more. He has suggested I go back to Wellington much sooner than I intended.' She turned to

Flora. 'So you see, I am more grateful than I can say for this invitation to spend time with you.'

'But this is a terrible shock,' Flora said. 'When did it happen?'

'Oh, right from when I arrived. When he met me in Tilbury I could sense something was wrong. It hasn't gone right since. In fact, the last two weeks have been awful.'

'I must say, you did seem to spend a lot of time on your own.'

'Of course, he *is* very busy. I know that. His work consumes him but he did write, no, *begged* me to come over. What has happened since he wrote the letter I don't know and he doesn't say. I just think he realizes that he is no longer in love with me; perhaps in some way I've changed and am no longer the person he proposed to which was, I must say, at the time quite unexpected. He simply feels he has made a mistake. Which he won't admit to me – not yet, anyway. I suggested we got married here, but he said his family wants a big wedding and anyway he hadn't enough money to support me. I told him I'd work, and that I'd do anything to be with him. That it would be fun to be young and in love in London!' Her eyes shone, not with tears, but with the sheer joy of how things might have been, might still be if only Hugh would change. 'But he admits now that he might be here for years and has no plans to return home.'

The euphoria of the moment lifted and Lottie looked so downcast, so desolate that Flora put a comforting arm round her shoulder. 'This is awful for you, Lottie, but can you be sure?'

'Oh, I can't be sure. I hope I'm wrong. It's his manner, his attitude. Sometimes you feel he is trying so hard. He wants to make it work but can't. He took me dancing and . . .' She looked with eyes brimming with tears at Flora. 'We made love, in bed, you know, properly, for the very first time. It was wonderful and meant so much to me, I was ecstatic; but I don't think it meant anything to him. In fact, I think he regretted it because he has avoided doing it again or even referring to it, as though he wished it had never happened. It's left me feeling horrible and somehow sordid.' Lottie vigorously brushed the tears from her eyes. 'The thing is I still love him, Flora. I adore him and I would give anything for him to change. But now I feel he won't, which is why I decided to come away with you. I had to see where Mr Hardy lives, and when I get back to London I'll see about a passage home, unless Hugh has done it already.

'You see, Flora, I am not as well educated as Hugh and the rest of his family. His sister was my teacher and she took me under her wing, anxious for me to study and succeed, and was very good to me. We were a poor family – not like the Carsons. My father drove a truck and then he went to war in Europe and came back an invalid. A few years later my mother deserted us and I had to leave school as we had no money. Miss Carson, Hugh's sister, did a lot for me and my family. Her father was the doctor who helped my father to get better and got him a job. I used to visit their home where I met Hugh and he started courting me.

'We had a wonderful, glorious six months when I learned to dance, ride, sail, swim and improve my tennis. We went to balls and ate at lovely restaurants until I felt I was every bit the equal of the Carsons and I learned to enjoy life for the first time and realized how good it could be. To my joy, my astonishment, Hugh, my partner in all this, asked me to marry him, then he went off to England supposedly only for a year, and when he came back a big wedding was to be planned. A big wedding which now won't happen.' Lottie turned despairing eyes to Flora. 'Maybe I was wrong to give in to him. He said he didn't know I was a virgin. Maybe he was testing me and I've disgusted him.'

'Oh, that is a *silly* thing to say,' Flora protested. 'That idea is so out of date and old fashioned.'

'Not in New Zealand,' Lottie replied, sombre-voiced. 'Not where I live.' And suddenly hating this conversation, giving so much of herself away, she jumped up and ran down the hill in the direction of the sea, desperate to hide her real distress from her friend.

Flora, deeply compassionate, understood and held back, but when at last Lottie came slowly back up the hill Flora held out towards her the welcoming, loving hand of friendship.

The Anderson family had a lot in common with the Carsons, Lottie decided. There was the same comfortable, even affluent set-up. A large red brick house in a tree-lined avenue with a tennis court and a well-tended lawn and garden. Mr Anderson, too, was a professional man, a solicitor of some standing in the town and Mrs Anderson the same kind of friendly motherly woman like Mrs Carson, who bustled around directing the fairly large staff, more than the Carsons, and keeping her brood in order. A big hug for Lottie when she had arrived followed a searching look into her eyes, as though she knew instinctively almost all there was to know about her and what kind of life she had led. How much Flora had told her in advance she didn't know.

There were three other siblings, all boys, one at university and two still at school. In the evening they all sat round the dinner table, Mr Anderson, a jovial kindly man sporting a large moustache, at the head.

They were interested to hear about New Zealand and both gratified and impressed by her enthusiasm for their most famous citizen who Mr and Mrs Anderson had met but made no claim to know well. From the ring and also perhaps because Flora had told them, they knew that Lottie was engaged and made polite but not intrusive enquiries about her fiancé. It seemed that the son at university wanted to be a doctor too.

Lottie felt engulfed by the kindly, comfortable, welcoming Andersons and would like to have prolonged her stay, but there was that urgency to get back and be with Hugh, whose former ardour she still so desperately hoped to rekindle.

Maybe when she got back Hugh would tell her that he had realized how much he missed her and everything would change.

On the last day of her stay Flora, as she had promised, drove Lottie to see the cottage where Hardy was born. After she parked the car they followed a path through a wood that led to the small thatched cottage which again, like the big house, they could only see from a distance being partly obscured by trees.

Once again Lottie could only stand and gaze at it while Flora looked on.

'One thing more to tell Madeleine,' Lottie said as she rejoined her friend. 'It is such a beautiful, peaceful spot. She will be very envious.'

'As a boy he walked to Dorchester every day to school and back, quite a distance.'

'He was working class like my family,' Lottie said. 'He knew about heartache and hardship. Does anyone live there now?'

'I'm not sure. His sister, maybe. Daddy will know.' She tucked her arm through Lottie's and they strolled back to the car. 'I want to take you in another direction today,' Flora said. 'There is a sweet little village called Plush. It is a pleasant drive and we can picnic on the way.'

So they headed north up over rolling hills and past fields full of sheep and cattle to Plush, tucked in the hills, smoke gently spiraling from the country inn on the edge of the village. They then pressed on further until they selected a spot which overlooked Plush and the way they had come, and once again rugs were spread on the grass, Flora opened the picnic basket and they began to eat.

'I'll miss this a lot,' Lottie said when she had finished eating, lying back on folded arms and gazing at the sky. 'It is so beautiful and how lucky we've been with the weather. I've completely fallen in love with Dorset, as I knew I would. I can't wait to tell Hugh what he's missed.'

'And have you missed Hugh?' Flora produced a pad and began sketching Lottie as she had done several times during her visit, swift, deft outlines which showed considerable skill, capturing various aspects of Lottie's personality.

'Of course I have. I love him as much as I ever did and I hope when I get back he will show me just how much he's missed me. Or am I being silly?'

Flora tactfully didn't reply, but put down her pad and pencil and looked across at Lottie. 'I would very much like to do a portrait of you when I get back to London. In fact, I'm quite sure a number of students in my class would like to as well. How would you consider being a model – clothed, of course,' she added hastily. 'And there would be some payment. It may help while you think things over and maybe extend your stay a little, if not for good. Help to tide things over with Hugh. Who knows?'

'Well, it's something I'd certainly think about, depending on how long I'm going to stay and that does depend on Hugh, but certainly long enough for you to paint my portrait. That would be very flattering.' She didn't add whether or not she thought Hugh would approve.

At first on her return things did seem to go well and Hugh had given her a warm, if not exactly loving, welcome. He seemed pleased to see her. He had hugged her briefly and kissed her cheek, taking care that their lips didn't meet. She had sent him a telegram with the time of her return and when she got back to the digs mid afternoon he had left a message with Mrs Smith that he would be back at about 7 p.m. to take her out to dinner. It had all seemed very promising and she had felt enthused and excited, and had dressed with care, hoping to seduce him all over again.

Now they sat facing each other across the dinner table in the restaurant he had taken her to after she first arrived. She took the lead by talking enthusiastically about her trip: the beauty of the Dorset countryside, the wonder of seeing the places where Thomas Hardy not only lived now but was born, the kindness of the Andersons. She went into raptures about the Dorset countryside. Above all, in view of his opinion of Flora's allegedly loose morals, their *respectability*, Mr Anderson being a prominent lawyer in the town and a member of the town council.

Impulsively she reached across the table for Hugh's hand. 'One day I hope we'll go there together. I'd love you to see it. Maybe . . .' She paused and gazed at him. 'Did you think any more about marrying here, Hugh? I love England so much and would be very happy to stay for a while. I know your family want a big wedding but I don't mind, I . . .'

Abruptly he withdrew his hand from hers and averted his eyes. Then, seeming to come to some decision, he raised them, his gaze fastened unfalteringly on hers, his face solemn, unsmiling. 'Lottie, I was hoping to tell you in a gentler way but I can't find one. I know it will be hard for you and, believe me, it is for me . . .'

'You don't love me any more,' she butted in, her expression bleak.

'Listen,' he went on urgently. 'It's not that I don't love you, but . . . I have met someone else. It was totally, utterly unexpected, and the last thing I wanted in the world, but that's how it is.'

His gaze faltered again while hers had become fixed on his face, as if her whole body had turned to ice, frozen her to her seat. Her heart was beating rapidly, uncontrollably; the shock seemed overwhelming and then everything fell into place, the whole thing from the arrival in Tilbury until this moment. Lottie had known something was wrong but wondered how she could have been so blind, such an ass as not to have recognized it before.

'I can't understand,' she said slowly, evenly, as if spacing her words, 'why you let me come. Would this not have been kinder in a letter before I left home?'

'It was all so sudden. It happened after you'd sailed. I had met her but not fallen in love. She is a doctor at the hospital. Her name is Sylvia. It was just like that for both of us, a *coup de foudre* as the

French call it. I can't explain it, Lottie, and I am dreadfully, dreadfully sorry, but I couldn't go on deceiving you, and as it is I do feel bitterly ashamed. I tried to fight it and so did Sylvia because I told her about you; she knows the situation completely – everything. We both feel bad about it, but we just can't help ourselves.' He lowered his head as if, even now, he was ashamed of what he was doing to a young woman who at his suggestion had come halfway around the world to be with him. In a whisper he added: 'I've asked Sylvia to marry me.'

Rage now supplanted shock and, with an irony she didn't know she possessed, Lottie said, 'So you are currently engaged to two people.' Slowly, she took the ring from her finger and put it on the table in front of him. 'Well, as of this moment you're not, so you can give this to Sylvia.'

'Don't be too hard on me, Lottie.' With his finger Hugh tried to edge the ring back towards her. 'We're both – Sylvia and I – very distressed, but for me to go on with you would be unthinkable, the worst kind of hypocrisy. I would be living a lie. I tried several times to tell you before, but I lacked the courage.'

'Knowing all this I can't think why you had to go to bed with me. We had resisted for so long, so what was I supposed to think? That was unforgivable, too.'

'I know it was. But I am a man and you are a very desirable girl, and I've had to control myself several times in the course of our relationship because it was obvious to me that you were a passionate woman. But I didn't know until it was too late that it was the first time for you, and I felt utterly ashamed and miserable, which is why I couldn't let it happen again. It was despicable and throughout all this I have behaved despicably. My family will think so, too.' He looked as though this admission made him feel better and leaned towards her. 'If there is anything, *anything* at all I can do to ease the pain of this please tell me. Anything.'

'No, there is nothing.' Lottie had made a superhuman effort to recover her self-control. She felt she owed it to herself, to her pride, not to break down in front of him. 'Nothing I can think of except to say that perhaps Sylvia is the woman for you – a doctor, undoubtedly a better class, more like your family, the sort of people you're used to, Hugh. Maybe coming from the wrong part of Wellington with the wrong sort of family I was never right for you.'

'Please don't say that, Lottie. It is completely untrue. You were beautiful, fun and I fell in love with you. I am still deeply fond of you and we have many very lovely memories of our time together. I did love you and my family love you and will, I know, be deeply upset and angry with me.'

'Oh, so you haven't told them yet?'

'Of course not. I don't think they'll be pleased. Madeleine and Violet adore you.'

'And if you didn't think I was a virgin – something I find extraordinary – did you expect me to be like Flora, someone you think has "loose morals" which, incidentally, I can tell you isn't true because I got to know her very well on the trip and she has a steady boyfriend, a fellow artist.'

'Good, I am very glad to hear it and I never thought you had loose morals, but I knew you had seen someone else. Only I didn't want to sleep with the woman I was going to marry. I didn't think it was right. Now, Lottie, what can I do to ease this? I would like to remain friends and I would like maybe to show you round London? I can take a few days off.'

Lottie felt the rage rising up in her. 'What about your suggestion that I go back to Wellington?'

Now that anger had supplanted grief, at least for the time being, she attempted to keep the sarcasm out of her voice.

'I have made some enquiries and, if you agree, there is a ship sailing from Tilbury next week, the *SS Ceramic*.' His face reflected his relief that she was being so reasonable, so understanding, so like Lottie and the sensible girl that she was. 'I'm sure we can get a berth, first class of course, and all on me.'

'I shan't be on that boat, Hugh. I am going to stay on in London for a while. Flora wants to paint me and has invited me to model for her class.' Then, seeing his shocked expression: 'Oh, don't look scandalized, Hugh, I'll have *all* my clothes on. I'm going to wire Flora and ask her if she knows somewhere I can stay and then I'm going to move out of the digs. Yes, I'm distressed, I'm shaken, it is not as I'd hoped, but I'm going to try and make the best of what is left of my time in London.'

She looked up at the waiter hovering over them and shook her head. 'I'm sorry, the food is lovely but I don't think I'm hungry any more,' and, rising from the table, she walked steadily and with dignity out of the restaurant and then quickly along the street towards the digs, sobbing uncontrollably as one for whom the effort had been all too much.

The wire said '*Flora, come at once*' and like a good friend, the sort everyone needs, Flora came. In a day she had Lottie out of the digs in Lamb's Conduit Street and lodging with a friend in Mecklenburgh Square, not too far away, but far enough from the treacherous Hugh, who Lottie felt she never wanted to set eyes on again.

The house in Mecklenburgh Square was owned by a fellow artist of Flora's, an older woman, Magda Feldman, who was married to one of the tutors at the Slade. They didn't let rooms, but occasionally were willing to put people up for a short time out of friendship and Magda had immediately responded to Flora's request to house Lottie, who she was told was going to model for a while before she went back to New Zealand.

Lottie took to Magda immediately. She was a large, untidy, comfortable-looking woman with a pronounced German accent and a cigarette dangling permanently from the corner of her mouth. She kept flicking the ash off her full bosom in a gesture which was both comic and somehow endearing, as if her appearance meant nothing to her, which clearly it didn't. She apologized to Lottie for having only a tiny room at the top of the house because they had friends visiting from Germany and the studio she shared with her husband Curt occupied the whole of the second floor.

Lottie felt grateful, embarrassed, confused at the rapid exit, almost an escape, from Lamb's Conduit Street, which took place in daylight the day Flora returned from Dorset. She told Mrs Smith that there had been an emergency at home, but did not say goodbye to Hugh, who she had not seen since the night she heard about Sylvia.

Despite her misery she felt now that she had entered an entirely new, uncharted world, that of Bohemia which was quite strange to her but not unpleasant, something new and even exciting if she could get over her distress. At least it took her mind off the damage that had been done to her self-esteem though she doubted if anything would help her entirely ever to forgive or forget Hugh. You can't be desperately in love and then, at a moment's notice, not be, whatever the wrongdoing on the part of the beloved. Love, being irrational anyway, is not like that, but eats at the fabric of the heart, the very core of the emotions.

At times she seemed completely overwhelmed by grief and depression at his rejection of her. Although she wanted to go home she also dreaded it as it was humiliating to leave as someone loved and soon to be married, then to return alone as a jilted woman no longer loved or desired.

The easy-going nature of the Feldman residence enabled her to come and go as she pleased; no questions were asked as to why she was there and, left to herself, she whiled away her time indulging her passion for exploring London, that vast metropolis, mother of a vast Empire of which New Zealand was but a tiny part. She loved the Georgian terraces not only of Mecklenburgh Square but the surrounding streets of this area known as Bloomsbury; the uniformity of the tall houses fronted by iron railings through which one peered down into dark, mysterious basements doubtless occupied by servants; the number of squares filled with majestic trees and shrubs, with nursemaids pushing prams, elegantly dressed ladies walking dogs and bowler or top-hatted gentlemen in formal attire hurrying through in a businesslike fashion. In addition there were numbers of idlers occupying the park benches, many with lost or vacant expressions perhaps indicative of the fact that they were out of work because of the disastrous economic consequences of the war, which had led to widespread unemployment. Evidence of poverty was everywhere if one ventured beyond the comfortable parameters of Bloomsbury to the back streets surrounding King's Cross or Euston railway stations. Here there were children playing, scruffy dogs running wild and lines of washing hanging across the street while working-class women in overalls gossiped in doorways, occasionally stopping to soothe a crying baby or box the ears of a young miscreant who had got out of hand.

She discovered not only the treasures of the British Museum but also of the Royal Academy and the National Gallery, magical places offering hours of enchantment and enlightenment to an unsophisticated uncultured colonial like herself which, while giving pleasure, only seemed to emphasize her lack of sophistication, culture and general knowledge of the world. She realized how empty and barren most of her life had been so far and wished that she had time and above all the leisure to learn and discover more. Her reading though extensive seemed ephemeral and she had hardly touched the classics.

Although well educated, Hugh had not been one for cultural pursuits and she had learned more about riding, sailing, dancing and playing tennis from her association with him than she had about art galleries or museums. Perhaps it was not too late. She had always loved literature, thanks partly to Madeleine, and Flora, in their many conversations in Dorset, had introduced her to other topics, mainly artistic, of which she had hitherto been ignorant.

However, she was aware that in fact she was now living on borrowed time, that money was getting short and there was no real reason to prolong her stay in England. She also worried about her family, especially about leaving Bella for so long, and realized that she had been rather selfish in placing so much emphasis on her own happiness to the exclusion of that of those near to her. She had even been prepared to stay here with Hugh indefinitely and now, belatedly perhaps, she was consumed by guilt. There was, however, the wish to have her portrait painted as a memorial, if nothing else, of this experience which had not turned out as she had expected.

Flora had told her to relax and be herself. She was sitting on a comfortable chair dressed in her normal clothes, face slightly in profile so that she was able to see out of the window on to the square, which once again was filled with sunshine, though with the beginning of September there was an autumnal chill in the air.

As term had not yet started at the Slade Flora had asked the Feldmans if she could use their studio and she had already made her preliminary sketches and started the painting.

Lottie was a good sitter, patient and obedient. She was also much more relaxed than she had been when she first arrived at the house in Mecklenburgh Square. She had soon made friends with the Feldmans, who insisted that when she wished she joined them at mealtimes, and would not think of accepting payment.

'I don't know what I can do to thank them,' Lottie remarked, trying to be careful not to change her position.

'Don't worry, they don't expect anything.'

'Maybe I can send them something when I get home.'

'Any idea when that will be?'

'No. I love it here, you know. London is the most amazing place. I can understand how Katherine Mansfield didn't want to go back to New Zealand once she had been in London.'

'Katherine Mansfield. She's quite famous. Did you know her?'

'No, but Hugh's family did. They lived almost next door to her family, whose name was Beauchamp. New Zealand is very proud of her – now that she's dead.'

'Isn't it always the way,' Flora murmured. Then, 'Just keep your face there, Lottie. I know it's difficult, but try not to move.'

'Sorry.'

'Many artists are only appreciated when they're dead.'

'I'm sure that won't happen to you. You'll be famous in your lifetime.'

'Oh, I don't know.' Flora put down her palette and stretched. She wore her usual exotic attire: this time loose, baggy oriental-type trousers under a purple painter's smock and smoked constantly as she painted. 'That's enough for today. I think you can relax.'

Lottie got out of her chair and took a peek at the painting. It was odd to see oneself captured on canvas and she gazed at it critically for a few moments while Flora cleaned her brushes.

'Too early to give a judgement,' Flora said, noting her expression.

'No. I quite like it.' Lottie stepped back. 'If anything it flatters me.'

'Well, artists see their subjects in a way often unfamiliar to them.' She gazed appraisingly at Lottie. 'You have a very vital, interesting face, Lottie. I've told you this before. But it has changed slightly since I first met you. Still beautiful, still interesting, but sadder, greyer, a little haggard. That's bloody Hugh for you, I expect.'

Lottie acknowledged that she might be right with a shrug but said nothing.

'Understandable.' Flora tapped her shoulder. 'Look, I'm going to a party tonight. Why don't you come? It'll cheer you up.'

Why not? Lottie thought. Better than sitting alone in her tiny room or pacing the streets of London full of gloomy thoughts about her uncertain future. 'That would be nice,' she said. 'I'd like it.'

'Good.' Flora finished tidying the studio in case others wished to use it, putting her canvas in the corner of the room and covering it with a cloth. Then she stood up. 'Look, there is something I should tell you. The place we're going to tonight belongs to my boyfriend, Rufus. I mentioned him briefly to you in Dorset, remember, but things have progressed since then. I'm moving in with him but I don't want my parents to know – they would be shocked. I hope you understand.'

'Of course I understand,' Lottie said. 'And I wouldn't dream of telling your parents, even if I were to see them again, which is unlikely. When the picture is finished I will have to contact Hugh about a ticket home. I've hardly any money left.'

'I can let you have some.'

'I may take advantage of that to avoid seeing Hugh, but I'd rather not. I can't avoid going home and I'm anxious about my father and Bella, from whom I've heard nothing despite my letters. Of course I also dread it, but it has to happen sometime. Life has to go on.'

'And one day I hope you'll come back and see me. I shall miss you.'

'And I you.' Impulsively Lottie kissed Flora firmly on the cheek. 'You are such a good friend and I'm so lucky to have you. I simply don't know what I'd have done without you. I will never, ever forget you and all you've done for me.'

The party was in a rather grand four-storey house overlooking the canal in an area known, perhaps because of this, as Little Venice. It was a wealthy, elegant part of London that Lottie hadn't visited before, though they approached it at nightfall and only the lights in the houses reflected on the water gave her any idea what kind of place it was.

It was also the first time she had met Rufus, who occupied a flat on the first floor that apparently belonged to his parents, whose main home was in the country. The party was in full swing when they got there and Rufus was already rather drunk, as were most people in the room, which was in semi-darkness. To the music from the gramophone couples gyrated on the floor, from which the carpet had been rolled back, their arms entwined, lips and faces touching.

Rufus was a tall, lean redhead and anything else about his appearance was difficult to make out as he swept Flora on to the dance floor and enveloped her in a bear-like hug. Lottie immediately felt out of place in the melee and, wishing she hadn't come, sought rather desperately for a means of exit. As if sensing her distress a man who had been leaning against the wall, glass in hand, viewing the scene, approached her.

'Would you like a drink?' he asked.

'Well.' Peering through the gloom at her saviour, Lottie nodded. 'Just a small one. Thank you.'

'There is champagne. It's Rufus' birthday.'

'Oh, I didn't know that. Yes, a glass of champagne would be nice.'

'Stay here, don't move,' he said and vanished into the next room, emerging after a few moments with a glass for her and his own refilled.

'I see you don't know anyone.'

'No, I'm a friend of Flora's. Do you know Flora?'

'Everyone knows Flora.' The stranger took a sip from his glass. 'Look, the next room is quieter. Would you like to go there?'

'Yes, I can hardly hear you.'

They slipped out of the room; Lottie was glad to leave the noise behind and relieved to find that the adjoining room which contained the bar was not only quieter but almost empty. It was comfortably furnished, obviously the lounge of the flat, whereas the one with the gramophone was possibly the dining room with the table pushed back against the wall. Lottie felt hot and flustered and brushed back her hair, aware of the stranger's interest by the way he scrutinized her face.

'Are you an artist?' he asked.

'No, I'm . . . well . . . nothing much. I'm on a visit here from New Zealand.'

'I thought I recognized that accent,' her companion said triumphantly. 'I'm Adam.'

'I'm Lottie.' It seemed silly and rather formal in the circumstances, but they shook hands then laughed in an embarrassed way, and Lottie felt an immediate rapport with him.

'I've only just got here myself,' Adam said, 'which is why I am one of the few sober people here, besides you, of course. Tell me, how do you come to be here with Flora?'

'It's a long story,' Lottie said, 'but, briefly, I met her in the digs I lived in when I first came to London. She was very kind to me and has become a very good friend.'

'You know she's going to move in with Rufus?'

'Yes. Are you an artist, too?'

'Yes. Well, I sculpt – same thing.' His feet started tapping. 'Look, do you want to dance?'

'I might as well now I'm here,' Lottie said and she left her half-empty glass on the table and went into the room next door, where there was some energetic jiving going on into which she and Adam entered with gusto.

The evening, which had seemed to start badly, got better. Adam was not only a good dancer, but remained sober and proved quite an interesting companion, although there was little chance to have a conversation. He was solemn and scholarly, dark-haired and dark-jowelled with an aquiline nose, deep-set eyes, tall and bespectacled. Not strictly attractive, not dashing in the way Hugh had been, but interesting enough to engage her attention, even her interest. In the slow dances he didn't attempt any undue intimacy, such as was commonplace among the other couples locked together on the tiny square that was the dance floor; she respected him for that and took it as a sign that he, in turn, respected her.

Various couples kept on disappearing amid gales of giggling, she supposed into a nearby bedroom or bedrooms judging by the size of the flat, but she and Adam went on dancing, chatting between numbers as if they were old friends, had another glass of champagne and some birthday cake when the time came for Rufus, who surprisingly was still on his feet, to cut it. By then Flora had introduced him to Lottie, was glad that she had acquired a partner and introduced her, as far she could in the melee, to one or two others who were too far gone to take much notice.

It was hot, noisy and eventually Lottie began to flag.

'I think I should go home,' she said as she and Adam were dancing a slow foxtrot, feeling more familiar now, their bodies growing closer, the firm grip of his hand on her back tightening as his lips brushed her cheek.

'Where's home?' he murmured, his mouth touching her ear.

'Mecklenburgh Square.'

'Oh, the Feldmans. I'll take you there. You can't possibly go alone.'

Lottie had indeed been rather fearful of venturing out into the dark and she had no idea of the time.

'Well, if you're sure.'

'I'm sure,' Adam said. 'Let's go. No one will take any notice.'

'Shouldn't we say goodbye? Won't we seem rude?' Lottie looked around, but there was no sign of her host or of Flora.

'I think they're busy,' Adam said with a wink. 'We'll send our apologies.'

Outside it was cool with a welcome breeze, still warm for September. It seemed natural for him to take her hand and they walked slowly along the side of the canal in the direction of Edgware Road, where he hailed a cab and gave the address.

'You know the Feldmans quite well?' Lottie asked, sinking gratefully back against the seat.

'Carl is my tutor. I stayed there, too, when I was looking for a place.'

Still clasping hands in an atmosphere of warm intimacy they fell silent as the cab made its way through the London streets. Gazing out of the window Lottie thought of Hugh and of the night they returned from Ciros and how different the end had been from the one she had been anticipating. How they'd stood outside her door and all she got was a peck on the cheek instead of an embrace, and instead of love there was that cold feeling of rejection. She should have known then. It had been wrong from the start.

The cab stopped and the cabbie looked back at them enquiringly.

'Thanks.' Adam jumped out and held out a hand for Lottie before paying the driver.

'Aren't you going home?' she asked, looking surprised.

'I thought I'd say hello to Carl. Do you mind?'

'Not at all if he's up, but it is late.'

'Carl won't mind. He's like that.'

Lottie let herself in with the key and as she anticipated the house was in darkness. As she started groping for the light switch Adam closed the door and followed her in and then suddenly, gently, with no roughness or sense of compulsion, he pressed her against the wall of the hall and began kissing her passionately, not clumsy, and with great skill. She felt her body yield quite willingly to him and there was no doubt what he wanted. With the memory of that fatal, unfulfilled night with Hugh in mind, she knew that it was what she wanted, too.

Eleven

Looking around at the people dancing, Lottie was quite happy to sit this one out with Adam, who had his arm around her waist. He did dance but he didn't enjoy it much. It was her birthday, a night out spent celebrating it with Flora and Rufus and inevitably in a moment of reflection her mind went back to the last one spent with the Carsons, after Hugh had left for England, when she was treated as a future member of the family. How would they regard her now?

'You look pensive.' Adam gazed at her surreptitiously.

'Just thinking,' Lottie replied. 'Wondering where I'll be this time next year.'

'And where were you last year?'

'With the Carsons. Hugh's family.'

His arm tightened round her waist, but he said nothing. Adam was very tactful. She had told him about Hugh; it was inevitable and she had to. Altogether he was a really nice man, kind, thoughtful, clever and above all considerate. In a short time he had taught her more about love than she had ever learned from Hugh, which was not surprising. But he wasn't Hugh and she wasn't in love with him. Not yet, anyway. Perversely she still yearned for Hugh. So she supposed that she was using Adam, who answered that desperate need that Hugh had inspired for completion, for a fuller sexual experience. Their love-making was good and happened often. But she knew it wouldn't last and when the money ran out, as it nearly had, even with aid from the generous Flora, she knew she would have to go back to New Zealand. But Adam helped to ease the pain of her rejection by Hugh, even if it wasn't completely assuaged. Also, the Feldmans were making polite noises that they might require her room.

It was late and she was tired, but didn't want to spoil the fun. However, when the music stopped and Rufus and Flora came back to the table, indefatigable dancers as they were, they confessed they had had enough too.

'It's been a lovely evening,' Lottie said sincerely. 'Thank you for it.'

Adam and Rufus got up to pay the bill and Flora reached over and clasped her hand. 'I'm glad we could share it with you and only by a fluke discovered it was your birthday.'

Lottie smiled. It was a fluke. Now that term had resumed she had started modelling for the art class, and when Flora suggested an outing Lottie had told her it was her birthday and immediately a trip was arranged to a small club, tucked away in the bowels of Soho, that did dinner and had a small dance floor. In many ways it had been a perfect evening – four people, well suited and relaxed and at ease in one another's company.

'I was wondering where I'd be this time next year. Last year I was with Hugh's family. I told Adam when he asked me, but he didn't mind. He is very sweet.'

'He *is* sweet,' Flora replied, 'and I also think he is very sweet on you.' She carefully examined Lottie's face. 'It's too soon after Hugh, isn't it, to know how you feel?'

'I do like him,' Lottie faltered, 'but not like Hugh. Not "in love". In a way I feel I'm using him.'

'I don't imagine he minds.'

'But I have to go home, Flora. I can't stay here forever.'

'Why not? What is there to take you back home?'

'My family. My sister, especially. I worry about her and also leaving Dad for too long. They are poor letter writers and I have had hardly any correspondence from them.'

'But if they're not missing you it's a pity you have to go back just when you are settling in here, earning a bit of money and, well, beginning to enjoy life, which you richly deserve after what you've been through. Think of Katherine Mansfield.'

'Yes, but I'm not Katherine Mansfield. I once thought I'd write books, but I have no desire now, no real talent. I *am* enjoying myself. I love it here but, well, I'll have to think about it.'

Lying awake next to Adam in his small bachelor flat just behind the National Gallery and Trafalgar Square, high up overlooking Nelson's Column, Lottie thought back over the conversation with Flora, the fun they'd had that evening and the fact that she was enjoying the kind of Bohemian student life that she was gradually being absorbed into more and more and loved. She knew she could never be like them, she was too ignorant and naive, but she did listen a lot. Above all, she observed, and now that she was modelling, she felt she was becoming more like them. Besides, Adam had taught her so much and not just about love.

He showed her places in London she could never have visited without him: Hampstead Heath, Greenwich, the River Thames at Richmond, Hampton Court, the gardens at Kew and even tourist spots like the Tower of London, Westminster Abbey and Buckingham Palace. He taught her much more about art in the various London galleries. He had no interest at all in sport so in every way could not be more unlike Hugh, who he had never questioned her about until gradually she had begun to reveal, little by little, her background with the Carsons carefully, hesitantly, because when one considered it, it was so dauntingly grim.

Adam stirred beside her in the cramped bed and groped for her, then, opening his eyes, blinked hard. 'You awake?'

'Yes.'

'Thinking?'

'Yes.'

'You're always thinking.' He heaved himself up in bed and looked at his watch. 'It's only five o'clock. Did you have any sleep at all?

'A bit.'

'Tell me what you're thinking about.'

'I have to go home, Adam. The Feldmans want my room. I have to see my family. It's a very uneasy situation.'

'You could always come back.'

'I could.'

'I wish you would, Lottie. I'm beginning to – well, it must be obvious. I'm falling in love with you.'

She put her hand on his but continued to gaze ahead into the semi-darkness. Ahead of her stretched a future as uncertain as the kind of day it would turn out to be, sunshine or cloudy? The climate in London was not unlike that in New Zealand and one never knew what weather to expect.

'You could always move in with me while you make up your mind. There's not much room, but . . . Or I could move and get a larger flat. Or would that be too much of a commitment?'

She turned to him, gripping his hand. 'You're so good, Adam,' and impulsively she leaned over him, positioning herself comfortably and invitingly in the bed as he moved towards her and locked her in a strong embrace.

He was too good. Much nicer than Hugh, but she knew it was too early to make any kind of commitment to someone she had only known a short time. She knew how things changed, how people changed. The Hugh in London – cold, remote – had been unrecognizable from the man she fell in love with in Wellington. He had become a completely different person, quite cynically making love to her when he knew he was in love with someone else and about to ditch her. Yet now she was sure he would disapprove of her relationship with Adam. He would consider her a 'loose woman', rather in the way he had condemned Flora, who obviously had entertained Rufus in her bed in Lamb's Conduit Street. Not many men, just one, and Hugh had jumped to his own conclusions. But then men and women were supposed to behave differently. A woman who gave her body too often was loose, but for a man it was considered normal, even expected.

She had jumped on a bus going up Tottenham Court Road and then, after alighting at Russell Square, sat for a while in the square thinking over what Adam had suggested: to stay in London or to go home for a visit and then return, maybe forever, rather like Kathleen Mansfield. It was an appealing prospect, but then there was Bella and her father who she felt now she had let down, even neglected. Their silence worried her. She had written a letter only a few days before, one of many regular letters which unfortunately took so long to arrive.

Arriving in Mecklenburgh Square she let herself in and went straight up to her room to prepare for the day. She had a modelling session in the afternoon and Flora wanted to try and finish her portrait back here, where she would have time to talk to her about her future, relishing the prospect of Flora's good common sense to help her in her dilemma.

She was about to take off her clothes ready for a bath when there was a knock on the door and she opened it to find Magda standing outside. 'Oh, Magda,' Lottie said apologetically, stepping aside. 'Do come in. I was going to take a bath.'

Her heart sinking, she closed the door as Magda, expressionless, came in, fearing that she was now going to get her notice.

'This came for you, Lottie,' Magda said, handing her a buff envelope. 'I think it came from your former digs and they had trouble finding you.'

'Oh, thank you.' Lottie reached for the envelope, her heart now racing. A wire could only mean bad news and she tore open the envelope.

She was right. Scanning the few words she slumped on to her bed and handed it to Magda, who read aloud: 'We have trouble at home. Please come back, Dad.'

The two women stared at each other as Lottie said, 'What can I do? This sounds awful.'

'You could telephone him?'

'We don't have a telephone. They are not very common in Wellington. Oh, I know. Maybe the place where my father works. Could I use your phone, Magda?'

'Of course,' Magda said, putting a hand sympathetically on Lottie's shoulder. 'I'll do anything I can to help.'

Getting the telephone number of Sir Eustace, or his whereabouts, was not a simple matter and took time, and also then to track her father, and it was not until the evening of the next day, due to the time difference, that Lottie was finally able to hear the sound of her father's voice crackling over the wire.

'Is that you, Lottie?'

'Oh, Dad, it took ages to get to you. What is it, Dad? What is the matter? Are you all right?'

There was a silence and then the voice crackled again sounding nearer this time, maybe as he got used to the unfamiliar instrument and held it closer to his mouth. 'Lottie, it's about Bella. She is going to have a baby and we do need you here as quick as you can.'

Wellington

As she stood on the deck of the boat which had brought her all the way from England and now steamed slowly into Wellington Harbour, Lottie was once again reminded of Hugh and the day when they had crossed it in his small yacht and climbed the hill behind Eastbourne and ran down the hill hand in hand after their kiss. Such a small but significant beginning had marked the start of a relationship which she had eventually come to think would endure.

Eventually her gaze turned towards the city of her birth with very different feelings from the ones she had had nearly five months before when she had said goodbye. Then it was a time of excitement, of hope, of anticipation. Now there was nothing but despair and anxiety on account not only of her sister, but the condition in which she found herself: no money, no job, nothing to look forward to.

When she left not only Bella and her father but the Carson family had come *en bloc* to see her off. Now she was sure there would be no familiar face on the quay.

And she was right.

Her baggage unloaded, she took a cab to her house, fortunate that she had a key as the door was locked. No one was in. She was pleased about this, pleased and sad as she put her case down in the sitting room and looked instinctively at the chair her father had so often occupied in the corner, glad that there was no longer a sad, weary figure sitting there, something positive that had come from her association with the Carsons. But everywhere was just as she had left it and, to her surprise and pleasure, tidy. But, of course, they knew she was coming.

She had cabled her father that she was on her way, but deliberately gave no exact time of her arrival and was glad she had left it vague.

Even her room was as she had left it. Next door Bella's bore signs of recent occupation: an unmade bed, clothes on the floor, stuff scattered about. But her room looked as though it would remain unoccupied for some time, as though the occupier had left for good.

Tired, as she had had little sleep the night before, she lay on the bed and gazed up at the ceiling. There was an ache in her heart on account of so many hopes dashed, and tears welled up which she furiously blinked away, angry with herself for this show of emotion. After all, she had had many weeks during the long voyage to try and rid herself of her bitterness over Hugh and concentrate on the good things that had happened since. Unexpectedly Adam had found a place in her heart – not love but gratitude for his friendship and affection. She had found a new friend in Flora and more than that she had seen something of a country some people still thought of as the motherland, the hub of a great Empire.

She must have drifted off to sleep because she was awakened by the voice of her father. 'Lottie, is it you? Are you there?'

And quickly she jumped off the bed and flew down the stairs and into the arms extended towards her. 'Oh, *Dad.*'

'Lottie,' he crooned, as though she were a baby, stroking her head. 'We've missed you. We needed you.' Then he held her away from him and gazed at her. 'Tears?' he asked in some surprise.

'Emotion, Dad.'

Lottie also stepped back and, once again angry with herself, brushed them from her eyes. 'I should never have gone away. I missed you.'

'And we missed you, Lottie, and needed you. But I suppose you wanted to be with your fiancé and that was understandable.'

He lit a cigarette with hands that shook, and sat down in his chair. 'You have your own life to live but you should have told me when the boat was due and I'd have met you. Or did the Carsons meet you?'

Lottie shook her head. 'Tell me about Bella? How is she?'

'She is very well, but of course I am very worried, frightened. She is a terribly young girl to be in the family way.'

'And who is . . . the father?' Lottie sat down by the table.

'Well.' Desmond stroked his chin. 'That seems to be a matter . . . Well.' He glanced nervously at his daughter. 'Actually, we don't know.'

Lottie looked at him in amazement. 'Does Bella know?'

'Lottie, a lot has been going on that I know nothing about. I fear that Bella may have been seeing a number of men, boys, call them what you will. I don't really know. She doesn't confide in me.'

'We didn't supervise her enough,' Lottie said. 'We never asked where she was. We are both to blame, Dad. I was so occupied with Hugh, thinking of myself. I blame myself, more than you.' She crossed the room and, perching on the arm of his chair, took his hand.

'Above all,' Desmond said angrily, 'I blame your mother for leaving us as she did.'

'Does Mum know?'

'Not that I know, but Bella has become a dark horse, very secretive. I can't watch her all the time. I don't even know where she is now.'

'But isn't she at work? At the salon?'

'Oh, no, they dismissed her as soon as they found she was expecting. It's becoming very obvious now, Lottie. They said she was a disgrace and a bad example to the other young girls. And I'm afraid she is. It is also a drain on me, Lottie, to have to keep her. I don't like to suggest it, but I wonder if you can help in any way. What exactly are your own plans?'

Desmond looked up at her, a hopeful expression on his face as though he was relying on her to ease some of the burden from his shoulders and make everything all right.

Sadly she had to disabuse him and for the next half hour or so she told him in some detail about her disastrous visit to London and her rejection by her fiancé.

Some hours later Lottie lay on her bed cuddling her little sister, whose tears had practically ceased, but every now and then her body was shaken by huge sobs and Lottie's arm tightened around her comfortingly, protectively. Then all movement ceased and Lottie thought she had fallen asleep.

Bella had arrived home shortly after Lottie finished telling her doleful tale to her father and when she saw Lottie she'd practically collapsed in her arms. An emotional reunion had followed, some food was eaten, mostly by Desmond, who had to go out to drive Sir Eustace to an evening appointment, and the sisters had been left alone talking endlessly until it was time to go to bed. Then Bella had crept in with Lottie and the tears had started all over again.

She did know the father of her baby, but had been reluctant to tell her father, fearful of the action he might take. He was a boy called Len a little older than her and he worked on the wharves. She had not told Len because she thought she didn't like him very much and was frightened of his parents. He had been quite rough and forceful with her – she was rather afraid of him and had decided not to see him again. And, no, she had *not* had sex with anyone else. Her father was quite wrong to suspect her of something like that. She hadn't liked it at all and never wanted to do it again. She only realized she was pregnant when her periods stopped and she went to see the doctor who, fortunately, was a woman who was very kind to her. Lottie resolved to go and see her as soon as she could.

It was a sad, sad story, Lottie thought, for a girl of just fifteen and without any real adult help. She felt guiltier than ever that she had left her to go to London in pursuit of her own pleasure. In retrospect it seemed terribly selfish and the thought of returning to London was now quite out of the question. She had a lot to atone for by leaving her sister alone.

Bella was pretty and vulnerable and she should have known that she would be prey to unscrupulous male attention and too weak to resist. Bella had thought of telling her mother, but was too shy and fearful of what she might say. Bella's life recently had been dominated too much by fear and she had been terribly alone, but now Lottie was back she had someone to look after her.

As if this message penetrated her consciousness Bella stirred, opened her eyes and her arm around Lottie tightened. 'I'm sorry,' she said. 'I've let you down.'

'I let *you* down.'

'What will Hugh say?'

'Hugh won't know.'

'When is he coming back?'

'I don't know.' She looked down at her sister. 'The romance is over, Bella. Hugh found someone else he loved more than me.'

'Oh, Lottie. How awful for you. Were you very upset?'

'Yes.'

'Do you still love him?'

'Yes. Sadly, I think I do. I despise myself for it. I don't mean to but I do think of him a lot. However, he is staying in London and I'm here and I'm here with you, Bella.' Her tone suddenly changed and she turned and looked her sister straight in the eyes. 'You're not thinking of keeping your baby, are you?'

Bella's eyes grew round. 'How do you mean?'

'It will be very difficult for you, for us, to look after a small baby.'

'Well, I'm not going to give it away, if that's what you mean.'

'Have you thought about this seriously, Bella? I mean, seriously.'

'I am not giving it away. That's all I know.'

Bella's hand went to her stomach and rested there as if she were protecting the vulnerable unborn. 'Never, ever,' she said firmly and her eyes began to close again. Lottie lay for a long time next to her sister, as if conscious of that other heartbeat next to her, as though there was a third person in the bed.

She knew she would support Bella, whatever she did. She would never let her down again and if that meant the end of her dream to return to London, so be it.

* * *

Mr Harvey had seemed pleased to see her and her hopes were high. She had dressed carefully and suitably in one of the frocks she had bought during her heyday with Hugh, the glorious six months when everything was going well and they were both in love.

He had enquired politely about her trip and was sorry to hear of her broken engagement. She felt she had to tell him the truth. But she tried to give an impression of cheerful optimism, as if the past was behind her. So it was a shock when, at the end of it, Mr Harvey crossed his hands on the desk and shook his head regretfully. 'I'm sorry, Lottie, but I can't offer you your position back or any other in the firm. I do feel you let us down and that is not an attitude we encourage at Harveys, where we place a high value on loyalty.'

'But . . .'

He held up a hand. 'No "buts", I'm afraid. It's a fact. You told me you were going to get married and I said I was sorry that you gave us so little notice.'

'I didn't have much myself.'

'Well, then, maybe that was rather an impulsive thing to do and all in all your behaviour is rather impulsive. That is not the kind of employee we wish to have here. Who knows that you won't do the same thing and change your mind *again*, perhaps?'

With an emphasis on the word 'again' he stood up. 'I did have a word with Mrs Morgan when I got your letter and she was quite adamant about your attitude. In fact,' he managed a bleak smile, 'it might have been kinder not to see you, but I liked you and I felt I owed you an explanation. I once considered that you had a very good career ahead of you and you were well thought of but, for whatever reason, you let us down. Promise not fulfilled I'm afraid, Lottie, but I wish you well.' And he extended his hand and shook hers, while showing her politely to the door.

She supposed they all thought that was what happened to a jumped-up woman who had the nerve to aspire to marrying a Carson. She'd got what she deserved. She didn't feel she wanted to see Mavis, who doubtless would have rubbed that in with some glee. Instead she took herself for a long walk by the waterfront, trying to think constructively, but no constructive thought came and it was in a mood of profound pessimism that she returned home, where she found her father unexpectedly back early and making himself a cup tea.

'Didn't get the job, any job,' Lottie said disconsolately, sinking into her father's chair. 'In fact, Mr Harvey gave me what you might call a good talking to. I am apparently unreliable and not the sort of person they want to employ.' She looked up at her father with a kind of despair. 'Never mind, I'll go on trying. I'll find something, anything.'

Her father put a hand on her shoulder. 'That's very unfair of Mr Harvey. You are not at all unreliable. If he knew what I know about you he'd realize that you are the most reliable person in the world. A rock.'

'I did go off to London and leave my young sister at the mercy of, well . . . anything. My mind was too focused on myself, Dad, and Hugh.'

'It doesn't mean you're unreliable. It means you were in love and that can happen to anyone. Even Mr Harvey. Cup of tea, dear?'

'That would be lovely, Dad.' Surprised and gratified that her father was now apparently capable of getting his own tea, she put out a hand and clasped his. 'You're my rock. Where's Bella?'

'She went out with Gertie from next door. I think they're just going for a walk.'

Lottie took the tea cup from her father and sipped it thoughtfully. 'What are we going to do about her?'

'I suppose she will have the baby adopted. Did she say anything to you?'

Lottie nodded. 'Oh, yes, she definitely wants to keep it. She is very firm, if a little woolly-minded, as if she likes the idea of having a small baby to care for – rather like a doll, I expect. Something to play with.'

Bella had always been a girl who liked playing with dolls. She was a very girlish girl, unlike her sister.

Her father slumped in the chair opposite her, tea cup in hand. 'How can we look after a baby as well as Bella?'

'We'll have to manage somehow, Dad. We'll cope.'

'Oh, this came for you, a letter from England. Maybe from Hugh?'

Her father turned to the table and passed her an envelope, and momentarily Lottie's heartbeat quickened with the fleeting, irrational thought that maybe Hugh had changed his mind. But the handwriting was unfamiliar and she tore open the envelope, drew out a couple of sheets of paper, and looked at the signature.

'Oh, it's from someone I met in England. I'll read it later,' she said and hurriedly stuffed it in her pocket. 'Bella rather liked the doctor she saw, a young woman, so I thought I'd go and see her and ask her advice, though if Bella wants to keep her baby I'll support her, even though at the moment I don't know how I'll be able to.'

Desmond finished his tea and got up. 'I must get back to work; take Lady Frobisher to some meeting or other.'

'Oh, you drive her around too?'

'All the family. Sir Eustace is in court all day. Lady Frobisher does a lot of charity work. Oh, by the way, Lottie, Sir Eustace and Lady Frobisher are having a big party in a couple of weeks. Maybe you could help out waitressing? I know the firm who are doing the catering – I could see if there'd be room for you? Would you mind that? It would be paid, of course.'

'Anything, Dad.' Lottie got up. 'That is, if I don't get a job before. I'll go to Kirkcaldies tomorrow and then just try around.'

After her father had gone Lottie went upstairs and, lying on her bed, read the letter from Adam. Its tone surprised her. It was quite passionate and he told her that he realized he had fallen in love with her, missed her and wanted her back again. Finally it ended:

I know you love London and there is so much for you here, Lottie. You were a great success as a model and a lot of the students have asked after you. I hope if you solve your family problems you will give some thought to my suggestion. Don't worry about money or accommodation. It will all be taken care of.

Yours ever devotedly,

Adam

P.S. Flora sends her love and wants to finish her portrait of you. It's very good.

Lottie put the letter on one side and gazed out of the window. The only view it offered was the tops of the houses opposite and the sky. Not like the tops of the trees swaying in lovely Mecklenburgh Square or Admiral Nelson atop his statue as seen from Adam's tiny flat.

London. A place of enchantment, of adventure, and an introduction to a new kind of life, new opportunities. She knew she had been a success in the art class and though she had so far refused to pose nude there was plenty of work, especially to those who wished just to draw or paint her face, usually in profile. Also, having seen how decorous the nude models were and how professional and respectful the students, it had crossed her mind that one day she just might consider posing in the nude and earn a lot more money as well.

She felt that in Flora and Adam she had made two new, good friends in London and, when the time was right, in her heart of hearts she knew she yearned to go back, away from unwelcoming cold Wellington with all its unhappy memories, to the chance to mix in the kind of Bohemian environment that so appealed to her, a chance to start a new life.

Twelve

Ada looked different: younger, her face softer. She had something that Lottie had seldom seen in all the years that they'd been together: a pleasant smile on her face. On first sight she could almost be described as happy and there had been little in her former life to justify that. Was it four or five years since she'd seen her mother? Lottie couldn't remember, but they had been hard, difficult years for her and those she had left behind.

Her mother lived in a very pleasant though small cottage in the grounds of a much larger house in Island Bay. No wonder she'd left home. Next to her stood a tall young man who must be Jack. There was no embracing, no kissing and, after Ada opened the door and let her in, not even a handshake. They simply stood looking awkwardly at one another.

'Hello, Mum.'

'Hello, Lottie.'

'Hello, Jack.'

''lo.'

Lottie wanted to kiss the little brother, now grown so tall, who she hadn't seen for years, but then she drew back remembering that, as a family, back when their mother lived with them, they didn't kiss.

'Jack, you pop off and finish your homework,' Ada said, giving him a little push, and he disappeared without another word.

'He's grown,' Lottie said.

'You look different too, Lottie.' Ada put her head on one side, appraising her. 'Quite pretty, in fact.'

Lottie took this as a compliment. 'You also look different, Mum.' But she didn't say how.

'Sit down, Lottie,' her mother said, indicating a chair by a window with a view of the pretty garden. It seemed a long way from Broadway Terrace. 'Now what brings you here?' She sat down in the chair opposite Lottie. 'I don't suppose it's just a social visit.' Shades of the old acerbic Ada here.

'It's about Bella, Mum. She's going to have a baby.'

Ada's pleasant expression promptly vanished and she looked startled. 'Is she married?'

'No.'

'Well . . .' Ada sat with her hands in her lap, fingers restlessly plucking at her dress. 'I don't know what to say. How did this come about? Bella is only . . . Why, she must be sixteen now.'

'Not quite, Mum. I'm afraid I've been in England for a while and, well . . .' A feeling of hopelessness overcame her at the inadequacy of explaining this to her mother.

'And I don't suppose your father was much use looking after her. I hear he has a job now. So she was just left to roam about on her own I expect and get into bad company. It was selfish of you to leave her with her father, who is quite incapable of looking after a young girl like that. But typical of you, Charlotte. You only ever did think of yourself.'

Because she needed a favour from her mother Lottie bit back any retort she wanted to make. She also noticed that her full name was back on her mother's lips, always a sign of disapproval. How quickly an old habit had instinctively returned, despite the passage of years.

'I did think she'd want to keep in touch with me after I saw her in town but she didn't,' Ada continued. 'Got a job with a hairdresser. Good thing as education is a waste of time – it gives people ideas above their station. Look what it did to you. Well, Lottie, what do you want me to do about all this? I suppose she will have the baby adopted and then try and get on with her life?'

'No, Mum. She wants to keep the baby. The thing is, I want to go back to England. I like it and have more opportunities there for work. There is not much for me in Wellington as I never got my School Certificate, thanks mainly to you leaving us, Mother.'

'I couldn't stand it any more,' Ada said defiantly. 'I'd had enough of slaving with that worthless father of yours sitting in a corner coughing his heart out all day. What happened to your fiancé, Charlotte?'

'It fell through. We're no longer engaged.'

Ada's eyes were lit by a malicious gleam of satisfaction. 'I'm not surprised. Everyone was astonished at a Carson getting engaged to someone like you.'

A hot flush sprang to Lottie's cheeks and she bit her lips hard again, determined to stay in control, and began hesitantly: 'I wondered, Mum, if you could give Bella a home? She was always very fond of you and . . .'

'Not a chance, Charlotte.' There was nothing hesitant about the way Ada sprang rapidly out of her chair. Her pleasant, relaxed expression had entirely vanished and the hard, sour, embittered look of old was back. '*Me* take Bella expecting a baby and not married? Mrs Ellis would give me notice immediately for bringing such shame on the family and I'd lose my job and this lovely house. And this is to say nothing of the effect on Mr Porter, the gardener here, to whom I will be engaged to be married when I have got my divorce from your father, which should be soon, and who has the strictest moral standards. It would completely destroy my life and I have made enough sacrifices for my ungrateful family, slaving after you for all those years. It is perfectly ridiculous for Bella to consider keeping her baby. It will ruin her life. She should put it up for adoption and forget about it. Then I might consider having her live with me if she still wants to and you can go off to wherever you want and well rid of you, I say.'

She pointed towards the door. 'You had better go now, Charlotte, before I lose my temper with you completely. I think you have a real nerve coming here to see me after all this time and trying to foist on me a pregnant *unmarried* daughter just in order to relieve you of the responsibility and satisfy your own selfish ends so that you can run off abroad. Just like you, Charlotte. You haven't changed one little bit and I'm not surprised Doctor Carson wanted to be rid of you once he found out what you were really like behind that attractive exterior.'

Burning with humiliation and anger, Lottie rose from her chair and was about to leave. Suddenly, however, she changed her mind and, crossing the room, looked down at her mother, who remained seated. 'Bella is your daughter, Mother, and her baby will be your grandchild. You have always made life hard for me, but there is no need to take it out on Bella who was close to you, loved you and was grief-stricken when you left. She was young, vulnerable and still is. Yet she can't turn to you when she is in trouble because you deserted her, and instead turns to Dad, who you treated abominably, too. You walked out on us all without a word of explanation. You are a most unnatural mother, harsh and unfeeling and I pity the man you expect to marry if he should become ill or in any way dependent on you. I feel this is something I should have told you before and I'm telling you now because I sincerely hope I never set eyes on you again.'

Without waiting for a reply from her mother, whose expression had gradually been transformed from righteous indignation to one of shocked surprise, Lottie turned on her heels and let herself out of the front door.

On the way to the main gate she passed a tall, lean man with a large walrus moustache, doubtless Mr Porter, he of the strictest moral standards, leaning on a hoe watching her indifferently, though he must have known who she was. Once on the road she hurried along to the tram stop, still shaking with emotion after her outburst, and consumed with rage and hatred for a woman she knew she never wanted to see again.

Lottie carried out her duties as a waitress with her customary skill and confidence, blending in easily with the crowd at Sir Eustace's summer garden party. It was in honour of his and Lady Frobisher's ruby wedding anniversary and the best of Wellington society were there in full: lawyers, doctors, politicians, prominent and successful business men all with their spouses. It was to be expected that the

Carsons would be there too and they were, the whole family as far as Lottie could see from the perch near the serving area where she first spotted them. She had anticipated that this would be the case when she took the job. However, because she needed the money so badly, everything else having failed, she knew an encounter was a risk she had to take.

As far as she could she took care to confine herself to another part of the lawn, well away from her erstwhile fiancé's relations, a family who had once come to regard her as one of them.

Perhaps she thought her waitress uniform of black dress and white apron would serve as a disguise. However, with the sun shining on her golden hair, which was only partly obscured, perhaps even enhanced, by a black velvet band, she attracted much attention, especially from the older generation of men who maybe indulged some private fantasy inspired by her striking good looks coupled with an air of docile servitude.

She also attracted the attention of the heir to the Frobisher fortune and baronetcy and if she did not at first remember him he remembered her. He had stood for a long time watching her, noticing her as soon as she started to move round the crowd carrying a silver tray full of glasses of champagne.

He stepped forward as she returned to the station to restock her tray. 'You don't remember me, do you?' he asked.

Startled, Lottie looked up. The face was familiar but she couldn't place it.

'We met briefly at Madeleine Carson's wedding.'

'Oh, yes.' Lottie felt confused. 'Yes, I do remember, vaguely.'

It was very vague indeed. He had the sort of pleasant but nondescript looks that could pass in any crowd. She, however, was worried about keeping her job and looked anxiously at the manager restocking her tray, who was also the boss. But he smiled and indulgently waved a hand.

'Don't let me take you away from Mr Frobisher, Miss O'Brien. Have a break for a few minutes. You've been very busy,' and, handing the tray to another functionary, he smiled obsequiously at Mr Frobisher while whispering in Lottie's ear, '*Sir Eustace's son.*'

Sir Eustace's son? She looked blankly at the man in front of her, who said apologetically, 'I'm sorry if I interrupted your work, but I never caught your name.'

Lottie felt annoyed at this intrusion, but if he was her father's employer's son she knew she mustn't show it. 'Lottie, Mr Frobisher. My father is your father's chauffeur,' she added pointedly.

Now it was Mr Frobisher's turn to look surprised. 'You are Mr O'Brien's daughter?'

'Yes, I am, sir. I don't want to be rude, but do you think I might get on with my work? We are very busy.'

She smiled at him politely and, abashed, he stood back. 'Of course.'

Puzzled, she watched him limp away into the crowd. Then she recalled Hugh introducing him at Madeleine's wedding and telling her how he had nearly lost his leg in the war.

'Sorry about that,' she said turning to her manager.

'So you know Mr Frobisher?'

'Only vaguely. We met at some wedding,' and she held out a tray expectantly.

As she made her way back, weaving in and out of the fashionable, well-dressed throng, Lottie felt increasingly uncomfortable, as if she was here under false pretences, wondering who else she might know or not know, who might recognize her from the days that she had some kind of status as Hugh's fiancé. She thought that lots of their friends must be here and her disguise was insufficient to protect her from the past.

Did it matter? No. It didn't matter because she had nothing to be ashamed of. She was cross with herself for even caring. If anyone should be ashamed it was Hugh and, besides, she needed money to help support her sister and, perhaps, a baby later, both of whom she would have to care for.

So she moved about quite freely, dispensing champagne and canapés, aware of the lecherous glances of some elderly men but trying to avoid any more embarrassing contacts that might remind her of how different things would have been had she still been Hugh's fiancé, or even, by this time, perhaps, his wife.

The Frobisher house was a large mansion set in extensive grounds with a manicured lawn and beds of exotic flowers. It was situated higher up on the hill, not far from the Carsons. From the front aspect there was a wonderful view of the harbour and the mountains beyond. There was a marquee on the lawn where luncheon was served, followed by speeches while the staff cleared up and transported dishes back to the house where other staff were busy washing up. There was much fetching and carrying to be done and Lottie remained largely out of sight, relieved that most of the waiting at the luncheon was done by waiters in tails. All in all it must have been a costly exercise and there was no doubt that Sir Eustace was a very affluent man indeed, maybe even richer than the Carsons.

Lady Frobisher was a tall, elegant woman. Her white hair was fashionably dressed but in a style befitting an older woman with an interesting arrangement of feathers projecting from a gold band. She wore a beautiful long gown of golden brocade and carried a fan which she occasionally used because of the heat.

Lottie didn't speak to her at all or have any contact with her, and she began to feel increasingly tired as the afternoon wore on. Finally some of the staff were given a break in relays by the side of the house away from the crowd in the marquee.

Lottie was in the act of re-entering the house by the side door when a woman she recognized immediately appeared around the corner from the front.

There was no ignoring Madeleine, who came up to Lottie and, to her surprise, greeted her warmly with a kiss on the cheek while reaching for her hand and squeezing it. 'Lottie,' she said, 'it is so good to catch you at last. I have been looking for you and I didn't want to disappear before I had the chance to speak to you. You see, I am expecting a baby and as it is so hot in that marquee I've asked Andy to take me home.' Madeleine was speaking rather breathlessly, emotionally. 'I saw you in the crowd and searched for you and now I've found you.' She let her hand fall. 'I didn't know where you were, if you'd come back and I did so much want to see you and say . . .' She was struggling to find the words. 'Lottie, I am so *terribly* sorry about Hugh. I did want you to know how badly we as a family feel about the whole thing. We feel he has behaved disgracefully and, and . . .'

Lottie interrupted her. 'There is no need to talk about it, Madeleine. Please. What happened happened and it is over now. And, look, Madeleine, I have to get back to work, so if you would excuse me . . .'

'But, Lottie, is there anything we can do, anything at all? We are so fond of you and don't want to lose touch and . . .'

'Absolutely nothing, Madeleine, and thank you. Look, I must

go now. Goodbye.' And with a wave Lottie quickly went inside the house where, for a moment, she leaned breathlessly against the wall in the corridor, trying to control the emotions that this encounter had released in her. One thing she knew for certain was that she did not want to have anything to do with the Carson family again. Although doubtless well intentioned there was still something patronizing about Madeleine's approach which she deeply resented. After a moment Lottie recovered, but was enormously relieved when the function finished, the occasional staff like her were paid off and dismissed and she could escape and make her way home.

As Bella had said the doctor was a sympathetic, obviously capable and practical young woman of about thirty. She belonged to a relatively new breed of women emerging from the confines of domesticity to train as doctors and take their place in society. Dr Barbara Preston was English, had trained in London and only recently arrived in New Zealand. Lottie liked her and thought that Bella would be safe in her hands.

She sat to one side while the doctor examined Bella behind a screen before emerging to pronounce that everything was satisfactory and returning to her desk, where she made a few notes. 'Now,' she said, smiling encouragingly at her patient who had taken a seat next to Lottie. 'I will arrange for your delivery in hospital and then . . .' She paused and looked at Lottie. 'Have you decided what you are going to do?'

'In what way?' Lottie asked.

'Bella is very young . . .'

Lottie interrupted her. 'Bella wants to keep her baby. There is no question of her giving it up and I am prepared to accept responsibility and look after her.'

'I see.' The doctor studied her notes. 'I don't wish to interfere, but you are not very old yourself, Miss O'Brien. Is this a sensible thing to do? There are many people unable to have children themselves and only too anxious to adopt small babies. I wonder if, as a family, you have thought this through. Bella gave me to understand that your mother didn't live with you – indeed, that you were estranged, and that you yourself were engaged to be married and lived in England.'

'No, I do not live in England. I was there to visit and I am no longer engaged. My home is Wellington and I'm going to stay here and take care of Bella and her baby. My father is also at home with us and between us we will support Bella in whatever she wants to do.'

'Fine.' The doctor got up. 'Then that seems very satisfactory to me. I only felt I should point out the pitfalls, but I can see you are a very capable person, Miss O'Brien, and have taken all this into consideration.'

She extended her hand and shook Lottie's. 'I'll see Bella in a month's time for a check-up and after that . . . After that Bella will soon be a mother.'

Bella soon to be a mother. The idea, now that reality had set in, seemed incredible. Lottie wondered if Bella had really considered the implications of what she was doing and whether she might change her mind when the time came? She had tried to talk seriously about it, but Bella was concerned with the present and the immediate rather than the distant future, and having a baby to hug maybe answered some deeply felt need she had for mothering, especially after Ada left home, taking the child with her she favoured most over Bella.

When they returned from the visit to the doctor, Bella went upstairs to rest and Lottie got on with the housework until her father came home and immediately slumped in his corner chair and opened the paper, just like old times.

'You OK, Dad?' Lottie asked nervously.

'Perfectly OK.' Desmond put his paper down. 'It's just nice to be looked after again, rather than having to do the looking after.' He extended a hand. 'It's great to have you back, Lottie, and to be spoilt by you.' His expression became anxious. 'I do hope you won't go away again. You seem so restless and we did miss you. I know England made a deep impression on you and my fear is you will be on that boat again and disappear forever.'

Lottie sat down in the chair opposite her father. 'I won't be going away again, Dad – not for the time being anyway. I did like England and think there were more opportunities there, but Bella says she wants to keep her baby and I think she means it. I would never leave her. We saw her doctor today, who tried to advise her to have it adopted, said there were lots of nice couples who couldn't have children, but Bella was adamant and I want to support her in what she wants to do. She is my little sister and I owe it to her.'

Desmond thrust his paper to one side. 'But, Lottie, I can't believe this. When she first broke the news to me she indicated that she did not want to keep it. She wanted to be rid of it.'

'Well, she has changed her mind and as long as it remains that way I will be here looking after her and the baby. I think I may have got a job with Kirkcaldies again. I saw them yesterday and they remembered me. Nothing much, just helping out in haberdashery where I worked before. Very junior.'

'Then Bella will be all alone here with the baby.'

'I may sometimes be able to get back at lunchtime, and maybe you could help occasionally, Dad. We'll work it out.'

'I'm not happy about it. The only thing that makes me happy is if it persuades you not to go away again. That makes me very happy. Didn't you want to work with the catering firm, Lottie? I heard they were very happy with you.'

'I don't want to go on doing that, Dad. I met or saw too many people I knew from the time I was with Hugh. I want a clean slate. Anyway, there is something demeaning about it, catering to the whims of rich people.'

Desmond chuckled. 'That's what I do all the time, Lottie. They have their uses. By the way, someone else was asking about you.'

'Who was that? The Carsons?'

'No, Edward Frobisher, Sir Eustace's son. He said he'd met you before. I didn't know that.'

'That's what I mean. People from the past. I met him briefly at Madeleine Carson's wedding but I hardly remembered him.'

'Well, he remembered you. Asked me a lot about you.'

Lottie bridled. 'I hope you didn't tell him anything.'

'Nothing to your disadvantage, my dear. I only told him what a fine person you were, how you'd supported the family when your mother left us and how I was very proud of you. He did know that you had been engaged to Hugh Carson and asked me if you still were, but I told him that was all off and he didn't ask anything more. Mr Edward is a very nice man. I sometimes drive him.'

'Is he married?'

'He has been, but it didn't work out. His wife was very pretty – rather flighty – I heard, and I think she left him for another man and they are now divorced. He suffers a great deal from the gammy leg he got as a result of the war, is in a lot of pain and I think he relates to me because he says we have a lot in common. He talks about the war and how it affected him to me in a way he says he can't with other people who wouldn't understand what we went through. And it's true. They don't. No one can possibly understand who wasn't there. Your mother never understood and never wanted to.'

Lottie got up, started preparing the tea and, with a smile of satisfaction, Desmond resumed his perusal of the paper, happy that things were almost back to normal again.

1926

Somehow it seemed like the rolling back of time when she heard a voice saying 'Hello, Lottie' and looked up to see Violet Carson, beautifully dressed as usual and carrying a number of packages, beaming at her.

Lottie had been doing a stock inventory, head bent over the counter in the haberdashery department of Kirkcaldies and there were no other customers around. She was dressed demurely in a uniform black dress with a white collar like the unimportant shop assistant she was.

'Hello, Violet,' she said, hiding the surprise and also the dismay from her voice. Somehow, she seemed destined to be pursued by her past.

'Any chance of a cup of tea?'

Lottie shook her head and indicated the ledger in front of her. 'I have a lot to do. Also, I'm alone for the moment.'

'Look, Lottie.' Violet deposited her array of parcels on the floor by her feet. 'Despite what has happened, we all love you. We can't change just because,' she lowered her voice and took a cautious look around, 'Hugh behaved so despicably. We remember the good times, the parties, the dances, the tennis matches, all the fun we had. Just because you are not going to be part of the family it doesn't mean we have to lose touch. Remember all the fun we had?'

Yes, she remembered. She smiled across at Violet. 'I do.'

'Look,' Violet said purposefully, 'on Sunday I'm arranging a tennis match at the club. I'd love you to come along. You are such a good player.'

'I haven't played for ages.'

Out of the corner of her eye Lottie saw her superior emerging from the door behind the counter. 'I have to get on with my work now, Violet.'

'I'll pick you up. Sunday, two o'clock, no excuse. Right?'

'I suppose so.' Lottie shrugged, but had no intention of going.

'And while I'm here,' Violet said loudly, 'please could I have a couple of yards of a pale blue ribbon. See . . .' She took a dress from the bag at her feet. 'To go with this.'

Lottie tried to put Violet and her invitation out of her mind but somehow it lingered. She looked out her tennis things, washed her dress and socks, cleaned her white shoes, put them on one side, just in case. A game of tennis sounded wonderful. It would get her out of herself. But it meant engaging with the Carsons again, and that was something she had vowed not to do.

She was very bored, very lonely and, she realized, practically friendless as so much of her time had been taken up with the Carsons and their circle. Also, she had been a successful young business woman as well, highly thought of, given responsibility and destined for promotion. And, yes, she had enjoyed it. It was like inhabiting another fun-loving, carefree world that one thought would never change, so different from the grim years of the past. Now she was back behind the counter selling ribbons and bric a brac with virtually no prospects at all as New Zealand, together with the rest of the world, was entering a time of recession.

So those former grim years were well and truly back, and upstairs was a heavily pregnant and frightened younger sister as uncertain as she was about what lay ahead. There were days when Lottie sincerely hoped Bella would change her mind, have her baby adopted and then eventually she would be free to escape back to England. This unworthy thought she tried to banish, but it was still there.

When Sunday arrived, her one day off, Lottie decided that she could no longer resist temptation. The weather was lovely, warm summer sunshine, not too hot, a gentle breeze blowing from the sea. Her one worry was Bella, who declared she wasn't feeling very well, her stomach hurt, and spent the morning in bed; but by lunchtime she felt better, decided it had been wind and, uncharacteristically generous, urged Lottie to go out and enjoy her game. Her father was going off to his veterans' club for some beers and a few games of darts with the boys, so by the time Violet's horn sounded outside the house Lottie had her tennis dress on and her shoes and racquet packed in her bag.

'Sorry I'm a bit late,' Violet said as Lottie got in beside her. 'I'm glad you decided to come. I thought you might not.'

'I nearly didn't.' Lottie brushed back her hair and closed her eyes against the sun. 'But it's such a lovely day and . . .' She turned and smiled at Violet. 'You know how it is.'

'You can't go on ignoring the Carsons forever. Madeleine told me about her little chat with you at the party.'

'I was very offhand. I was rude. Please tell Madeleine that I'm sorry. I seem to say this a lot where you and your family are concerned.'

Violet's hand briefly touched hers. 'We understand. We really do. We wanted to get in touch with you, but didn't know where you were or whether or not you had come home. Hugh said you simply disappeared. We were a bit worried, to tell you the truth.' She paused and concentrated on her driving. 'I don't know whether I should tell you but Hugh and his woman, Sylvia's her name, have got married. She actually seems awfully nice . . . but not as nice as you,' she concluded hurriedly.

Lottie felt her heart give a lurch. 'How do you know? Have you met her?'

'No, but no one can be as nice as you. We all loved you and that didn't change just because Hugh . . .'

'Look, Violet. I don't want to appear to be rude yet again, but I wish you would stop going on about Hugh. He is completely out of my life and I have other things on my mind.'

'Honestly?'

'Honestly.'

'That's good. You are so pretty, Lottie. You'll soon have all the men running after you. Actually, there is someone I am very interested in and you will meet him today at the club.'

'Ah, that's why I'm invited?'

'Not at all, but . . .' Violet blushed. 'His name is Albert. Isn't that an awful name? But he is very nice.'

'Are you dating?'

'Yes, in a way. We've been out a few times.'

'I'm very glad for you, Violet. What does he do?'

'He's a teacher at the same school as me. I actually got a job teaching infants, mainly to please my sister. Albert teaches history in the higher school – very clever and academic, not at all the sort of man I thought I'd fall for but . . . But, well, you'll meet him soon.'

With that the car drew up outside the tennis club and Lottie, determined to put aside her shock at hearing that Hugh had tied the knot, was looking forward to meeting the man Violet was dating.

Albert may have had an 'awful name', according to Violet, but he was a good tennis player. He was also very amiable, natural and reasonably good looking, and Lottie took to him. Her own partner, Frank, who was a friend of Albert's, was also very agreeable. The trouble for Lottie was that she hadn't played for some time and was aware of the fact that she was missing too many shots and letting her partner down. Despite this, she was pleased she had come and for a while at least was able to forget her worries and the finality of the rejection by Hugh, now confirmed by the fact that he couldn't wait to see the back of her before marrying his new love. Perhaps, at last, she would be able to banish his memory entirely.

After the game, which Violet and Albert easily won, there was a break for tea in the clubhouse. When the matches started again, this time she and Frank had to sit it out while Violet and Albert played with the winners of the last game of doubles. Then she and Frank would play the losers of that match.

It was all a little more sophisticated than the games Lottie had played either at school or at the Carsons', and she knew she was rusty and had let her partner down, for which she apologized. He politely assured her he didn't mind and trotted off to refresh himself at the bar, and for a while Lottie sat watching the competing couples. Then, aware of a movement on the bench beside her, she turned and was greeted by a familiar face.

'Hello,' Ed Frobisher said. 'So we meet again.'

This was the last place Lottie expected to see a man with a gammy leg, but she managed to hide her surprise and returned his greeting.

'I saw you play,' he said. 'You were very good.'

'I was hopelessly out of form,' Lottie replied. 'I hadn't played for ages.' Then, because she was curious, despite her wish to discourage him, 'What brings you here?'

'I expect you're wondering because of my leg.' Ed touched his knee and gestured towards the stick by his side. 'Oh, I've been a member for years. I used to play a lot when I was younger. A pleasant place to come and socialize on a nice day when one has nothing better to do.'

They fell into a protracted silence, during which Lottie reflected on the fact that they had something in common. They both knew the Carsons and her father was employed by his, which is why she was determined to maintain the distance between them.

'It's nice to see you again,' she said politely and got up, ostensibly to go to the ladies' room, but in reality she wandered round the clubhouse to familiarize herself with it for a while, then she strolled out to the grounds again to see how the match was going. Ed had also disappeared, so she resumed her seat and watched to the end when she and Frank had to play the losers of the doubles on another court.

Violet and Albert finally won their match and came off the court to applause from the assembled onlookers. She took her seat on the bench beside Lottie, towelling her face which was covered with sweat.

'Now it's your turn,' she said, looking up at Frank, who had just reappeared. 'Go on and win.'

'Not much chance, I'm afraid.' Lottie rose reluctantly and looked apologetically at her partner.

Frank shrugged as though he didn't care, or didn't expect too much, which made Lottie all the more determined to put in an extra effort and, as she had innate skill, her game slowly improved and they won their match.

Violet, who had been watching her, joined in the general applause as she and Frank came off the court. Next to Violet Albert was busily chatting to a woman on his other side, and beside Violet was Ed Frobisher, bad leg stretched out in front of him, looking relaxed.

'Very well done,' Violet said enthusiastically as Lottie came up to her. 'I knew you could do it. Lottie, Albert and I have to rush off to another engagement, but Ed Frobisher has kindly agreed to take you home. I hope that's all right?'

Frank politely shook hands with Lottie, thanked her for the game and then went off to talk with friends on the far side of the clubhouse, while Lottie tried to hide her irritation with Violet behind a practised smile.

'That is perfectly all right by me. But it is not necessary. I can easily get a tram home.'

'Oh, please,' Ed said, getting to his feet. 'It will be a pleasure.'

Sitting next to Ed in the front seat of his splendid Bugatti, Lottie was reminded of the good times when she'd briefly risen above her origins and enjoyed life in the fast lane of Hugh Carson, his family and friends. She had never been in a Bugatti but there had been plenty of expensive cars, leisurely tennis parties, dinners and glamorous dances.

She could think of nothing to say to Ed, who seemed similarly tongue-tied, and they drove in silence towards her home.

One thing, though, had changed. She was no longer ashamed of where she lived and on his enquiring directed him to her home, expecting anyway that it was unlikely she would ever see him again.

'Thank you very much, Mr Frobisher,' she said, preparing to get out as the car stopped outside the front door. 'It's a beautiful car.'

'I don't suppose . . .' He began, but at that moment the door to the house was flung open and the neighbour from next door, Gertie's mother, hurried towards her.

'Lottie!' she cried. 'Thank heavens you're here. Bella has been taken bad . . .'

'Oh my goodness.' Lottie leapt out of the car and ran into the house, where she could hear loud groans from upstairs. She rushed up to the room, where she found Bella lying spreadeagled on the bed, face contorted with pain, clutching her stomach.

'Oh, Lottie!' she cried. 'It hurts so much. I thought you'd never come.'

Lottie sat by her side and put one hand on the heaving stomach, felt the wetness on the bed and said, 'We'll have to get you to hospital at once.' She flew down the stairs again, but Ed was already inside, his face registering concern.

'Is there anything I can do?' he asked.

'My sister is having a baby. I have to get her to hospital. Could you possibly . . .'

'Of course,' Ed said at once and, briskly putting aside his jacket, followed Lottie up the stairs and did not appear too disturbed by the sight that confronted him, which he instantly absorbed.

'Here, I'll carry her,' he said and, scooping her up in his arms, carried her carefully downstairs and laid her gently in the back seat of his beautiful car while Lottie, who had followed him with his jacket and a blanket, tenderly covered her.

'No time for anything else,' she said, turning towards Gertie's mother and the few neighbours who, hearing the noise and seeing the splendid car parked outside the house, had come to gawp. 'When my dad comes home, please could you tell him?'

And she jumped in the car next to Ed, turning so that she could keep an eye on her sister who now lay inert, shocked and terrified by the whole experience and the thought of what was to come.

It was a very long night. Bella had complications, a breach birth and at first Lottie went back and forth from the delivery room trying to comfort her, as she began to be surrounded by an increasing number of medical personnel, always returning to find Ed still there sitting in the bare waiting room, looking as anxious as if he had been the father. Somehow she was grateful for his company and had no time to feel embarrassed. She was moved and impressed by his warm human concern, as well as his efficiency in taking control of the situation which must have surprised, if not shocked him.

'There really is no need for you to wait,' she said, sitting down for about the tenth time by his side. 'There is nothing more we can do.'

'I think it's nice for you to have a bit of company,' he said. 'I'll wait until your father comes and if he doesn't I can take you home when it is all over. It is a very worrying situation for you. I can understand that.'

'It's extremely good of you, especially as you hardly know us. I can't think where Dad has got to. He was spending the day at his veterans' club but I thought he would be home by now. Perhaps Gertie's mother didn't tell him.'

'Don't worry. I'll stay until he comes.' And he pressed her hand but in a comforting, friendly way, not letting it linger.

Lottie went out again but this time she was not allowed in the delivery room and, although she was told nothing explicit, she understood that the doctors were fighting for the life of her sister and her baby.

This time she was visibly distressed and close to tears when she returned to the waiting room and flopped on a chair, holding her head in her hands. 'I can't bear it,' she said at last. 'I feel it's all my fault.'

'How is it your fault?'

'I was in England when I should have been looking after my sister. She is only just seventeen. What's more, I would never have come back if I had not had a wire from Dad, and by that time it was too late.'

'Is your mother not around?'

'She left home years ago. I did go and see her when I came back to see if she could look after Bella, but she said she was ashamed of her and wanted to have nothing to do with her. She is trying to make a new life for herself. You see, I desperately wanted to go back to England – that's how selfish I am, Mr Frobisher. And I have even thought that if Bella had her baby adopted I could still do that.'

'Well, she probably will have it adopted, won't she?'

'If it lives. If *she* lives. Imagine how I'll feel if she dies or loses the baby. It will haunt me for the rest of my life. But no she says she will never have it adopted.'

This time she succumbed to tears and Ed put a hand gently on her shoulder.

'Lottie, I am sure she is in good hands. Look, I'll go and try and use my influence to get us a cup of tea.'

While he was gone Lottie made a determined effort to compose herself. Confused and distressed by the situation, she was extraordinarily grateful that it was Ed who had brought her back and not Violet. Or supposing she had come by tram? The truth was she should not have gone to the tennis club when Bella was obviously feeling unwell, so once again she had to reproach herself. Perhaps her mother was right and she was someone who was too self-absorbed for her own good.

When Ed returned he was carrying two cups of tea and looked pleased with himself. 'I managed to extract these from a dragon,' he said, handing a cup and saucer to Lottie and apologizing for having spilt some of the tea. 'She seemed to think I'm the father, so it helped.'

'And did you mind?'

'Of course I didn't.' He gazed at Lottie. 'Why should I?' And he took a sip of his tea.

'I, we, seem to have put you in a very difficult position, Mr Frobisher. You can't possibly have expected a situation like this. I can't tell you how grateful I am. You have possibly saved Bella's life.'

And she stopped, feeling close to tears again.

'Well, you can show your gratitude for a start by stopping calling me "Mr Frobisher". My name is Edward but I'm known to everyone as Ed, so you must call me Ed like everyone else. Was this exaggerated respect because your father works for mine?'

'Partly, I suppose so. Yes.'

'And is your attitude to me, which is wary to say the least, because of this or because you don't like me?' His directness was embarrassing.

'I can't say I don't like you Mr . . . Ed. I really hardly know you. I certainly don't dislike you.'

'That's a start,' Ed said and sat back with a look of satisfaction on his face. Then, his expression more relaxed, he looked at her earnestly. 'Lottie, I don't know how much you know or want to know about me, but it may help if I told you that I have been around. I was in the war, wounded like Desmond, as you know. I have been married and I also lost a baby, so I know what you're going through.'

'And your wife?'

'She left me for someone else. We both never recovered from losing the baby, but it happened quite early in her pregnancy. I think it just showed the extent of the gulf between us and that we should perhaps never have married. She also didn't understand about the war – I married her afterwards, maybe to help me try and get over it, but it didn't. She never liked to talk about it, just enjoyed fun and having a good time, which I was ill-equipped to give her.'

'Sounds like what Dad said about my mum,' Lottie said. 'They didn't get on either after the war. In the end she had had enough and just left us.'

'And how old were you?'

'Sixteen.'

'Still at school?'

'Yes. I had to leave to look after Dad and Bella and get a job to help support the family. Dad just used to sit in a corner of the living room all day doing nothing except coughing and smoking. But

Madeleine Carson's father, Doctor Carson, helped him to recover and we owe them a great debt.'

'Which is how you know Violet?'

'And Hugh.' She looked challengingly at him. 'You know about Hugh. Dad told me.'

'Don't forget I first met you at Madeleine's wedding,' Ed said. 'I remembered you, but I don't think you remembered me, which is not surprising. I remember how lovely and excited you looked that day, prettier than the bride, and I envied Hugh, who was very attentive to you. I never expected to meet you again, certainly not in these circumstances.'

'I'm very glad you did,' Lottie said. 'Otherwise . . .'

She was interrupted by the door of the waiting room opening and a doctor came in still dressed for the operating theatre. Lottie looked up at him with apprehension, but was immediately reassured by the broad smile on the doctor's tired face. 'Your sister is fine, Miss O'Brien, and so is her baby, a very healthy but large boy, which is partly what caused all the trouble. Nine pounds four ounces. It was a very near thing.' And with the back of his hand he wiped some of the perspiration from his brow.

'Oh.' Speechless with joy and relief, Lottie gave vent at last to all her pent-up emotions and, bursting into tears, leaned heavily against Ed who, gently but firmly, put his arms around her and hugged her.

Thirteen

Ed Frobisher stood on the doorstep, a large bunch of flowers in his hands. Lottie stepped aside with an expression of surprise on her face.

'How nice to see you,' she said. 'Come in. Bella's upstairs feeding the baby. Please excuse me with my apron on,' and she began hurriedly to take it off, but Ed waved his hand dismissively.

'Please don't worry about me. I don't want to disturb you. It may be an awkward time to call.'

It was awkward, but then any time was, Lottie thought, deciding to keep her apron on after all. Ever since Bella had come home with the baby they were on the go all day.

There was a protracted silence as Ed took off his hat and placed it on the table with the bouquet. 'I won't stay long,' he said, 'I can see you're busy. Any name yet?'

'Not yet, she can't decide . . . you know.'

'On what?'

'Well, he is a beautiful baby, but she is very young and she realizes now how it will tie her down for life. I was just making tea. Would you like a cup?'

'Thank you. But tell me, how she is and how are you?'

'Bella is very well. Of course, she is young and she soon recovered though they kept her in hospital for a few extra days just to be sure. And we were very grateful to you, Ed.'

'Please think nothing of it, Lottie. I was only too pleased to be able to help. Tell me, are you working?'

'No, not working. Kirkcaldies have given me a few days off. I've told them my sister is ill. I can't tell them the truth, of course.'

'Of course not. But . . .' Ed's expression was grave. 'She will have to have the baby adopted, won't she? It will be an impossible situation otherwise.'

'It will be hard for us, but not impossible. He is such a sweet baby, and to give him up will be very difficult. There are lots of things we have to consider.' She paused. 'But look, I'll go and get tea and then tell Bella you're here.'

Lottie lingered for a while in the kitchen, trying to get her thoughts together. Ed's sudden appearance had disturbed her. He had promised to visit, said he would visit, but it was still unexpected. They had reached a kind of intimacy in the time they had spent together on that fateful night, which was impossible to forget or ignore. They had held hands as he tried to comfort her and she had rested her head on his chest in a fit of weeping after she heard that Bella and the baby were all right. He had sent flowers while Bella was still in hospital and through Desmond enquired regularly about her and the baby. Because of his help in getting Bella to the hospital and his concern, he had become part of their lives, and she wondered for how long.

When she returned to the sitting room, to her surprise Bella had come down and Ed was admiring the baby, making clucking noises and one of his fingers was clutched tightly by the baby's hand.

'He's an endearing little fellow,' Ed said, looking up. 'No wonder you can't bear to part with him.'

'We're not parting with him,' Bella announced firmly, looking up defiantly first at Ed and then at her sister. 'I'm not giving him up and I don't care what happens.'

A heavy silence fell on the room while Lottie put the tray on the table and began pouring tea. 'You're quite, quite sure?' she asked gently, passing Bella a cup.

'I've always been sure. I never said I'd give him up. It was you who suggested it, and Dad.'

'We just thought that, all round, it was for the best.'

'Best for who?'

'Well, maybe best for the baby and you,' Ed intervened. 'It is very difficult for a young unmarried woman to keep a baby. What will people say?'

'I don't care what they say,' Bella said stoutly. 'It's what I am going to do.'

And Bella began rocking the baby in her arms and looking lovingly down at him while the infant gazed adoringly at her and, at that moment, Lottie knew for sure that Bella was right.

She handed Ed his tea. 'Well, the decision is made,' she said. 'And I'm very happy about it.' She smiled encouragingly at her sister and planted a kiss on the baby's head. 'Now you must give him a name.'

'He's called Edward,' Bella said as firmly as when she announced she was keeping him. 'I've called him after Mr Frobisher because I know he saved our lives that night.'

'Well . . .' Ed looked embarrassed, but not unhappy. 'I don't know what to say. I am flattered. Very flattered indeed . . .'

And while he was still speaking, the door opened and Desmond came in.

'Dad!' Lottie said in surprise. 'You're early.'

Desmond took off his hat and put it on the table next to Ed's, ignoring Lottie and, turning to the visitor, said deferentially: 'I didn't know you would be here, Mr Frobisher. How good of you to call, sir.'

'Just came to see your grandchild, Mr O'Brien,' Ed said. 'He's very beautiful and I've just been told he is to be called after me. I feel very flattered.'

'Well, they owe you a lot, Mr Frobisher. They might not have got to the hospital in time.'

'It was just chance that I was there. Anyone would have done the same.'

'You did more. You stayed all night and supported me through a very difficult time. Otherwise I'd have been alone,' Lottie's eyes slid accusingly towards her father, 'having had *no* idea where Dad was . . .'

Desmond wriggled uncomfortably. 'I came home late and didn't know you weren't in bed until Gertie's mother knocked on the door at six and told me what had happened.'

'Well, it's past history now,' Lottie said, 'and the big news is Bella has just told me that she wants to keep Edward and is not going to have him adopted.'

Desmond plopped himself down in his chair, mopped his brow and looked across at his younger daughter. 'Well, it's her decision and she knows we will support her. He is a very fetching little thing.'

'Oh, *Dad*!' Bella cried and still with the baby in her arms, ran across to her father and hugged him. He then took the baby from her and placed him tenderly on his lap, studying his little face as if seeing him for the first time. 'You made the right decision, Bella. See the way he's looking at me. He knows. He's a dear little fellow, an O'Brien all right.' Then he turned again to Ed, who seemed mesmerized by this touching scene of domesticity. 'I'm afraid your father is not too well, Mr Frobisher, which is why I came home early.'

'Oh.' Ed started up anxiously.

'Nothing serious. I took him home to have a lie down. He's had one or two turns recently, dizzy spells. I told him he should see Doctor Carson and he's promised to. A bit of overwork, I imagine.'

'I'll pop in and see him on my way home,' Ed said. 'In the meantime, Mr O'Brien, I wonder if I could take Lottie out for a drive to get some air – that's if she wants to. Give her a little break.'

'*Now?*' Lottie said, startled.

'Yes, now if you like.'

'Would you like that, Lottie?' her father asked.

'Well, just for a little while. Yes, I'd like that a lot if it's all right.'

Yes, it was good to get out for a while in this luxurious car with the bonnet down, to feel the breeze on her face, the wind blowing through her hair. She stretched lazily and smiled across at Ed as they turned the corner at the end of her road and headed in a northerly direction. 'Very nice of you to think of this.'

'I thought you looked extremely tired. It is a difficult time for you.'

Lottie didn't reply so he continued: 'Is there anywhere special you'd like to go?'

'We can't go too far. I have to get back to prepare supper for Dad and Bella.'

'And I mustn't be too long because I want to go and see my father.'

'How about Petone Beach? It's not too far.'

'Good idea, and we can take a stroll along the beach.'

Sitting back, Lottie remembered the time she had gone there with Violet. What a lot had happened since then. It seemed like a lifetime ago.

Soon they came in sight of the beach and Ed parked the car. They sat looking out on to the harbour. 'I came here a long time ago with Violet Carson. I was thinking how much had happened since.'

'Yes, I can imagine.' Ed looked at her. 'Shall we have a stroll?'

He got out of the car and opened the door for her and they began to walk along the beach. 'We live in a very beautiful place,' he said, gesticulating to the scenery around them and pointing in the direction of the distant hills, 'don't you think?'

'Yes, I do.'

'But you'd still prefer England?'

'Not prefer, but I found London very exciting. Dorset's particularly beautiful.'

'Oh, you went to Dorset?'

'I wanted to see Hardy country. I was very interested in Hardy at school. I made a friend in London whose parents lived in Dorchester and she invited me to stay. I actually stood outside Mr Hardy's house and he was probably inside!' Her face glowed with excitement.

'And London?'

'London was fascinating. This friend whose parents lived in Dorchester was an artist and I met some interesting people. I began to model for students at the Slade School of Art . . . with my clothes on,' she said hurriedly, noting his expression. 'It was all *most* respectable and I would have stayed but for the wire from Dad and the news about Bella.'

'Stayed forever?'

'Not forever. I'd have come home to see Dad and Bella.'

'And your mother?'

'I never want to see my mother again,' she said coldly. 'And she knows it.'

'Isn't that a very sad state of affairs?'

'It is very sad, but my mother left us – walked out of the house without saying goodbye to me or my sister – and took my young brother with her. So I lost a mother *and* brother. I saw him recently and he scarcely knew who I was. Bella and my mother were quite close. My mother and I never got on. She thought I was useless and I thought she was very hard, particularly after Dad came back from the war. I understood she had a lot to do and I wanted to help her, but we always clashed and she wanted me to leave school to help support the family. At that time Dad didn't – couldn't – work and my mother was horrible to him.'

'And the Carsons helped you then, I understand?'

'Very much. Madeleine was particularly good to me. She did all she could to help me stay on at school; she thought I might be a teacher, but when Mum left home I had no option but to leave. You see, Ed, I missed out a lot in life. I am only half educated and yet I get to meet people like the Carsons and, well, you who went to Cambridge.'

'I'm not particularly well educated, Lottie. Don't misunderstand me. I did go to Cambridge but at my father's insistence. I studied law, which I hated, and got a poor degree. Then I went into the army and came out a wreck, sickened and embittered by war. My father thinks I'm useless, too, if you want the truth, and sometimes I think I am compared to him. I'm a partner in a law firm – I did actually manage to qualify as a solicitor – but I do very little. My grandmother left me enough money to make me independent, much to my father's disgust, so that I don't really need to work.

'So you see, compared to me you are a paragon; besides which, I admire you so much, the way you've looked after your family, taken mundane jobs when clearly you are very clever, and supported Bella, who in many ways would be an outcast of society forced to have her baby adopted.' Ed stopped abruptly and looked at his watch.

'Shall we get back and, look, I'd love to come and see Bella and my namesake and . . . and perhaps you also?'

From then on Ed became a fairly constant visitor to the O'Brien household. He would appear on the doorstep, always unannounced and always with flowers for Bella and usually a small toy, a rattle or a cuddly bear, for Edward. Lottie wasn't often in because she was working, or she would arrive home to find her sister and Ed chatting amiably, Bella having given him a cup of tea, and playing with the baby.

At first, Lottie had thought he might be courting her sister, but eventually she came to realize his interest was in her from the way his face lit up when she came through the door and his invitations to go for a drive which she generally refused on the grounds that she had to help Bella. Despite the bond that had undoubtedly been formed between them that night at the hospital and cemented during their walk at Petone Beach, she saw him as a friend, not a lover, and preferred it that way. Relying on his shyness and perhaps his gentlemanly good manners, she had no intention of getting too close to him and risking a repetition of her relationship with that other upper-class family: the Carsons.

Apart from that, Ed didn't attract her at all. She knew he was about thirty but he looked much older. In appearance he was non-descript, of medium height, with dark hair going grey, a pale complexion, and he wore gold-rimmed spectacles which he peered over as if he were short-sighted. Nor was he glamorous in the way Hugh was with his height, charm and striking good looks, nor artistic and self-assured like Adam. He didn't dance, sail or play tennis – his leg was too much of a handicap. He dragged it a little and always supported himself with a stick.

In short, he was rather a brotherly figure, pleasant and friendly, comfortable to be with and she appreciated what a nice man he was, just as her father had said. Besides, she was short on friends and it was good to have one like Ed, who was so natural that she could even forget at times that her father worked for his in a servile capacity. With Ed it didn't seem to matter.

Bella liked him a lot and was completely at ease with him and on the occasions she announced that he had been and left, Lottie was always conscious of a slight feeling of disappointment because she had missed seeing him. It was strange – unreal but not unwelcome.

Life had settled into a kind of routine. Lottie continued working in the haberdashery department at Kirkcaldies and got home as soon as she could to help Bella. Her father usually came in a short time after her. They had tea, played with the baby, she did household chores while Bella settled Edward for the night and her father read the paper. She was glad, eventually, to fall into bed, exhausted with the day where one had no time for fun or entertainment just because one had to keep going. And every day was like this for some weeks, even months, after Edward was born. There was no choice. Day after day it was the same.

One evening Lottie got in feeling more tired than usual to find Ed sitting on the carpet in his shirt sleeves playing with Edward. She looked at him with a weary smile and slumped into her father's chair. 'What a day!'

'That bad?'

He got to his feet and rolled down his sleeves, gently rescuing his spectacles from Edward who had somehow got hold of them and seemed to be trying to put them on.

'My boss is away and it seems to be the one day that half the populace of Wellington wanted to buy buttons or ribbons.'

'Oh, dear.'

Lottie rose from the chair. 'Where's Bella? I must start thinking of supper.'

'Bella's in the kitchen. We have got a little plan for you,' Ed said mysteriously, shrugging on his jacket while Edward started to bawl and reach up for his spectacles. 'I'm going to take you out to dinner. We both insist.'

'Oh, no, I can't possibly . . .'

'You can. Bella has already prepared supper for herself and your father so all you need do is get changed – that is, if you want to because you look pretty fine as you are.'

At that moment Bella appeared from the kitchen, wiping her hands on a cloth. 'Really Lottie, you must go. I think it is a very nice idea of Ed's. You haven't been out for weeks. You get no fun.'

'Nor do you.'

'Yes, I do. I have the baby all day and I meet my friends and go for walks in the park. I do all kinds of things while all you do is work, then rush home and look after us.'

'Well . . .' It was tempting and the very idea bucked her up and made her feel less tired. 'In that case I'll go and see if I have anything decent to wear. Is there anything I can do in the kitchen?'

'It's all done,' Bella said, giving her a push. 'Go away and enjoy yourself.'

'She is a very sweet girl, your sister,' Ed said, looking across the table at Lottie.

'She is a dear,' Lottie replied, 'and she has come on enormously since having baby Edward.'

'In what way?'

'Well, she's more mature. She used to cling to me a great deal. Now she has grown up, is more independent.'

She sat back and watched the waiter pour wine. It was the same hotel she had been to so often with Hugh and she even thought one or two of the waiters recognized her. They certainly recognized Ed and sprang to attention when he entered the dining room, taking him to one of the best tables and hovering attentively while he ordered.

Lottie wore one of the dresses she had worn in London and her hair glowed in the lamplight while her face shone with pleasure as she looked across at her partner. 'Thank you for this, Ed. It really is a treat.'

'It is a treat for me.' He paused and gazed at her. 'You look really lovely tonight, Lottie.'

'Thank you, Ed.' She smiled uncertainly, taken aback by the intensity of his gaze.

'There is something I want to ask you,' he said and paused while their waiters fussed around them again with their fish entrée. Lottie steeled herself, wondering what was to come and hoping it would not mean the end of a friendship.

'I would like to help you with Bella and Edward. I know it is a struggle for you and you have to work very hard, and although you look beautiful tonight there are still deep shadows under your eyes which shouldn't be there. I would like to give you an allowance which would enable you either to stop work or work fewer hours so that you can help Bella and relax more. I'm really doing this for Edward; please understand that.'

Lottie slumped back in her chair, feeling shocked but also relieved it had not been a proposal of marriage, which she had half expected given the occasion, the splendour of the best hotel in Wellington and the way he looked at her, which suggested much more than mere friendship. For a moment she stared at him and then, swiftly recovering her composure, leaned across the table. 'Ed, it is terribly kind of you but of course I can't possibly accept . . .'

'Please think about it,' he interrupted her. 'Don't decide now. It is not just for you. It is to help Bella and Edward, to whom I feel especially close. You have become a kind of family to me, Lottie. I have no brothers and sisters. My father is remote and unloving and my mother is caught up in all her good works, the many committees she is on. I don't want to embarrass you, but . . .'

'I can't, Ed. Believe me, I appreciate it because I know it is well meant. But my family has taken enough charity. I am perfectly able to work and help Bella. I would feel like a kept woman taking money from you. Remember we accepted help from the Carsons, and although extremely grateful because it was done with the best of intentions, I was a girl then and now I am a woman. It also caused a lot of trouble and awkwardness because for years I was paying back Madeleine. She never asked for it but I considered it a debt of honour. I don't want to go through all that again.'

'But from me it is a gift,' Ed began, but Lottie held up a hand to silence him.

'Between us Dad and I can manage perfectly well. We appreciate what you are doing for us and the kindness you have shown. Please don't spoil it, Ed. Please.'

And she reached over and took his hand, aware of the tiny shudder that seemed to pass through him as she did so.

Violet said, 'Isn't it ridiculous! I've got engaged to Albert.' She had been bubbling with some sort of repressed excitement ever since she appeared at Lottie's counter, laden as usual with masses of parcels, and asked her to meet her after work. Now they were sitting in her car outside the store, Violet's excited face turned to her companion.

'But why is it ridiculous?'

'Because of that silly name, but he *is* rather nice, don't you think? Did you like him?'

'Yes, I thought he was nice.'

'Only that?' Violet looked dismayed.

'Violet, I hardly know him. You and he rushed off after the game.'

'You don't think he's a bit dreary?'

Lottie laughed and clutched her companion's arm. 'How do I know? The point is, are you in love with him?'

'I think so.' Violet looked doubtful. 'I think I am. The family like him.'

'But the family aren't going to marry him. Maybe you should be a little surer before you accept.'

'But I've accepted. In fact, we're going to have an engagement party soon and I want you to come.'

Lottie shook her head impatiently. 'Really, Violet, I don't know what to say. That sounds pretty definite to me. I wish you every happiness, Violet, I really do, but I don't think I can come to the party.'

'Why not?'

'Well . . .'

'Because of Hugh? But he won't be there. All that is in the past. Besides, Ed Frobisher will be coming and you like him, don't you?' Violet glanced at her slyly. 'I know you're seeing each other.'

'Well, not exactly *seeing* each other. I mean, not in that way. We're not romantically attached, not a bit. Look, I'm sorry but I must get home,' and she made as if to get out of the car.

'I'll take you,' Violet said and put the car into gear. 'I *want* you to be at the party. Then you can tell me honestly what you think.'

'About what?'

'About Albert.'

'But you're engaged to him. You're having a party.'

'Yes, but you know, Lottie, what you think matters a lot to me. I think you're a good judge of people. You're so sensible.'

'I wasn't very sensible about Hugh.'

'Hugh behaved horribly and it was not your fault.'

'Well . . .' Startled, Lottie didn't know what to say.

'Come, I'll ask Ed to pick you up.'

As the car came to a halt outside the door of her house, Lottie said, 'Do you know about Bella, my sister?'

'What about Bella?'

'Bella has had a baby. She is not married and Ed has been extraordinarily kind. The day he drove me home after the tennis match we found Bella in labour. Ed drove her to the hospital and she had a complicated labour – she could have died or lost the baby. He stayed with me all night and often comes to see Bella and the baby and . . . occasionally we do go out. But it is pure friendship, nothing more. He is simply a really nice person.'

'Oh, he is, but he is quite shy and withdrawn; maybe because he had such a difficult time with that horrible wife of his.'

'You knew her?'

'Yes, we knew her, but she behaved very badly and went off with someone else. She lost a baby and it seemed to unhinge her. She was a notorious flirt and hurt him a lot. He deserves someone better.' Her pretty violet eyes stared straight into Lottie's face. 'Someone nice like you. I think he's a little in love with you, maybe a lot.'

'Oh, now that is ridiculous.'

'No, it's not. He asked me to set up the tennis match so that he could see you again.'

'Then why didn't you tell me?'

'Because I know you. After all, we've got to know each other pretty well and I know how hurt you were by Hugh. But Ed isn't Hugh. Or maybe that's part of the problem?'

'Maybe it is,' Lottie said a little wistfully. 'Would you like to come in and see the baby?'

'I would love to come in and see the baby but I have to meet Albert. In fact, I'm late already. Shall I tell him you'll be at the party with Ed?'

'If you like,' Lottie said. 'But you'll have to ask Ed.'

'I don't imagine he'll refuse,' Violet said slyly. 'I don't think you realize how lucky you are to have all the men fall in love with you. You've got something special Lottie and you don't know it. But that's what makes you so nice.' And impulsively she leaned over to kiss Lottie's cheek.

Having an escort did make a difference. Otherwise, she was sure she wouldn't have gone. As it was she looked stunning, having splashed out and bought a new dress of aquamarine silk taffeta in the fashionable flapper style of a straight tubular column, sleeveless with a dropped waist and scalloped hemline reaching just below the knee. Ed had presented her with a magnificent corsage made of white orchids when he picked her up and she had pinned this to the left of the scooped neckline. She wore flesh-coloured stockings and T-bar shoes with buckles and a very slight high heel so as not to be taller than Ed.

He looked rather good, too, in a tuxedo and there was something different about him, an air of confidence, an energy as he opened the door for her and made sure she was comfortable in her seat. Yes, she did like Ed. She had been annoyed with him for offering her an allowance, with its echoes of Carson patronage, yet she got over it because there were differences, because she felt he had Bella and the baby's interests at heart as much as hers. She only hoped he didn't bring it up again.

So they exchanged glances as he got into his seat and then he patted her hand.

'Happy?'

'Yes, why not?'

'You look perfectly lovely tonight, Lottie. All the men will be after you.'

'Don't be silly.'

'You underestimate yourself.' Ed started the car and the perfect machine purred into life. 'That's what Violet says. And she's right.'

'Oh, you talk about me with Violet?'

'Of course.' He chuckled.

Yes, there was definitely something different about Ed tonight.

'How do you like Albert?'

'Well, I don't really know him. Do you?'

'No, but she doesn't seem too sure if she is in love with him.'

'Oh, that's Violet. She's crazy about him if you ask me. Otherwise, she wouldn't be giving a party, would she?'

'No, I suppose not. I'm rather nervous about seeing all the family again, to be truthful.'

'Violet knew you would be, that's why she asked me to escort you and I jumped at the chance. There is no need to be nervous with the Carsons. They are very nice people and from what I hear are very fond of you. Just be perfectly natural with them and everything will be all right. Besides, you have me.'

And suddenly to Lottie that seemed important. Someone she could lean on.

The room was already thronged with people when they arrived at the Carsons' house, which was ablaze with lights, to be greeted by Violet and Albert standing at the door, looking happy as engaged couples should. Violet threw her arms round Lottie, whispering,

'I'm so glad you came. I didn't think you would. You remember Albert? Ed, you know Albert?'

'Of course.'

Ed and Lottie shook hands with Albert and then, while Violet greeted another guest, wandered into the crowded room, Lottie rather nervous, Ed seeming quite self-assured and greeting a number of people with a nod or by name.

Looking around her Lottie again recalled the many times she had been there, first as a nervous schoolgirl, then almost as a member of the family, feeling completely at home. Now she felt anything but and her misgivings returned when she felt a tap on her back and turned to see Madeleine with a broad smile on her face, who greeted her with a kiss.

'Isn't it lovely about Violet?'

'Lovely.'

'And Albert is so nice.' She turned to Ed. 'Ed, your mother was asking after you.'

'My mother?' Ed looked about him with surprise. 'I didn't know she was coming. Is my father here, too?'

'No, your mother says he's not so well.'

'Oh, dear, again? I'd better have a word. Lottie, come and meet my mother.'

'I see you had your baby.' Lottie smiled at Madeleine.

'A darling girl, Cherie. I do hope you will come and see us now that we have found you. You know we really missed you, Lottie.' She smiled at her understandingly. 'Are you working?'

'At Kirkcaldies, for the time being.'

'We must get together. We must try to arrange something. We live not too far from Ed, though Andy may have to go overseas.'

'I'd like that . . .' And then Lottie felt Ed tugging her hand. 'I'd better go. I'll see you a bit later.'

Lottie felt nervous about meeting Ed's mother. She didn't know why, and followed him reluctantly across the room. She was sitting in a far corner glass in hand talking to a number of other women of about her age who had found a nice place where they could sit and gossip and watch the younger people, rather like a scene from a Jane Austen novel. Among them was Mrs Carson, who rose to greet Lottie and kissed her warmly.

'How lovely to see you again, Lottie. And how pretty you look tonight.' She turned as Ed bent towards the distinguished-looking grey-haired woman who Lottie recognized from the wedding anniversary party, bent and kissed her.

'Is Dad not well again, Mother?'

'I don't know what's the matter with your father. He gets tired so easily. I left him resting, but Gerald Carson is keeping an eye on him and can't find anything seriously wrong.' As she spoke to her son her gaze was on Lottie.

Ed drew her forward. 'Mother, I'd like you to meet Lottie.'

'How do you do?' Lady Frobisher said with a smile, outwardly charming, but studying her face carefully. 'I feel I've seen you somewhere before.' She extended her hand and Lottie shook it.

'It was at your wedding anniversary party, Lady Frobisher.'

'Oh, were you there?'

'I was one of the waitresses.'

'Oh.' Lost for words, Lady Frobisher looked at her son and then added in a distant voice, 'How interesting.'

'Lottie is a great friend of our family,' Mrs Carson said and then a penny seemed to drop and understanding dawn.

'Oh,' was all Lady Frobisher said again, and she kept her eyes fixed on Lottie, as though trying to peer into her soul.

Then Lottie knew that she knew who she was and probably all about her, that they had probably discussed her already and they were all trying to be kind but were in fact patronizing. Again, she wished that she had not come. It was always a mistake to try and revisit the past.

'Your mother doesn't like me,' Lottie said in the car on the way home. 'Or at least doesn't approve of me. I could tell.'

'I don't know what makes you think that,' Ed said. 'I thought she was perfectly pleasant. It was difficult to hear yourself think with all that noise.'

'Perhaps you're right,' Lottie said but she knew he wasn't.

'I thought it was a very good party.'

'It was good. The food was fabulous.'

A silence fell between them as if each were absorbed in their own particular thoughts.

And she had enjoyed herself after that brief encounter with his mother. Ed knew quite a lot of people to whom he introduced her, and they had danced a little. Lottie also danced with some other men including Albert, while Ed sat it out and watched. But all the time, whoever she was with, she was aware of those penetrating eyes of his mother, although unseen, observing her somewhere from a distance.

When she left Ed went to see her off while Lottie remained talking to Violet and Albert. She had spent some time with Madeleine, renewed her acquaintance with Andy and, yes, she did remember those tennis matches when they had first known one another and she was a schoolgirl.

Dr and Mrs Carson sought her out, Dr Carson kindly enquiring after her father, but there was always lurking the feeling that somehow she was on trial, she didn't belong, and as Hugh's ex-fiancée she was an embarrassment. Better to have stayed away. Ed belonged. It was his crowd and she was an interloper.

Ed stopped outside her door. The house was in darkness. Ed looked towards it and she hesitated. 'I'd ask you in, but it is very late.'

'It is late. Do you go to work tomorrow?'

'Yes.'

'Perhaps you could have dinner with me tomorrow night?'

'Not tomorrow, Ed. I have a lot to do.'

'The weekend, then. Sunday? We could go out somewhere along the coast?'

'That might be nice.'

'Shall I call for you around ten?'

'All right, then.' She looked at him, sensing something in the atmosphere, and then he leaned towards her, slid his hand around her waist and very gently but firmly kissed her.

Fourteen

It was late afternoon on the day following the party and Ed sat for a long time by the side of his father, who was resting in the conservatory on the far side of the house. He was worried about him. He did not look well and, his mother had told him, kept on coming home exhausted.

Throughout his life Ed, as the only child, had had a difficult relationship with both his parents. He knew that his father felt he had failed him, that he was not destined to become the top-notch lawyer he was, or in any way emulate his success. It was, they thought, a pity he had inherited so much money from his maternal grandmother because it made him independent of parental control and, above all, advice. The war had changed Ed and so had his disastrous marriage – and not in the way his parents had wished for. His mother loved him, he knew, but in an obsessive, rather than caring way, wanting to control everything about his life which Ed had always firmly resisted.

As if aware of his presence, his father suddenly woke up, raised his head and looked at him. 'Ed, how long have you been there?'

'Not long, Father. Mother said you weren't too well.' Sir Eustace struggled to a sitting position.

'That's nonsense. I am perfectly well. Doctor Carson said I am as fit as a fiddle, but I have a heavy workload at the moment and I get tired. Perfectly natural at my age. I shall soon be retiring, you know.' He produced his heavy timepiece from his waistcoat pocket.

'Ah, time for my whisky. Go and get it for me will you, Ed, there's a dear?'

And his father sank back on the sofa and closed his eyes again while Ed crept away.

He was measuring the whiskies for his father and himself from the table in the dining room when his mother came and took off her stole, tossing it over a chair. 'Ed, darling, how lovely to see you.' She flopped on a chair and began removing her hat, shaking her head as if glad to be free from its restriction.

'Busy day, Mother?'

'Busy as usual. All these committees are so exhausting.'

He turned to her. 'Whisky for you?'

'Lovely,' she said, smiling at him. 'Thank you, darling.'

'Dad doesn't seem too great, Mother.'

'He's not great at all. I'm very worried about him,' and she took the whisky from Ed and sipped it gratefully while he sat opposite, his own glass in his hands. There was a tension in the atmosphere. He thought he knew why and shifted uneasily.

'That was a very nice party last night, Ed.'

'Yes, Mother, did you enjoy it?'

'Very much. The Carsons always give a good party.' She stopped to sip from her glass as though measuring her words. 'About that girl you introduced me to, Ed?'

'Yes, Mother?'

'She is very pretty. I knew I'd seen her before, but . . .' Ed knew there would be a 'but', '. . . Evelyn Carson tells me she is the *daughter* of O'Brien and, furthermore, her sister has an illegitimate baby. Did you know that, Ed?'

'Of course I know it, Mother.'

'I imagine you were taken with her at our party, so have you been seeing a lot of her?'

'Yes, a good deal. However, I met her long before our party, at Madeleine Carson's wedding. I was very taken with her then.'

'Oh, she was there?' Lady Frobisher looked surprised. 'As a waitress, I suppose?' His mother held up her empty glass and asked her son to refresh it, which he was glad to do as he was beginning to fume inwardly and knew he would have difficulty controlling his temper.

'She was a *guest*, Mother,' he said, handing her the glass. 'Violet introduced us. She was a friend of the Carsons and later became engaged to Hugh.'

'Oh, *that's* the girl.' Lady Frobisher's brow cleared as understanding dawned. 'Evelyn didn't tell me that. No wonder. But, Ed, do you really think she is the sort of girl you should be associating with?'

'Why not? This is New Zealand in the twentieth century, Mother, not England in the nineteenth.'

'I am quite aware of that, Ed, and I don't think anyone would call me a snob. I am associated with a number of organizations which are concerned with those less fortunate than ourselves, including unmarried mothers. I am therefore considered very compassionate.'

'Then you will like Lottie very much, Mother, because so is she. She has had a very hard life and has come through it with flying colours. The Carsons, who knew her through Madeleine, appreciated this and she became a good friend of theirs.'

'I'm not sure Evelyn did, the way she spoke to me.'

'Then I'm surprised.'

'Hugh Carson saw through her, too.'

Ed's voice rose. 'What do you mean by that, Mother, "saw through her"?'

'Well, he broke off the engagement, didn't he? She went all the way to England after him and he probably realized she was after his money. There is more to a girl than good looks, Ed – it is upbringing and breeding that matters. Don't forget one day you will be a baronet and extremely wealthy. Do you honestly think that Miss O'Brien, from a poor family, who worked as a waitress and now I understand works in *a shop* with little prospects, is unaware of this? Why, it would transform her world if after being rejected by Hugh Carson she managed to ensnare you . . .'

Ed stood up with a sharp exclamation, put his glass firmly down on the table and glared at his mother. 'I'm fed up with these insinuations, Mother, which are unworthy of you and completely unfair to Lottie. Furthermore, I am perfectly capable of making up my own mind of who I see and eventually who I marry . . .'

'Well, you weren't very clever with Sophie, were you, Ed? You didn't see through her until it was too late. I sincerely hope that your intentions towards this young woman are not serious, but if they are, and I do think you are very gullible, I'm warning you as your mother who loves you, to get out before it's too late and you land yourself in another disaster, in which case . . .'

But Ed interrupted her. 'I'm not listening to any more of this, Mother. Would you please give Father his whisky when he wakes up?'

And without a farewell he left the room, aware that some sort of watershed in his life had just been reached.

Ed's house in Wadestown was some distance from his parents only a mile or so from central Wellington. It was attractively set on a quiet hillside among trees not far from Kaiwarra Park, and afforded spectacular views of the harbour. It was a large colonial-style building which he had bought before his marriage to Sophie Whiteside and, despite its association with that unhappy part of his life, he loved the house and the peace he derived from its beautiful surroundings, its panoramic views of the water and the hills on the far side.

He was both exhausted and distressed from the interview with his mother. She was the only daughter of a wealthy upper-class English family and had met his father, the young lawyer from New Zealand, when he was reading for the Bar in London and had subsequently made her life with him in Wellington. She yearned, however, for the old country and still had many of the mannerisms and prejudices of her class. He should have known how she would feel about Lottie.

Ed poured himself a large whisky when he got home and slumped into a chair, from which he had a panoramic view through a large picture window of the myriad lights from Wellington reflected in the still waters of the harbour. It was a beautiful and calming scene of which he never tired. The unhappy encounter with his mother had brought to the fore a number of issues troubling his mind, or rather one major issue: his feelings for Lottie, with whom he had been obsessed ever since his first meeting with her at Madeleine Carson's wedding. Since his bitter divorce Ed had never been interested in women or even looked at one until he saw Lottie. She had stood out, even in that crowd where there were a number of beautiful young woman, not only for her looks but for her air of graciousness and a kind of detachment from it all. Despite her air of elusiveness he felt he could relate to her. He was mesmerized by her from the start and then she was gone, and he never even knew her name. Then some years later miraculously she reappeared again as a waitress at his parents' anniversary party, where he learned she was the daughter of the family chauffeur. From then on he had devised means to meet her and get to know her better. But she was elusive and evasive, qualities that had attracted and at the same time haunted him. She was certainly not after his money. He thought of how her pride and horror of being patronized by people like the Carsons, who also had the power to hurt her, had made her determined to discourage him and she had – until the kiss. She had responded to the kiss and he had been borne aloft by a sense of elation ever since until the conversation with his mother had brought him sharply down to earth.

Lottie was a complex person, but he thought if she wanted anything it was not to ensnare him – if so she had gone about it in a very funny way – but to escape from the dreary monotony and routine of her life. This is why she had loved England so much and he was determined one way or another to take her there.

Lottie got home from work, weighed down by shopping bags in both hands, more tired and exhausted than usual because she had had a number of difficult customers, one of whom had complained about her and she had been summoned to the manager's office. The complaint had been that she was offhand which Lottie considered unfair as she had again been left alone in the department, had been serving several people at the same time and this woman had been particularly demanding and difficult, even rude. She had been told that she had an 'attitude' problem which she should do her best to correct, otherwise . . . The warning had been clear and the last thing she wanted was to be out of a job.

It was true that she hated it. The dreary routine was mind-numbing for someone who had no interest in haberdashery and knew that in the economic circumstances she had little or no chance of promotion, especially now in view of her interview in the manager's office.

Lottie pushed open the front door and was confronted by a scene of domesticity she had not expected. Baby Edward was sitting on a rug on the floor, clearly delighted by the attention being paid to him by two people, Bella and a man, who were dangling various toys in front of him and making baby noises, 'boos' and 'ahs' which he seemed to find extremely amusing.

Bella, face alight, jumped to her feet as Lottie staggered in, relieving her of her shopping, some of which she had done on the way home and some during a severely curtailed lunch break as there had been so much to do in the store, which also meant she had no time to eat.

The young man suspended his baby play and got sheepishly to his feet. 'This is Len,' Bella said, 'Edward's father.'

'Oh.' Lottie was momentarily lost for words, then she nodded. 'Hello, Len.'

'Hello,' Len said, wiping his hands on the sides of his trousers. 'Sorry, my hands are sticky.'

'Yes.' Lottie laughed. 'Edward does dribble a lot. Well,' she looked at him appraisingly, 'how nice to meet you.'

'He's a nice little fellow,' Len said, looking down at the baby rather fondly, Lottie thought. Affection, perhaps, mixed with shock at how easy it was to produce a living human being like this and not even know about it.

'We do love him,' Lottie said firmly.

There followed a very awkward silence until Bella said, 'Let's take these things into the kitchen and get a cup of tea. Len, you keep the baby entertained.'

Whereupon Len, who was a tall, ungainly chap, obediently got down on his knees again and started playing with Edward who, resentful at so suddenly being neglected, had begun to whimper.

As soon as they got into the kitchen Lottie shut the door and stared at her sister. 'Explain,' she said. 'I thought you didn't *like* him!'

'Well . . .' Bella started to take things out of the bags and put them away. 'He's not so bad after all.'

'When did you meet up with him again?'

'A while ago. In town. We bumped into each other. He was just passing and stopped when he saw me. Started chatting. It was very awkward, really. He said "I didn't know you had a baby" and then when I said nothing he looked at me as if he had begun to understand. Then he said, "Is it mine?" and I said that yes it was and he asked me why I hadn't told him and, well, it went on from there. I didn't tell you because I thought you might be angry.'

'Me, angry? Why should I be angry if the baby's father makes an appearance?'

'Because of what I said about him. Maybe I was wrong. He came to see Edward a few days ago and now today. He wants his parents to know.'

'You said you were frightened of them, Bella?'

'I know, Lottie, but it is a long time ago. A person can change their mind, can't they?'

'Certainly, and in this case I am all for it but I want you to be careful, Bella. No jumping into bed with Len.'

'Oh, no nothing like that,' Bella said primly. 'Well, not for now,' and she smiled shyly at Lottie who, not sure whether she was telling the truth, thought not for the first time what a devious little thing her sister was.

'Better take the tea in,' she said, pouring water into the pot, 'or Len will wonder what's happening.'

'I hope you like him, Lottie. He was very scared of meeting you.'

'I hope I do, too,' Lottie said. 'But that's not the important thing. You and especially baby are important and I don't want you rushing into anything just because Len has acknowledged that Edward is his son.'

'I just think I handled the whole thing badly,' Lottie said to Ed as they sat in his car looking out on to a rain drenched scene. The idea had been to drive round the harbour, possibly as far as Days

Bay or Eastbourne, but now they had stopped by Petone Beach and were reconsidering what to do. She had decided to unburden herself and found Ed immediately understanding and sympathetic.

'How did you handle it badly?'

'By my attitude. I was also stiff and awkward with Len. After all, I don't want to put him off.'

'Did you like him?'

'He was all right. I mean, I found nothing offensive about him apart from what Bella had previously told me, which was not very complimentary. She said he was rough – with her, I imagine – and she didn't want to see him again and was afraid of his parents. Apart from that he seemed very mild to me, polite, obviously nervous. He is also quite good looking and I can see why he attracted my young, impressionable sister.' She gazed out of the windscreen. 'Drat this rain. I was looking forward to a nice drive.'

'Look, would you like to go back to my house for some lunch?'

'Well . . . Why not? That sounds very nice.'

'If it brightens we can go out later but I think the rain has settled in.'

After a short drive they arrived at Ed's house, so picturesquely set among trees and Lottie was immediately captivated by it.

'It's lovely,' she exclaimed as she entered the wide hall and looked around through doors opening into spacious rooms and windows everywhere, with views to the sea or the bush-clad hills behind the house.

In the dining room the table was already laid for two people and Lottie looked at him curiously. 'I see you planned this?' she said teasingly.

'Well, when I saw what sort of day it was it did enter my mind that we might have lunch here. My maid left everything ready. Cold cuts in the larder, lots of salads.'

'Does your maid live in?'

'No, but you are quite safe with me, Lottie.' His tone was also jocular and then they looked at each other as if recalling that kiss after he had driven her home, when a boundary had been crossed, promising unfinished business.

'I feel safe with you, Ed,' she replied. 'Very.'

'Not too safe, I hope, but come on, let me show you the rest of the house.'

As they wandered from room to room, chatting and stopping to admire the views, Lottie experienced a feeling of security, of familiarity, as if somehow she had visited the house before, only of course she hadn't.

In the kitchen the food had been nicely set out in a cold larder and only needed to be put on a hatch that separated the kitchen and dining room. Lottie then helped to carry dishes to the sideboard and they helped themselves. Ed produced a bottle of wine which he poured into tall glasses.

'This is a lovely surprise,' Lottie said, raising her glass and silently they toasted each other. 'Tell me, how long have you lived here?'

'I bought the house before I married Sophie.'

'So it was her choice?'

'Together we decided we liked it.'

'How long were you together, Ed?'

They had never discussed his marriage. Probably the time was now ripe to do so. 'Four years. I came home from the war in 1917 and married her two years later. We had known each other before the war. Our parents were friends. Her father was also a barrister. She didn't become pregnant immediately and then she lost the baby at five months. It was a bitter blow for us both, but we had not been getting on too well before that. In fact, we should never have got married. I was too wounded, mentally and physically by the war, much older than my years and she was too young to sympathize or understand; she was only nineteen when we married. Very, very pretty. We thought the baby would cement our marriage and when she miscarried she blamed me and we had no sexual relations after that. The marriage had completely broken down. Then she met somebody else – well, I think she had known him quite some time, and that was it. Sophie was never very sympathetic or particularly kind to me. I irritated her. She was dismissive of my war experience and intolerant of my war wound. A bit ashamed of me, I think. Didn't like to be seen out with me and I limped quite badly in those days. I really don't know why she married me and, frankly, Lottie, the whole thing left me feeling very bitter.'

'I don't wonder,' Lottie said. 'I can sympathize with how you felt because Hugh left me feeling the same: somehow diminished by the experience, as if it was my fault.'

'And after Hugh? Has there been anyone?'

'Yes.' Lottie nodded, thinking that if it had to come out it might as well be now. 'There was a man called Adam in London. Very nice – an artist. But I was not in love with him and in a way I suppose I used him to try and get over Hugh, which I'm a bit ashamed of. Hugh was such a shock. Adam did, however, offer a new kind of life. I met him through another artist called Flora. Flora was lovely.'

'Ah, that's how you became an artists' model?'

'Exactly. They were very nice people and I liked the Bohemian lifestyle, mixing with artists, writers and so on. There were a lot of parties. I told you I am only half educated, Ed, and they taught me a lot. They both lent me the money to come home when my father called me, so that I never needed to see Hugh again. I have repaid them.'

'And Adam? Do you keep in touch?'

'Adam wrote and I replied, but it was a half-hearted correspondence that petered out. I don't think he was really in love with me either. We were just good friends and liked each other. I knew I had no future with Adam, even if I did succeed in going back to London, so I stopped answering his letters.'

By now they had finished their meal and Ed rose from the table. 'Let's take our wine into the lounge and see if the weather is clearing up.'

He took her glass and led her to the chairs in front of the picture window where he had spent so much time recently contemplating his future. They sat for some time staring out into the rain, which almost completely obscured the view.

'We were right about the weather,' Lottie said, stretching her legs and feeling thoroughly relaxed after a nice meal and a couple of glasses of wine.

'What was the weather like in England?'

'About the same. Maybe a bit worse. It was cold in Dorset, but then I was there in the summer which is now when we have our winter. In fact, this time last year I was in London.'

'Would you like to go back to London?'

'Yes, one day. Maybe when Bella is older and more able to look after herself.'

'And what about me?'

She looked surprised. 'You?'

'Do I figure in your life at all, Lottie?'

'Of course. Of course you do, Ed.'

Ed swallowed hard and leaned slightly forward in his chair, tiny beads of perspiration on his forehead. 'I wondered if you would like to go back to London – on a honeymoon, maybe?'

Taken completely by surprise, Lottie could only stare at him. He got out a handkerchief and wiped his forehead while a dark flush stole slowly up his cheeks.

'I know I am putting this very badly, but you must know how I feel about you, Lottie. You must know by now. Maybe that was a very awkward way of saying it, but I am asking you to marry me.'

As Lottie still failed to respond he hurried on. 'I know you don't love me, Lottie, but I think, I hope, you care for me and one day, perhaps, could love me?'

His obvious discomfort moved her so much that Lottie felt a surge of affection for him and, reaching across, took his hand and squeezed it tightly. 'Ed, I like you so much and yes, I do care for you. You really are the nicest person I have ever known. But marriage is a very big step and, well, I'm not ready for it yet. I have to think of Bella and my father, particularly Bella and the baby, and they have to come first. They would be lost without me.'

'I thought we could give a home to Bella and Edward. There is lots of room here. I've already thought about it.'

'Ed, that is so typical of you and so kind, but I am really not ready for it. I am still very young and things change. My parents married young and what a disaster that was. You make it sound so tempting – all my worries taken away – but not yet, Ed. It wouldn't be fair to you.'

'Then it's not absolutely no?'

'It's not absolutely no,' she said slowly.

'Then I'm going to ask you again,' he said, his face alight with hope, 'and again and again. I want to make you happy, Lottie and I know – I absolutely know for sure – that I could.'

That night Lottie lay on her back in bed, wide awake but dreaming, dreaming of the great changes which would take place in her life if she agreed to marry Ed. Her dreams were constantly interrupted by the sound of Edward crying in the next room until, after frequently getting up to help Bella soothe him, she took him into her own room in his cot and put it beside her so that at least Bella would be able to get some sleep, even if she couldn't. She didn't think she would get much sleep anyway.

Perhaps worn out by his exertions, Edward seemed to settle and was soon asleep so that, for the time being at least, Lottie could continue uninterrupted with her inner debate.

To be taken care of. It was very tempting. It would mean the end of a life of drudgery, a life without fun. Moreover, she would be able to give up a job she hated, have her sister and her baby also looked after, have a nice, even grand house to live in. Hadn't it been what she had always aspired to, striven towards, since she was a young girl? Always longed to get away from Broadway Terrace and better herself? At last she would be free of money worries and enjoy a lifestyle such as she had only begun to envisage during the heady days that preceded her engagement to Hugh, when she was not only in love but she had almost became part of the Carson family.

Anyone, knowing her circumstances now, would say she was a fool turning down such a tempting offer. But in her heart Lottie knew it was also wrong to agree to marry a man she liked but didn't love simply for gain. Ed was just too nice to treat in that way.

Ed was a rock, steadfast, wholly admirable. But with Hugh she had experienced that something extra, glimpsing just how exciting life could be. Not only had she been deeply in love with him, enthralled by him and his good looks, but she liked all the things he liked and Ed didn't, or couldn't, because of his handicap: sailing, dancing, tennis, horse riding and parties. For her there had also been the glamour of being an accepted member of the Carson family – of being at last equal with them, one of them.

In London she had also discovered something completely new and there was always the possibility that she could return there and resume the Bohemian lifestyle all over again; maybe study, go to university, complete her education and put herself on equal footing with her peers rather than a permanent hanger-on. She would not have to work in a store, she could earn her living as an artists' model and, compared to all this, life with Ed, though safe, would be dull.

The only thing that would change would be that if, in time, she could somehow return the feeling that good, kind Ed who had so much to offer had for her and somehow learn to love him, too?

Fifteen

In many ways it was a re-run of Madeleine's wedding. Same place, same guests, a beautiful hot spring day, a marquee on the lawn, a small string orchestra quietly playing, fantastic food. Only the bride and groom were different and, as expected, the bride looked stunning, radiant. Studious, bespectacled Albert seemed very happy, if not handsome the way tall, martial Andy had been.

Lottie, back home among the Carsons, for once felt happy, too. Happy for her friend, who had even overcome her resistance to her new husband's Christian name by calling him Al, which he seemed not only to accept but even like.

Yet so many things were different from Madeleine's wedding. Lottie was no longer alone but had an escort in the faithful Ed and after the ceremony at the church she walked more confidently into the house to be greeted at the door by the line-up of Violet, Albert and close family: Madeleine, her husband and Dr and Mrs Carson, all of whom greeted her warmly as an old friend.

As they moved through the hall on to the lawn there were a surprising number of people who Lottie knew, either through Ed or the Carsons. For Madeleine's wedding she had borrowed a dress from Harveys; now she wore a simple but stylish one she'd bought from a little boutique on the far side of town. She did not wear a hat and Bella had used her hairdressing skills to create a fashionable bob with soft finger waves brushed back from her forehead. As usual, there were many admiring glances cast her way from women as well as men. But Ed was never far away – attentive and courteous, steering her expertly through the throng.

'I didn't see your parents in church,' Lottie said, accepting a glass of champagne from a passing waiter.

'Didn't I tell you?' Ed said, casually doing the same. 'They're in England. Father is attending some function to do with his old Inn. They're making a holiday of it, thinking the sea trip would do Dad good, also visiting family as my mother is English. I thought your father might have mentioned they were away.'

'No, he didn't. He is out such a lot I hardly ever see him. I think he must be courting.'

'Seriously?'

'No.' Lottie smiled. 'Just guessing.'

There was no particular reason to feel a lightening of spirits, but Lottie could not help but remember that cold, penetrating stare the last time she had seen Lady Frobisher, and was very relieved that she was away.

Moving among the crowd she exchanged words with some of Hugh's friends with whom they used to play tennis or go dancing. But mostly she stood listening and smiling while Ed greeted acquaintances, some of whom Lottie knew but most of whom were strangers. However, it didn't matter. In this familiar environment she felt that now she was accepted, an outsider no more.

After drinks and canapés the guests sat down to the wedding breakfast in the huge marquee and she and Ed were on a table that included people she knew and people she didn't, one of whom was a woman sitting across from her who was elegant, stylish, beautifully dressed and who kept on staring at her in a curious and rather disconcerting way while the speeches were being made.

Afterwards the dancing began, led by the bridal couple, and one of the first people to approach her was Andy, Madeleine's husband.

'May I?' he said, gesturing towards Ed who nodded amiably and, sitting back in his chair, lit a cigarette and puffed away at it contentedly. 'You are the most beautiful woman here,' Andy said as his arms closed round her and the foxtrot started.

'What about your wife?'

'She's beautiful, too.' He was obviously a bit drunk, but pleasantly not objectionably so. 'Enjoying yourself?'

'Very much,' Lottie said. 'It takes me back to your and Madeleine's wedding and what a lot has happened since.'

'Hasn't it just?'

'I'm dying to see the baby.'

'You must come round with Ed.'

'Ed and I are not a couple, you know, Andy.'

'Oh, sorry, I thought you were.'

'We do go out and are good friends, but I am still an independent woman.'

'Then you must come by yourself if you prefer.'

'I may just want to talk to Madeleine.'

'True, but come soon because I am due to be posted abroad.'

'Any idea where?'

'Not sure, maybe India.'

'Will that be nice?'

'I think so.'

She leaned closer to him. 'Andy, do you by any chance know the name of that woman sitting over there?' She discreetly indicated the table they had just left and the woman who had been staring at her so fixedly, now talking to her companion.

'Oh,' Andy said, seeming surprised, 'didn't you know?'

'Know what?'

'Well, that's Hugh's wife, Sylvia.'

'Hugh is *here*?' Lottie was grateful for the crowd and the music to disguise her shock.

'I think he's coming. He was supposed to be here, but something has detained him at the hospital. It must be important for him to miss his sister's wedding. It's all right now about Hugh, isn't it? Violet thought . . .'

'Of course,' Lottie said carelessly. 'Perfectly all right.'

Only she knew that if she'd been told beforehand she would have made an excuse not to come and that the sudden acceleration of her heartbeat was not just due to the music.

When they returned to the table Sylvia had gone and she and Ed started to dance. Ed was a slow, clumsy partner but she was grateful for his presence and nestled up to him while his arm tightened around her and he murmured in her ear, 'You know I love you.'

She wanted to say 'I love you, too' and she thought that in a way, now seeking protection with him from Hugh, maybe she did.

They strolled back to the table and as she was about to take her seat some impulse made Lottie look towards the entrance of the marquee and there she saw him, urbane, elegant and handsome as ever, greeting his sister with a kiss, his arms extended and a regretful grin on his face, as though he was busy apologizing for being late, using his charm to make excuses. Next to him was Sylvia, who had perhaps left the table to wait for him.

Hugh wore a suit not morning dress, perhaps indicating that he had come from work and had no time to change.

Lottie braced herself and accepted a fresh glass of wine to steel her nerves just as Hugh strolled across to the table, hand in hand with Sylvia, and made straight for Lottie almost as if it had been planned. She then realized that Sylvia must have known who she was and had gone ahead to warn Hugh.

'Lottie!' Hugh exclaimed. 'Isn't this a splendid occasion? And how lovely to see you.'

He stooped to kiss her on the cheek. 'I don't think you've met Sylvia, my wife?'

Lottie rose and, although disgusted with the whole charade of pretence, nevertheless felt she must participate in it or risk making a fool of herself. 'Hello, Hugh.' She then turned to Sylvia. 'How do you do?' she said, as if she had never seen her in her life before, or been aware of her stare across the table.

'And Ed.' Hugh shook his hand vigorously. 'Very good to see you again. This is my wife, Sylvia.'

Glancing at him, Lottie was unable to divine his feelings except that he seemed to accept the situation with his customary aplomb as he greeted Hugh and politely shook hands with Sylvia.

'I haven't got long,' Hugh said, glancing at his watch. 'I'm on duty. So no drinking but I think I have time to steal a dance. May I, Ed?' and he reached out for Lottie's hand as the music started again and drew her on to the dance floor.

She felt angry but helpless. This wasn't the place to cause a fuss and spoil Violet's day, but somehow it seemed typical of Hugh to think he could do such a thing and get away with it.

'Is this all right?' Hugh asked earnestly.

'Is what all right?' she said crossly.

'Asking you to dance? I had to explain things to you.'

'I certainly don't think this is the place or the time to do it.' It was impossible to keep the anger from her voice.

'I don't mean about the past, but about today. Turning up like this.'

'Hugh, it is your sister's wedding and I would expect you to turn up for it. I had no idea you were in the country and frankly, Hugh, I don't care, either.'

'But Lottie . . .'

'What happened happened a long time ago. All over.'

'Well, I'm very glad you have that attitude. I told Violet you might feel awkward, but she thought that as you now had Ed you wouldn't mind.'

'She is quite right. I don't mind and by the way I do not "have" Ed. We are just friends.'

'That's not what I hear.'

'Then you are remarkably badly informed.'

He simply smiled in his superior, nonchalant way and drew her closer to him. Her pulse quickened. His proximity reawakened not only memories but small vestiges of the desire for him which annoyed her as she thought, hoped, they had gone forever.

Lottie wondered how much of what he was doing was deliberate to gauge his effect on her and she tried to disengage herself, aware of an infuriating, knowing smile on his face.

'I am so relieved to hear that,' he murmured. 'I know I behaved badly and believe me I felt very guilty about it, especially when you disappeared. But Flora seemed to think you were coping. And I know you, Lottie. You are so strong. I always knew you'd be all right.'

Oh, yes, 'strong Lottie', she could always cope. Inwardly she forced herself at least to maintain the pretence of being polite though she was seething, longing for the dance to end, conscious of the fact that both Ed and Sylvia must be watching them.

'Sylvia is very attractive,' Lottie said. 'No wonder you fell for her.'

'It wasn't just that. You're attractive, too. There were other things. Oh, I can't explain,' and he looked rather guiltily, she thought, towards the wife he had chosen over her.

'Like breeding, education . . .' she murmured, but she didn't think he'd heard as the tempo of the music increased and his head was still turned away. She immediately regretted saying it anyway, and said instead more loudly, 'How long are you here for?'

'Maybe for good. I have a temporary job at the hospital, but it depends if they let me go on developing my paediatric surgery. I still have exams to do. And we're hoping Sylvia will also get work there, too. If not we might go back. At least six months, I would think. Maybe we'll see one another?'

'Maybe,' Lottie said indifferently as the music finished and to her great relief they went back to the table to rejoin their partners. There was no more conversation between them and shortly afterwards Hugh and Sylvia left and Lottie and Ed continued eating, dancing and socializing as if nothing had happened to spoil the pleasure of the day.

But it had. It had introduced a jarring note. Hugh's appearance was unexpected and unpleasant. She felt Violet might have warned her, or perhaps she guessed that if she did she wouldn't have gone. Lottie knew Ed was upset and she, too, felt uncomfortable. Not only uncomfortable but annoyed. Enraged, in fact, by the whole artificial, contrived performance on the dance floor, which in some way she felt had been engineered by Hugh, maybe to make his wife jealous. All the way back to her house they maintained an awkward silence which was hard to break.

'How did you feel about seeing him again?' Ed asked at last as he stopped the car outside her house and sat back in his seat.

'I felt nothing. Why,' she reached out for his hand, 'were you worried?'

'Of course.'

'You needn't be. Frankly my only feeling was one of extreme annoyance. I didn't want to dance with him, but to refuse would have caused a scene as he was the bride's brother.'

'What did you talk about?'

'Trivia.'

Then, spontaneously, she leaned across and kissed him, looked up into his eyes and said, 'You are a much, much nicer person than Hugh Carson will ever be, dearest Ed.'

And he was, much, much nicer. Reviewing the events of the day as she usually did, lying in bed almost too tired to sleep, her jumbled thoughts were about the impact of seeing Hugh again, and comparing him with Ed. It was silly pretending they were not a couple. They were, so why was she denying it to herself as well as everyone else? In the months that had passed since he had proposed they had been together regularly. He often came to see Edward and took her out for excursions round the harbour and occasionally, for days at a time, even further afield to places like Rotorua, with its hot springs and bubbling mud pools, where the Te Arawa Maories from Polynesia settled a thousand years before. They had spent several days exploring the vast Tongariro National Park, an area of exceptional beauty and diversity with its three snow-capped volcanic mountain peaks and astonishing range of plants and exotic bird and animal life. They stayed in good hotels – separate bedrooms, of course, as Ed wanted to conduct his courtship, as Hugh had, on proper, acceptable lines and not put pressure on Lottie. His wish was to seduce her by love, not lust.

To Lottie, who had never left Wellington until her trip to London, these trips were magical as well as instructive about her native land. She also got to know Ed in a much deeper way and realized the extent of his knowledge, intellect and skills as a teacher – not patronizing, just instructive. He was a revelation to her as, once he got going on a subject that interested him, he was not at all dull, quite the opposite. It was on one of these trips, staying in a luxurious hotel on the edge of the National Park to celebrate her twenty-first birthday, that as he'd promised he again proposed.

Once more she had refused, despite the fact that it was such a nice occasion, at dinner in the hotel's beautiful restaurant with the snow-capped mountain range in the distance and champagne to toast her majority.

Yes, Ed was very comfortable to be with, easy-going and undemanding. If, for the moment at least, she didn't want him as a husband, she cherished him more and more as a friend.

Sixteen

1927

Gradually the days of summer passed and autumn set in. Edward had his first birthday and Lottie organized a small celebration, to which Len and Ed also came.

Len had been a regular visitor to see his son and take him out with Bella, and they had become a couple, rather as Lottie and Ed were, despite Lottie's attempts to resist it. She now no longer denied it and there were frequent outings with Violet and Al and other friends of Ed's, and excursions to some more interesting places:

Hawkes Bay, Lake Taupo and the Bay of Plenty where Captain Cook arrived in 1769 in the course of his expedition to map the entire coast of New Zealand, being only the second European to discover it.

One day Violet appeared unexpectedly at the haberdashery counter, as she sometimes did, but this time she whispered that she had something important to tell her. She hung about until Lottie had her lunch break and they went to the restaurant round the corner they often used, as staff were not encouraged to be seen with customers in the restaurant in the store in case it lowered the tone.

'Well?' Lottie leaned across the table.

'I'm having a baby,' Violet said, her expression one of excitement tinged with fear.

'That's wonderful news.' Lottie clasped her hand and squeezed it. 'You must be thrilled.'

'Thrilled and scared,' Violet said with a tiny shudder. 'It's a bit soon.'

'Is Al pleased?'

'Al's pleased, the family pleased. It's all a bit, well, unexpected. I didn't know much about it . . . *that* or anything at all before I got married. Do you know what I mean?'

'I think so. You mean sex?'

'I was unprepared for it, really. So was Al. I was his first as he was mine. It was all rather horrible to start with. A shock.'

'I wonder why Madeleine, or even your mother, didn't prepare you. After all, your brother and father are doctors.'

'I know, that's what's all so silly. I didn't like it at all, frankly, and I still don't, but if that's what one is supposed to do to get a baby then I suppose we'll have to continue because of course we want more than one. If only there was another way.'

She gazed thoughtfully at Lottie. 'Do you . . .?'

Lottie paused, the question hovering. 'No. If you mean do Ed and I sleep together, the answer's no.'

'But Ed must know about it. He's been married.'

'I know about it, too.'

'Oh.' Violet's eyes widened. 'With Hugh?'

'Mainly with another man I met in London, after Hugh. It seemed natural. He was an artist and the people he mixed with were very Bohemian. He was a good teacher and I liked it. I was lucky.'

'Does Ed know?'

'No, at least he knows about Adam but not that we went so far, and I don't think he'd approve. He is very conventional.'

'Do you love him? I know he's crazy about you.'

It was a question Lottie had anticipated but was reluctant to answer. 'I do like him very much. I don't know about love. I don't think so. Not yet anyway.'

'He's very different from Hugh.'

'Yes, he is.'

'By the way, Hugh's going back to England. He and Sylvia have decided it's where they want to be. More opportunities for qualifying as a senior surgeon. Also, Sylvia misses her family.'

Lottie said nothing, but applied herself, though with little real appetite, to the food on her plate. 'I don't suppose you want to see him again?' Violet continued. 'He did mention that he would like you to remain friends.'

A surge of anger swept through Lottie as she put down her knife and fork and looked straight into Violet's eyes. 'Look, Violet, I want it to be clear that what happened between Hugh and me is over. I know it is difficult for you, as his sister, and that's why I was nervous that this might come up, but I have no interest in Hugh and, no, I don't want to see him.

'I should never have gone to England. For that I don't altogether blame Hugh but myself for falling so badly in love that it made me selfish. Bella didn't want to be a teenage mother and that was partly my fault, although we love little Edward and wouldn't want to be without him. So, no, I don't want to see Hugh again. I was once very much in love with him, yes, but at your wedding I realized I was no longer.'

'I'm really glad of that,' Violet said, leaning across the table. 'In fact, I'm glad we've had this conversation, though I'd have loved to have you as a sister-in-law.'

It had been a very difficult meeting with Violet and in the course of the long afternoon that followed Lottie found their conversation largely occupied her thoughts in between the tedious business of looking after difficult customers. She was so tired of trying to remain patient while they sorted through countless boxes of buttons or endless samples of ribbons, discarding first one then another before deciding to go back to the ones they had liked in the first place and ending up by not buying anything at all, in which case she was blamed by her supervisor for not trying hard enough to clinch a deal. Many times she was on the verge of losing her patience, but she also wanted to keep her job in order to maintain her dignity and independence as other jobs in this time of recession would be hard to find.

As usual, she had done a little shopping on the way home and when she got there she was surprised to see Sir Eustace's Daimler outside the door of the house. Her father seldom brought the car home unless he had another appointment in the evening.

She opened the door and her eyes were immediately riveted by the sight of a strange woman sitting bolt upright in her father's chair, looking very uncomfortable, her eyes fixed on the door like a startled rabbit. Her father, looking similarly ill at ease, stood by the fireplace smoking a cigarette, which he was not supposed to do and was usually a sign of inner turmoil, even agitation.

'Ah, Lottie,' her father said as she entered the room, putting her purchases down on the table. 'There you are. We were waiting for you.'

Lottie's eyes were still on the visitor who stood up rather awkwardly now, a nervous smile on her face. She was of medium height and wore a brown coat and a pink felt hat. The first thing Lottie thought was how much she resembled her mother, handsome but with an edge to her, the hint of an uncertain temper.

'Lottie, I want you to meet my friend, Mrs Walker.'

'How do you do?' Lottie said politely, managing a smile.

'Nice to meet you,' Mrs Walker said, almost with a little bob as though Lottie were royalty, and giving her a limp hand to shake. She was clearly extremely nervous.

Desmond puffed out his chest importantly. 'Lottie, Mrs Walker and I became engaged today and I wanted you to be the first to know.'

'Engaged!' Lottie gasped, her gaze going rapidly from her father to Mrs Walker, whose pale face was gradually changing colour.

'I know it's a surprise.' Desmond went across the room and put his arm protectively around his intended's shoulder. 'But Mrs Walker – Maude – and I have been seeing a good deal of each other for several months now. She likes a run in the Daimler, don't you, Maude?'

He and his lady love exchanged conspiratorial glances. Lottie could see him passing himself off as a gentleman owning a Daimler and Mrs Walker enjoying the experience of being in the passenger seat, not unlike her, if she was honest, with her affection for the Bugatti. Her father went on: 'Maude is the widow of a gentleman who sadly was wounded in the war and I met her through my veterans' club. Now that I am divorced from your mother I was able to ask Maude to do me the honour of marrying me.'

'Well, I'm very glad for you, Dad,' Lottie said, recovering. 'It's just a surprise, you never having mentioned Mrs Walker before.'

'Well, I wanted to be sure before I announced anything. You see I was nervous of bringing her here, I'll be honest with you, because of Bella. I thought Maude might not approve . . . you know, about Edward, but she has been most generous and understanding.' And clasping her hand, he looked lovingly at her.

'I'm looking forward to meeting them,' Mrs Walker said, regaining her composure. 'Your father is very fond of the baby.'

'It will be a surprise for Bella, too, but no doubt she will be pleased for you, Dad. We're both pleased for you to have a companion.' She smiled warmly at Mrs Walker, feeling it was too soon to call her Maude, and suggested she made a cup of tea.

Bella was anything but pleased with the news of her father's engagement and took an instant dislike to Mrs Walker. She said she 'smothered' her, whatever that meant, but doubted her sincerity. She objected to her coming to the house when her father was not there and generally giving the impression that she was just waiting to take over by making plans for the future.

Lottie thought Bella was being difficult again and kept on nagging her about doing more round the house. When she got home in the evening now there were unmade beds, unwashed dishes and she had to set to cleaning the place while Bella pleaded preoccupation with the baby. Even the baby's clothes were unwashed and there were dirty nappies in a bucket outside the kitchen door. Lottie suspected she did it to annoy Mrs Walker, who in turn complained to her father and it all came back to Bella and of course Lottie who, as usual, seemed to bear the brunt of the trouble.

And it was trouble. It had not really dawned on Lottie that Mrs Walker would be moving in when she became Mrs O'Brien, and although she had nothing against her she had not warmed to her – mainly, she thought, and it was no fault of the poor woman – because she so resembled her mother both in looks and, she gradually discovered as Mrs Walker made her presence felt more and more, in character, too.

In fact, Desmond was marrying Ada all over again.

The situation came to a head a few weeks after Desmond had introduced Mrs Walker to the family. Lottie had come home from work early and the first thing she heard when she opened the door was the sound of Edward screaming his head off. She dashed upstairs and found Bella lying inert on her bed, eyes closed, and Edward standing up in his cot beside her leaning against the bars, rather dangerously, Lottie thought, fist in his mouth, face puce, eyes bulging and trying to get his mother's attention.

'Good heavens, what on earth is this?' Lottie exclaimed and swiftly took Edward in her arms, only to discover that, in addition to whatever else was wrong, he was also soaking wet. Holding the wet baby on her knee – thankfully he had stopped crying as soon as he saw his aunt – she sat on the bed and firmly shook Bella with her free hand.

'Bella, Bella,' she said gently. 'Wake up.'

'I'm awake,' Bella murmured without opening her eyes.

'Are you ill? Edward is soaking wet.'

'I'm having another baby,' Bella said, choking back tears. 'I want to get rid of it.'

At that moment, Lottie felt this was news she couldn't cope with and got off the bed with the baby. 'Look, let me deal with Edward and I'll come back quick as I can.'

In a house with no bathroom and an outside toilet ablutions were never easy, but all who lived in the house had a lifetime of coping with the inconvenience of washing in the kitchen and Lottie hurried down, removed Edward's nappy, put it in the bucket outside the back door with the rest and then washed him down and took him back to Bella's room where she quickly got a clean nappy and put it on together with clean clothes. Then, with him still on her knee, now gurgling with pleasure at being dry and safe with his aunt, she sat down on Bella's bed and put a hand on her shoulder.

'*When* did you know this?'

'I saw that nice doctor.'

'*Why* didn't you tell me?'

'I was scared.' She opened her eyes and looked fearfully at her sister. 'I was really scared, Lottie, of what you'd say after what you told me.'

'What did the doctor say?'

'I told her I didn't want it. She said she couldn't help me with that. She wants me to go and see her with you. Maybe if I can't get rid of it I will have it adopted. Oh, Lottie, I don't know what to do. I really don't know what to do.'

And Bella succumbed to a paroxysm of tears while Lottie tenderly put Edward, sleepy and exhausted by his tantrum, into his cot again. Then, feeling overwhelmed, she sat staring disconsolately at her sister.

'It is Len's, isn't it?'

'Of course it's Len's.' Bella looked at her indignantly. 'Who do you think? He said he knew what to do . . . you know, about not having babies, but obviously he didn't.'

'Have you told him?'

'Yes. He said his mother might know someone who could get rid of it. I don't think he really wants to, but we didn't know what else to do.'

'You mean, Len would like to keep the baby?'

'I think so. He loves Edward and he says he loves me.'

'And you love him?'

'Of course I do – why would I go with him otherwise? What sort of person do you think I am, Lottie?' The look she gave her sister was one of injured dignity. 'If we could, Len and I would like our own little place to live together with Edward and the new baby; we can't live here with that awful woman coming and there is not enough room in his house with all his brothers and sisters. He shares a room with his brothers as it is.'

'You mean you might like to get married?'

'Yes, of course I would. He didn't ask me, but I think he might be talked into it. But we can't afford to so there is no point in thinking about it, and that's the truth. Maybe he should ask his mother about . . .'

'Look, abortion is illegal in this country. It is also horrible and if it is done by an unqualified person it can be very dangerous. You know, Bella, until recently you've been a very good mother. You seemed happy and looked after Edward well. But just lately you've been a mess and the house is a mess. How long have you known you were pregnant?'

'Not long, a few days, but I thought I was . . . you know, for ages.'

'Your periods stopped?'

'Yes. I told Len what I was scared had happened, especially as he said he knew what to do, so it was his fault, really, not mine. I was afraid to tell you, Lottie, because I knew you'd be cross. I hoped it wasn't true and then I went to see the doctor and she said it was very true, I'm about three or four months gone, which really scared me so I knew I had to tell you.'

'I am cross and upset,' Lottie admitted, 'but I am your sister and I love you and you must *never* be afraid of me – you can tell me everything. Do you understand that, Bella? *Everything*, and I will always do what I can to help.'

'It's that woman,' Bella said fiercely. 'I can't stand her. I simply can't live with her in this house.' Impulsively she leaned forward and kissed her sister and Lottie took her in her arms, stroked her head and made soothing noises, as if it were she who was the baby.

When she got downstairs Lottie set to tidying up and cleaning the house, her mind working overtime. Bella stayed in her room and was still there when Desmond came in, a broad smile on his face as he looked around.

'Oh, nice and clean,' he said. 'I would imagine this is due to you, Lottie. I don't know what's wrong with Bella these days. She's not herself.'

'She's pregnant,' Lottie said. 'That's what's wrong.'

Her father sat down with a bump, the smile abruptly vanishing from his face. 'How did that happen?'

'The usual way, Dad.'

'Is it Len's?'

'She says so.'

'He's a nice enough lad. I've got quite fond of him, but a thing like that . . .'

Her father got up and put one of the forbidden cigarettes, which somehow he always seemed to have about him, in his mouth. 'What's to be done, Lottie? You see . . .' He stroked his face nervously. 'You see, Maude doesn't really want Bella here with the baby. She hasn't really taken to her and says Bella is never very nice to her which, I must say, I have noticed. She says the place has got very untidy, and it has, and Bella is sloppy all of a sudden. They would never get on. It would never do and I don't want to lose Maude.'

'I suppose it is since she thought she was pregnant. She is about four months, the doctor thinks.'

'Well, Maude can't be doing with it and, frankly, Lottie, it is a problem because we have now set the date.'

'You've set the *date*!' Lottie said furiously. 'Without consulting us?'

'I had no option. You see, Maude has to leave her house. It belongs to the army – her husband was invalided home and died eventually from his wounds only a couple of years ago – and now they want it back. My divorce from your mother is complete and yes . . . in about a month's time.'

'Then what about me, Dad? Did you think of me in all this?'

'Oh, I don't think Maude minds you. In fact, she quite likes you, Lottie. She thinks you have class.'

'Dad, do you seriously think you can drive my sister and her baby out and I'd stay here looking after you and your new wife?'

Desmond looked at her with surprise. 'I don't see why not? Where else would you go? Isn't there a place Bella could go for a while? A home for unmarried mothers, that kind of thing? I know Lady Frobisher is a patron of such a place and might agree to use her influence. She is a very nice person, Lady Frobisher. I'll ask her. I'm sure she'll understand.'

Ed opened the front door of his house and was astonished to see Lottie standing outside at eight o'clock in the evening. 'Are you all right?' he asked anxiously, reaching out for her arm and leading her indoors. 'You look all in.'

'I'm perfectly all right,' Lottie assured him. 'I just felt I had to talk to someone and who better than you?'

'Well, I'm very glad to hear that,' Ed said, taking her into the lounge and seating her in a chair by the window with its lovely view of the bay. 'Can I get you a drink?'

'I wouldn't mind. Whisky, perhaps?'

'I didn't think you drank whisky. Now I *am* worried.'

'Well, I need one now.'

Ed hurried out of the room, returning after a short while with two glasses, one of which he handed to Lottie and took the chair next to her. 'Tell.'

'My sister is expecting again and Dad doesn't want her in the house because he is marrying "that woman", as Bella calls her, in a month's time and she can't do with Bella. Mutual dislike, I think.'

'Well.' Ed took a gulp of his whisky. 'That is a drama.'

'But she doesn't mind me, apparently, because she thinks I have "class" – and also I suspect she thinks I'll keep the place clean. Bella has let things go. She's four months pregnant, but has suspected it for a long time.'

'And never told you?'

'She was too frightened. Makes me feel bad, and I told her she must always come to me, regardless of what happens.'

She went on to tell him the rest of the story, as Bella had told her, and then about her conversation with her father. 'He thinks your mother will help her get into a home for unmarried mothers.'

Ed looked nonplussed. Then: 'Well, I'm sure she would, but . . .'

'Exactly, Ed, do you think I'd allow such a thing to happen? To my sister, when I am here to look after her? Certainly not. Anyway, it wouldn't be fair on you.'

'So what do you think should happen? There is always a place here . . .'

'Ed, that's not why I came, to scrounge. It's very sweet of you, even to think it, but it is out of the question. I just wanted to try and clear my mind. I don't want to be away too long. Bella's alone, but I had to get out of the house or I felt I'd scream, what with Bella in tears, Edward having tantrums and Dad behaving like a caged lion until I persuaded him to go to his club or whatever or take solace in the arms of Mrs Walker.'

'What about Len?' Ed said thoughtfully. 'Would he marry her?'

'She said Len, who adores Edward, is very supportive, yet they have never discussed marriage because they can't afford it.'

'Obviously.' Ed stared for a long time out of the window. Then he stood up.

'Let's have them here for dinner. We can go through all the options and then decide what to do for the best.'

'They're very young,' Lottie said doubtfully.

'Yet they will be the parents of two children. Let's talk about it and see.'

'Ed, you're very good.' Lottie also got up and moved closer to him. 'And very wise. I quite honestly don't know what I'd have done without you.'

'I have my uses,' Ed said drily, stooping to peck her on the cheek. 'Let's drive you home.'

Bella and Len were suitably impressed by the size and grandeur of Ed's house, its spaciousness, the magnificent view of the harbour from its windows. Ed collected them with Lottie and baby Edward, not in the Bugatti but in a more down-to-earth family car, a Ford Model T.

It was a lovely, sunny evening and first of all they, including Edward, who was beginning to toddle but stayed mostly in his father's arms, had a short walk round the garden and admired the view.

They were an attractive young couple by any standards, Lottie had thought, as they sat down to a simple dinner of lamb and vegetables followed by trifle for dessert. Ed had decided not to serve wine. Len was tall and sturdy with bushy black hair and large brown eyes. Although he was largely monosyllabic Bella didn't seem to mind. Bubbling away, happy and secure in the company of her beau, she did most of the talking for him. Len wore a grey suit, obviously his best, with a white shirt and blue tie. Bella, pretty and petite beside him, wore a short patterned summer dress. It was hard to think of them as already parents.

Ed's maid, Betty, had stayed behind to cook and serve dinner and keep an eye on Edward who, now fed and all tucked up in his pram, looking the picture of contentment, gurgled away happily.

At first talk was of generalities, the weather, the progress of the baby and Len's job, which he seemed to be enjoying. Then Ed decided they should get down to business.

'You know,' he began, 'I have a personal interest in this family, which I have come to regard almost as a part of my own. I am particularly fond of Edward. You have asked me to be his godfather and I want to see him happy and well looked after.' He glanced at Lottie, as if seeking her approval, and she nodded encouragingly. 'Lottie has told me, Bella and Len, about the new baby you're expecting and also that your father, Bella, is to remarry and would rather you were not in the house.'

'And I don't want to be there either!' Bella said spiritedly. 'I can't stand that woman.'

'Yes, I am aware of that.' A smile flickered across Ed's face. 'What I want to know is how you two really feel about each other. I want you to be honest with me.' He sat back in his chair and Lottie could visualize him now in his role of a lawyer interviewing a client, sympathetic but firm, or maybe, like his father, staring at them from over the bench. She had never really imagined him in a professional role, mainly because he hardly ever talked about his work. But she suddenly felt proud of him, even slightly in awe, as though he had subtly taken on a new dimension, grown in stature and was no longer the importunate lover who she repeatedly, and maybe unkindly, rejected. What, she thought, if it was too late? What if Ed should suddenly reciprocate and reject her?

And it was then that Lottie realized to what extent Ed was an essential part of her life and how lost, even bereft, she would be without him, and how close it felt to loving him. If not being madly in love, it was a deeper emotion, more profound and, possibly, long-lasting.

His question, however, drew only silence from the young couple who looked at each other, apparently lost for words.

'Let me put it another way,' Ed said magisterially. 'Would you like to live together, provide a home for your children? In that case, do you want to get married?'

At this Bella nodded enthusiastically, while Len's tanned face slowly darkened.

'You, Len?' Ed looked at him, glancing first at Lottie, as though he was beginning to despair. The task of sorting out the problem of this couple was beginning to defeat even his legal skills.

When tongue-tied Len didn't reply he continued: 'The alternative, I believe Bella's father suggested, is that Bella should go into a home for unmarried mothers and perhaps have the new baby adopted. They can be taken away at birth, you know, so that you never need to get to know them.'

His tone changed and Lottie thought that, out of frustration, he was now increasing the pressure.

'Oh, we don't want that!' Aghast, Bella had finally found her voice. 'Do we, Len?'

'Well . . .' Len said. By now his face was puce; beads of perspiration stood out on his forehead, indicative of his torment. 'Well, we can't afford anything like that, sir,' he spluttered at last.

'If you could afford it is it what you would want? Do you want to marry Bella and take care of her and your two children *if somehow* it was possible?'

As the inarticulate Len still struggled for words, Lottie intervened, saying gently, 'Tell the truth, Len. No one will blame you if you say no. It would be wrong to get married if you didn't feel you loved Bella enough to want to spend your life with her.'

'What I am suggesting might be possible,' Ed said. '*Might* be possible, and that is to make a house available rent-free. Len continues with his job and, I assume, earns enough to support a wife? It so happens I own a house not far from here which is vacant. I am just offering you help, not charity, for the sake of Bella and Edward and the unborn baby – and you, of course, Len, if you think your relationship is strong enough? Do you?'

'Yes, he does!' Bella said firmly. 'Don't you, Len? You told me you loved me only the other day? Didn't you? Say yes, Len, because if you don't we'll never, ever have another chance like this.'

She stared at him, as if defying him to disagree. He nodded but his eyes were cast to the ground and his expression was not at all that of an eager bridegroom.

'Yes,' he said at last. 'I do love you, Bella, you know that but, well, it is all so unexpected. Gave me a bit of a shock.' And, producing a grubby handkerchief, he began agitatedly removing trickles of sweat from his brow.

'Oh, Len, I knew you did!' Bella threw her arms round him and kissed him fervently. Then, her face radiant but clearly close to tears of happiness, she turned to Ed. 'It's just that he has difficulty saying it,' she said. 'He never says much. That's just his way. But we're both very, very pleased, aren't we, Len?'

Len nodded.

It had rained the previous day and all night a storm raged, rain beating against the window panes, interspersed with loud claps of thunder. Occasionally Lottie woke up but fell back into a fitful sleep.

Now she woke to the early morning sunshine, peeping round the sides of the curtains, and the sound of birdsong. Gently she threw aside the bedclothes, so as not to disturb the sleeping Ed and, putting on a robe, crept out of the bedroom and down the stairs, along the corridor and into the garden.

Here she was, almost overwhelmed by the sheer new, fresh beauty of the day, revealing in all its pristine glory the splendour of the scene confronting her. The blue, almost translucent waters of the harbour shimmered in the rays of the morning sun, the ferry pulled away from the wharf and fishing boats chugged past on their leisurely way across the harbour out into the open sea.

Lottie began to walk slowly round the garden, thinking of all that had happened in the weeks since the dinner with Bella and Len. It was almost impossible to comprehend the change in their fortunes in such a short time, and so quickly.

Bella and Len had married and moved into their new house only the previous day, amid the downpour. The week before that she had moved out of the house where she was born, with few regrets, to begin her new life. It was, she reflected, like burying the past and looking forward to a new, exciting if uncertain future, where anything could happen.

She and Ed would also have a quiet wedding, quite unlike the spectacle that had been planned for her had she married Hugh Carson, which now she was so glad she had not. It would be hard to find someone kinder and more thoughtful than Ed, and Lottie had realized at last that she couldn't do without him, which in itself was a form of love, probably the best kind.

He would look after her, pamper and protect her and to someone who had lived the life she had, with all its setbacks and responsibilities, she had decided to give in, welcome it and enjoy it. It meant freedom from worry, financial insecurity and relying on another person, which had been impossible for as long as she could remember.

Above all, it would be mutual. She would look after Ed, take care of him and give him the sort of love he had wanted for so long. In turn she knew his sterling qualities as well as his sheer devotedness would guarantee her happiness. The fact was that he needed her as much as she needed him. Despite his years she knew he was shy, vulnerable and insecure in the shadow of his formidable and often disapproving and critical parents, sensitive about his gammy leg and his reliance on a stick. She would restore his confidence, give him that sense of self-esteem that he deserved. His mother in particular, who did not yet know of their engagement, would be firmly pushed to the background.

A honeymoon in England was promised where she could show him London, introduce him to her friends there and take him to Dorset to see Hardy's house and the glorious view of the English Channel from the surrounding hills, where she and Flora had once picnicked in such different circumstances. Maybe, even after all this time, Flora would want to finish her painting of her?

Ed knew a lot about gardening. She, brought up in a terraced house with a bare backyard, knew next to nothing. But she loved the parks in the city which she had often wandered round as a girl, and the lush countryside to which Ed had taken her. She had learned to appreciate the magnificent flora her native country had to offer, species of trees and plants grown nowhere else in the world.

In season Ed's garden was full of roses, hibiscus, red and white Kakabeak, the yellow Kowhai and the large, shiny broad-leafed Puka tree.

Drops of rain still glistened on the leaves, the heads of many flowers were bowed or broken, and branches torn from the trees were strewn on the ground. But after the rain came the sun bringing renewal which, she thought as she wandered contentedly back into the house, seemed a metaphor for her life. The bad, storm-tossed part was, she hoped, now over and the happy sunny part was only just beginning.